KILL HER TWICE

KILL HER TWICE

Jack Fredrickson

**SEVERN
HOUSE**

First world edition published in Great Britain and the USA in 2022
by Severn House, an imprint of Canongate Books Ltd,
14 High Street, Edinburgh EH1 1TE.

Trade paperback edition first published in Great Britain and the USA in 2022
by Severn House, an imprint of Canongate Books Ltd.

severnhouse.com

British Library Cataloguing-in-Publication Data
A CIP catalogue record for this title is available from the British Library.

ISBN-13: 978-0-7278-5063-8 (cased)
ISBN-13: 978-1-4483-0837-8 (trade paper)
ISBN-13: 978-1-4483-0836-1 (e-book)

For Susan
Forever

ONE

For an hour, maybe two, she was the most famous murder victim in America.

Because for that hour, maybe two, he was the most famous murderer.

Not for killing her, but for killing her again.

As far as murders went, the beginning of the story was somewhat ordinary – man goes nuts, kills girlfriend – and the press might not have reported it at all. But the news was slow that day, and it was close to Halloween, and suburban Weston was far enough west of Chicago to have never been bloodied by a stabbing. So the press ginned up the horror of it and sent it out in their broadcasts and newspapers.

It began around midnight. October had been parched, without rain, and a nervous wind hurled the last of the autumn's dead leaves, crackling like bits of bones, across the closely cropped lawns. Bikes and trikes and soccer balls and skateboards stopped some of them, but it was the red-brick and cedar single-story house at the dead end of the cul-de-sac that caught the full fury of the pelting, as if to warn her. But by around midnight, it was too late.

Only two other homes were still lit. The next day was a Thursday, a work day, and most people on that cul-de-sac were securely asleep. Even the pumpkins carved for next week's Halloween seemed to be dozing in the snug shadows of the darkened doorways.

The brick and cedar house was hushed like its neighbors. The bluish light of a television glowed behind drapes just to the left of the two-car garage. Farther back, a fluorescent light flickered faintly. Sara had yelled at him again that morning, to replace that annoying kitchen bulb, but as usual, Martin forgot, or was too busy, or was too tired, or whatever.

To the left of the bluish glow, the flickering fluorescence, and the darkened living room, the glassed hall along the front of the house lay, behind the drawn drapes, in the dim white mist of a night light, set so he could find his way to bed without disturbing her. Past the two closed doors of the guest rooms, the master bedroom was farthest left. Its door had been left halfway open, another precaution to keep him from waking her when he came to bed.

She sat on the floor, leaned back against the right side of the bed. The pale peach English comforter she'd purchased just the week before was pulled down beside her. It was of the finest goose down, cost a thousand dollars, and it was ruined.

Neither of them had good-paying jobs – Sara was the cashier at an independent grocery, Martin the day manager of a struggling hot-dog shack – but she racked up debt on her ever-growing packet of credit cards like she expected to win a lottery. Time and again, though always careful to speak calmly, he suggested he couldn't understand why she'd incur such charges, with their horrendous interest costs, for such expensive things like designer clothing, showplace furniture, and that English comforter. Even the walnut knife block set in the kitchen cost seven hundred dollars. She always screamed back that they had only one life to live, and she wanted to live it nice.

Amy Wilson, a neighbor two doors down, often heard Sara's rage. She was up late that night, absently listening to talk-show television set low as she hemmed curtains in her family room. Her windows were cracked open a couple of inches. She heard a woman scream. She set down her curtains and hurried out the front door. The cul-de-sac was silent. Only two other houses were still lit. Sara Jansen's place – for it was just Sara's; she made no secret of the fact that it was her money alone that paid for the place – had the blue light of a television on. Believing it was that television she heard, Amy went back inside, noticing the clock above the television as she resumed hemming. It was 12:07 a.m.

Forty-one minutes later, at 12:48 a.m., James Simmons put down his newspaper and stepped outside for his last cigarette of the day. Down the street, the lights in the Jansen house were being switched on behind the drawn drapes, room after room. He thought it odd, but then again, he thought Sara Jansen odd. She was a prickly thing, not accustomed to lowering her voice the way other folks did, and he often heard her tirades, even from a few houses away. No doubt, she was off on another tear behind those closed drapes, even at that late hour.

One hour and eighteen minutes after James Simmons finished his cigarette, at 2:06 a.m., the phone rang at the Chan house, down the same block. Lydia and Thomas Chan were asleep. Thomas fumbled the phone off the nightstand and put it to his ear. A man's voice he didn't recognize screamed to come over right away and then the phone went dead. Caller ID registered the caller's name as anonymous. Thomas called the number displayed. There was no answer. Instantly awake now, he slipped on jeans and a sweatshirt, and ran out the front door barefooted. He stopped and looked up and down the cul-de-sac, not knowing who'd called. Only two houses were still lit: the Wilson place, by a single lamp and a television behind curtains, and Sara Jansen's house, where every room was bright behind drapes. He would say later he couldn't very well knock on the doors of the two lit houses, not in the middle of the night. And so, he stood as still as he could, straining to listen for anything wrong, but after five minutes of hearing and seeing nothing unusual, he went inside and sat in his darkened living room, tensed for the phone to ring again.

Twenty minutes after that, red and blue flashing lights washed bright through the sheer curtains of the Chan living room. Thomas, still dressed, ran outside. Two Weston police cars, their spotlights searching the houses for street numbers, slammed to a stop in front of Sara Jansen's house at the end of the cul-de-sac.

Martin Tripp stood barefoot outside his open front door; one arm thrown up to shield his eyes from the glare of the spotlights. His blue jeans and white Ralph Lauren polo shirt were splattered with what looked like black paint in the harsh light. A light-colored towel, glistening and sodden by more black, was wrapped around his right hand.

Officer Rainey jumped out from one of the cars, Officer Lucas from the other.

'Small man, hat!' Martin Tripp yelled. 'Out back door, over the fence. Sara, bedroom at the end of the hall. I'm cut.' He held up the bloody towel wrapped around his hand.

Both officers drew their guns. Rainey ran around the right side of the house toward the back. Lucas shouted to Tripp to wait outside by his patrol car and stepped in through the open front door.

The house was bright with light, easy to see. Front windows lined a hall to the left. Lucas raised his gun and moved to the left and down it. He opened the first door and went into a bedroom. There was no bed. The dresser drawers had been pulled out and dumped, spilling hundreds of soaps and cosmetics onto the floor. The closet had been emptied. Women's coats lay on the floor amid the soaps and cosmetics.

The next bedroom was like the first. No bed, drawers upended of more soaps and cosmetics, closet emptied of the women's jackets and sweaters lying amid soaps and cosmetics on the floor.

The master bedroom was farthest left at the end of the hall. The door was open. Sara Jansen sat on the beige carpet, slumped back against the edge of the king-sized bed. Her eyes were wide and lifeless. One leg was crossed beneath her, the other splayed out. Blood, already drying, stained the front of her soft lavender nightgown, the comforter, and the beige carpet.

Lucas knelt to feel her carotid artery but it was only for protocol. He knew she was dead.

He scanned the room quickly. Like in the guest bedrooms, the dresser drawers had been pulled out and emptied onto the floor. A man's underwear and socks lay among a woman's sweaters and lingerie. Clothes from the two closets, most still on their hangers, lay scattered on the furniture and on the floor, their pockets pulled out as if by someone looking for valuables.

He went back along the glass-windowed hall. The dining room was at the back of the house, adjacent to the kitchen. The four drawers from the sideboard lay on the carpet, spilled of unused linen napkins, silver napkin rings, and two ornate candlesticks. Across the hall, the living room had also been tossed, the end table drawers dumped of leather coasters, small candles, and one deck of playing cards still sealed in its plastic wrapper.

Something there especially caught his eye. A wood panel lay beside an overturned end table. Glue lines along its edges matched those on the underside of the table. Lucas would later testify that the false panel might have been used to hide documents or currency.

The kitchen was in shambles, ransacked like the other rooms. Silverware lay scattered on shards of broken glasses, cups, and plates. Five carving knives had come loose from a wood block holder when it was thrown against the wall.

Lucas put on plastic gloves and tried the back door knob. It was unlocked but he did not go outside.

He went back to the hall. A den, at the front and between the garage and the living room, was ransacked like the other rooms. It had a door that opened to the two-car attached garage. He switched on the light. A spotless white Mercedes C300 and a dirty dented green Honda Accord were parked there. A quick look showed no one inside.

He returned to the front door and went outside. Rainey had come from behind the house and leaned against Lucas's car. He shook his head when Lucas walked up. There'd been no sign of an intruder.

Rainey had already radioed for an ambulance, supervision from one of Weston's two detectives, and the county's medical examiner and his forensics team. Neither Lucas nor Rainey spoke to each other or to Tripp in the back seat while they waited for the support units.

The ambulance arrived within minutes. Told that there were two victims, one dead inside, the other in Lucas's car, one of the EMTs knelt and taped and bandaged the still-bleeding long cut on Martin Tripp's hand and then, per protocol, joined his partner to wait next to their ambulance for the other units. Tripp's wound would be examined and treated more thoroughly at the hospital.

Detective Harry Slage, wakened at home, arrived eighteen minutes after the ambulance. After speaking briefly with Lucas and Rainey, he went inside for a brief look at the master bedroom and came out. The forensics team would examine everything when they arrived.

Slage opened the back door of Lucas's car, helped Martin Tripp get into the back of Slage's unmarked black Chevrolet Impala, and sat in the front. Slage began conducting a preliminary interview. He had little experience with murder investigations; only two murders had occurred in Weston in thirty years, and they were domestic disputes that escalated into a choking and a bludgeoning with a cast-iron frying pan.

Tripp was clearly shaken. His story, told haltingly, was brief. A small man, wearing a wide-brimmed hat and a long coat, and armed with a handgun, must have entered the home through the unlocked kitchen door. He confronted Tripp in the den, where he was watching television. He marched Tripp down the hall, pushed him into a guest bedroom, and told him to remain quiet or he'd be killed. He closed the door and continued down to the master bedroom where Sara lay sleeping. Slage asked how the intruder knew where the master bedroom was. Tripp replied that the curtains in the hall were usually kept open, and the intruder could have seen inside anytime from the street.

A few minutes later – Tripp couldn't be sure, exactly – he heard Sara scream and then go silent. Sounds of rooms being searched began to fill the house: drawers hitting the floor, closet doors banging open. It was madness, it was deafening, but Tripp assumed Sara's silence meant she was cooperating, and so he remained silent in the guest bedroom. Finally, he heard the kitchen door slam. He ran to the master bedroom and found Sara sitting on the floor, slumped back against the bed. He dropped to the floor to sit next to her and cradled her in his arms. Sometime later – he didn't know how long – he at last accepted she was dead and called the police.

The four-person DuPage County forensics team arrived with a member of the medical examiner's office twenty-one minutes after Slage and began their investigation in the master bedroom. Sara had been stabbed once, directly above the heart. Her body was removed by the ambulance personnel for a thorough autopsy at the medical examiner's office.

A forensics investigator went out to Detective Slage's car with a set of paper pants and top. Martin Tripp was covered in blood – the result, he said, of cradling his stabbed wife in his arms while he waited for the police. His clothes were bagged. Throughout, Slage kept pressing Tripp to go over his story again and again.

Tripp insisted the intruder was a short man wearing a long coat and a hat. He could only have entered the single-story house silently at the back, through the kitchen door, since it was always left unlocked, and had come to the den to confront Tripp where he was watching television.

'The sound was off?' Slage asked.

'No, just turned low. Sara was a light sleeper. She didn't like to be disturbed.'

Tripp said he couldn't remember sustaining the large cut on his hand, saying that the man must have cut him, though he wasn't sure when or where. Slage asked if he'd left the guest bedroom before the intruder left and Tripp said he didn't think so.

Slage pressed Tripp about the killer's means of entry. There were no signs of forced entry through the kitchen door. The door was always unlocked, Tripp said. Common enough practice in their neighborhood.

Detective Slage paid particular attention to Martin Tripp's demeanor. Tripp remained calm, occasionally smiling, perfectly relaxed. Slage asked whether Tripp had used drugs that night. Tripp admitted he'd used a little marijuana and perhaps an oxy or two, but except for not knowing how he'd been cut, his mind had been clear throughout. His attorney would later say he was in shock, disbelieving, and stoned out of his mind, and that was what accounted for his calm demeanor.

Of great interest to the forensics team was the thin trail of blood drops along the top of the high thread-count Egyptian-cotton sheet, leading to its edge. A quick lifting of the mattress revealed a bloodied ten-inch carving knife wedged between the mattress and the box spring, the sort of knife brought out for a Christmas roast or a Thanksgiving turkey. The tip of the knife was broken off. A subsequent examination of the knives spilled from the cutlery block thrown against the kitchen wall showed the presumed murder weapon to be part of the matching set.

The forensics team searching the kitchen found the jewelry that Martin said the intruder must have come looking for. It was stuffed in a bloodied plastic storage bag hidden behind the cookbooks on a small shelf at the end of the kitchen counter.

At dawn, Detective Slage had heard enough. 'Looks like you did it, Mr Tripp.'

'Looks like I did,' Tripp agreed.

Slage handcuffed Martin Tripp's unwounded hand to an anchor ring in the back of his car and drove him to the hospital, where his cut was stitched. He then drove him to the Weston police station to be interviewed by Slage and the town's other detective on video. Tripp demanded to speak with an attorney before being questioned further. He was fingerprinted and escorted to a holding cell.

It took Martin Tripp forty-eight hours to find someone to
represent him. More precisely, it took forty-eight hours for Tripp
to be found by an attorney desperate to represent him. Reginald
Aplon, a shiny-suit lawyer operating out of a storefront office in
a shopping center at the north end of Weston, beat it to the jail
because Tripp offered the opportunity to fathom a novel defense
and escape forever the indignity of practicing law next to a sub
sandwich shop in a strip mall.

Aplon just had to figure out how.

TWO

I t was hot that August afternoon, dog days hot. But the state
of my finances wasn't so hot, and so I was outside, two
hundred yards downriver from the cylinder where I live,
working a missing creature case. The mayor's mother's black cat
had disappeared and there was a hundred-dollar reward.

There was competition. All municipal hands were on deck.
Those cops, firemen, and other payrollers that could be found
upright, as the bars along Thompson Avenue had already been
open for hours, were dispatched to slap, tack, or stick reward
posters on anything inanimate or simply slow. Civilians had
joined the fray as well, poking under anything that might hide a
hundred-dollar cat. Upriver, those of the town's winos fortunate
enough to sleep indoors at the Rivertown Health Center had
tumbled out early to brave an unaccustomed sunshine as well,
lured by the wonderfully imaginable number of muscatel pints
a hundred dollars would bring. Even the city-controlled First
Bank of Rivertown's two employees, its compliant president and
his tottering mother, were poking under the shrubs around their
soiled stucco building as best they could.

Though it seemed as if all of Rivertown's citizenry who could
walk or crawl were out walking and crawling in search of the
cat, I was optimistic. I'd seen a cat, black like the whiskered
fugitive, skulking in the shade of my turret that morning. And
so, after setting out a bowl of milk, I was downstream along the

Willahock, jabbing the underbrush with the oversized pole net I bought to trap a drone, when my cell phone rang.

'Hold for Mr Brumsky,' the voice said. Soft Brazilian samba, perhaps Jobim, perhaps Gilberto, was playing in the background.

'You are Mr Brumsky,' I said to Leo.

'I know that, you idiot. I'm just testing out the message for when I get a secretary.'

'Are you contemplating hiring a secretary?'

'Of course not. Why would I need a secretary?' Leo was a provenance specialist, an expert in authenticating the histories of art auctioned by the major American houses, and from which he made hundreds of thousands of dollars. And because he respected the traditions of our youth, he was also a restaurateur, making almost nothing from running a peeling hot-dog trailer down the very Willahock River from where I was standing, looking for a cat.

He occasionally talked in riddles, he often said, to exercise his formidable brain and to try to confuse mine.

'Where are you now?' I asked, thinking that if he was at the trailer I'd zip over for a cool hot dog and a colder drink to wash it down. Leo lets me run a tab.

'No,' he said. 'The operative question for you to ask is: "Where have you been?"'

And so I asked, 'Where have you been?'

'At the barbershop.'

The conversation had descended into the third level of lunacy. Leo had been shaving the narrow fringe of his head that hadn't gone bald since junior year of high school. He had no need of barbering.

'Why were you there?' I asked.

'I was just passing by . . .' he said, prompting.

'And . . .?' I asked, obliging.

'I ran into Kowalski the Frenchman coming out.'

'He's back?' I said. 'Did he say why he left?'

'Nope, and as one shining dome to another, I didn't ask.'

Kowalski the Frenchman had become something of a minor mystery to those who paid attention to city hall. A longtime collector of street taxes from those bars, hock shops, and tattoo parlors not owned by the lizards that ran Rivertown, he'd disappeared suddenly the year before.

'You're saying his dome was shining?'

'No; that was a figure of speech,' Leo said. 'Even on such a hot day as this, he was wearing his beret.'

Some, less informed, figured Kowalski the Frenchman was at least half-French because he always wore a wool beret. The town's more devoted tavern habitués suspected different. They bought into the salacious rumor that had the totally bald Kowalski, a lifelong drinker of yeoman's dedication, passing out dead drunk in one of the town's honky-tonks some years earlier. The story had it that Kowalski's companions, equally hard drinkers but also men of mirth, thought it would be hilarious to gift Kowalski with a memento of his evening's drinking, and so they carried him, unconscious, to the closest of Rivertown's three tattoo parlors where the top of his bald head was adorned with a full color rendering of a man and a woman expressing horizontal affection.

The story further said Kowalski, at five-four even shorter than Leo, didn't become aware of the inking for several days, though it was obvious to even the most casual of taller passersby that the top of his head had become a naughty picture. It was only when one of the town's many hookers began shrieking in laughter that Kowalski became aware of his adornment.

It might, or might not, have been legend. What was certain was that even the town's most dedicated drinkers respected boundaries, and no one ever attempted to dislodge Kowalski's beret, even when the head beneath it was passed out on some bar surface. And when Kowalski disappeared, some wags opined that the constant fear of someone plucking away his beret had finally become unbearable, and that he lit out for more hospitable and perhaps permanently colder places where a year-round beret would not tempt curiosity.

But there was another rumor. He'd been the town's bagman, the guy in charge of collecting the cash-kickback street taxes that kept city hall fat from Rivertown's businesses, and some wondered if he'd been skimming from his collections and took off before he got caught. That rumor never got much play because he'd always been a loyal soldier and no word of missing money ever came from city hall.

'So what would the bald, bereted Kowalski need at the barber shop?' I asked Leo, doubling back to why he'd called.

'Why would *he*?' Leo asked, still riddling. 'I was intrigued. I went inside and with spectacular humor, said I wanted whatever Kowalski wanted. "Information," the first-chair guy said. "He just wanted information." "About what?" I asked. "About whether anybody else other than him had recently come home," the barber said. He said Kowalski asked it casually, but he might have been dead serious. Still, the barber didn't make much of it, thinking that Kowalski, having been away, wanted to reconnect with any old friends who'd also been away.'

A patch of black flashed out from beneath the scrub along the riverbank, fifty feet ahead. I yelled something into the phone about catching fur and clicked Leo away as I charged toward the fur racing up the rise toward the street. Pounding along the pavement, I didn't see the Rivertown squad car coming from city hall. It slammed to a stop.

'Hey!' the cop shouted out the open window, probably irate that he'd had to lift one of his feet onto the brake so quickly, so early in the morning.

'Jogging!' I yelled. I didn't want to be truthful, for fear they'd pull over, join the chase and, while not agile, still beat me to the cat.

I stopped at the edge of the park. Calling the ragged spit of land between my street and the thrumming honky-tonks and leering hookers along Thompson Avenue a park was, like most things uttered officially in Rivertown, a lie. There's nothing park-like about the decades-old tangle of fallen trees, snapped branches and mounded, rotting leaves. It might have been intended as a park once, but the lizards that ran the town never thought to spend to keep it clear, and so it had devolved into the sort of thorny bramble that could hide a black cat for hours, days, or even years. Or me, as it once had some long months before, when men with guns came looking for me.

I stood stock-still, breathing slowly, straining to hear any sound of a cat thrashing, but the only sound I heard was being made by other people poking in the brambles. The cat was gone. I gave up after fifteen minutes and went back across the street to the turret.

A man stood by my timbered door. He wore too-long blue jeans, weed-stained at the turned-up cuffs, and was sweating in a dirty tan trench coat that he might have slept in more than once. I'd

seen him around town two or three times in the past week, and
figured him as one of the denizens that slept under the viaduct.

He held out his hand. 'I'm a killer.'

'A killer?' I managed.

There was no telling what, gun-wise, was handy in the deep
pockets of his filthy coat. 'Then we'll sit on the bench down by
the river, where I'll have a chance of pushing you into the water
if you get to feeling murderous.'

He didn't smile. Neither did I. Closeup, the man looked
menacing enough to be a killer. About my height, reasonably
north of six feet, with dark hair and but the briefest lingering of
a shave done two or three days before, it wasn't his duds – the
dirty trench and the too-long jeans – that gave him the menace.
It was his eyes. They were dark, coal dark. And unblinking. They
were the eyes of a mad man looking out from absolute darkness,
a man who could see to kill without ever letting the light in.

We sat on the bench, him at one end, me at the other. 'Do I
look familiar?' he asked.

'You do not,' I said, angling to see if his coat pockets, now
that he was sitting, bulged from a gun. 'Though so many killers
are roaming around the Chicago area these days, it's hard to
remember them all.'

He nodded, didn't smile or blink his dark eyes. And, for too
long a moment, he said nothing more.

'What do you want?' I finally said.

'What are you doing with that?' he said, pointing to the pole
net I'd set down on the ground next to me.

'Chasing a cat,' I said.

'Your cat, or the black one whose picture is plastered on every
door, window, and windshield in town?'

'There's a hundred-dollar reward for that missing cat.'

'I'll pay you more.'

I looked more pointedly at his stained coat. 'Aren't you hot
in that thing?'

'You're asking if I have any money,' he said.

'It does come to mind.'

'I get chilled easily.'

'You don't seem cold now,' I said, tapping my forehead as a
gesture to the sweat beading on his.

'And you want to see if I'm carrying a weapon.' He stood up and took off the coat. He wore only a blue T-shirt underneath, ripped under one sleeve, and his jeans were tight enough to show he wasn't packing.

I gave him a nod and he slipped his coat back on.

He reached into the side pocket of the jeans and pulled out a rubber-banded tube of cash about the size of a fat cigarette. 'Two hundred dollars in twenties. You'd have to catch two cats to make that much.'

'To do what?'

'For openers, to tell me about your infamy.' He dropped the money in my lap.

My hand itched but I didn't reach for the dough. 'You'll pay me two hundred dollars just to hear about the Wilts case?' It was the only infamy I had, but it had been enough.

'Yes.'

'Why?'

'I need to be sure.'

'About what?'

'About you. If I am, I will pay you five hundred more, upfront, if you're willing to proceed.'

'I'll give you the short version for free,' I said, torn between not looking at the tube of money in my lap or the man's unblinking eyes. I focused on four empty milk jugs floating slowly by on the Willahock. Rivertown's recycler, a cousin of the mayor, operated upriver.

'I got accused of deliberately authenticating forged evidence in the trial of a crooked suburban mayor,' I said. 'I authenticated it, but I'd been fooled. It hit TV and the front pages, mostly because I was married to the daughter of one of Chicago's wealthiest industrialists. I got cleared within days, but news of my exoneration got buried in the middle of the papers and wasn't mentioned at all on television, so the taint stuck. My insurance investigation business tanked. I blamed my wife's prominence for my notoriety. I started drinking, became a self-pitying ass. She threw me out. I had it coming. I was living too large anyway – the Rolex, the used Mercedes.'

I gestured at the turret behind us. 'I'd inherited this stone cylinder because my mother's sisters didn't want its tax liability. It was the only shelter I had. I moved in, broke, a drying-out

drunk, thinking to renovate it, and myself, into something usable.'
I stood up, letting the little tube of cash fall to the ground. 'That's
what you get for free.'

'I really don't look familiar?' he said, remaining seated.

'You only look crazy, bundled up in this heat.'

'I have my own notoriety, though the reverse of yours. My
supposed crime didn't hit all the front pages, but my acquittal
made national news.' He paused, waiting for me to recognize him.

I shook my head. 'I don't know who you are.'

'They said I killed my wife,' he said, his eyes still hot on
mine. He smiled faintly. 'Even I said I killed her.'

'Yet here you are, walking around loose, after admitting you're
a murderer? Why walk to me?'

'You have experience with being falsely accused.'

'You just said you confessed. Nothing false about that.'

'You knew my girlfriend.'

'Who was she?'

'My name is Martin Tripp.'

Despite the summer heat, a sudden chill came over me, and I
clenched my fists to keep from shaking. 'I want nothing to do
with you,' I said. 'Your lawyer did what he signed on to do, but
I don't have to sign on for anything.'

I walked away from him, up the rise toward my door. Ahead,
the flashing neons of Thompson Avenue taunted me with their
vibrance – Rivertown thrumming, gaudy, wicked, bright, but most
of all, alive. Behind me, Tripp taunted, too alive as well. Life
was everywhere.

Except for Sara Jansen. Stabbed in life, scorned in death, she
was alive no more.

THREE

The case had been tried only four months before and the
outrage of Tripp's acquittal was fresh in my memory, as
it must have been in tens of thousands of memories across
the country. But like many in Rivertown, I had an even stronger

reason for being disgusted. Tripp was right; I'd known the victim, if only as well as I wanted to know her, which was slightly. Sara Jansen was prickly, hard to like, but she was a Rivertown girl.

Tripp's lawyer was Reginald Aplon by name but known as 'Apples' by many, and even more telling as 'Trail Apples' by those familiar with horse droppings. He was greasy, slick, and daring, and demanded speedy adjudication of Tripp's case, so anxious was he to try a novel strategy to put himself on the national map.

The trial of Martin Tripp, charged with first-degree murder, commenced a little over five months after the killing. The evidence against him was overwhelming. His hand was slashed in what prosecutors called an aggressive wound. His fingerprints – and his alone – were found, along with his blood, on the murder weapon secreted beneath their mattress. The cigarette-smoking neighbor who'd witnessed the house lighting up, room by room, almost an hour and a half after another neighbor heard a woman scream, had indicated a time delay needed to stage a ransacking before the police were called, to make the killing appear like a robbery gone bad. The bag of the purportedly stolen jewelry containing Tripp's fingerprints – and again, Tripp's alone – that was found hidden in the kitchen. And finally, and most damning, Tripp's own confession that he had, in fact, stabbed Sara. The evidence pointing to Tripp's guilt was monumental, and most in the legal community were confident that Apples Aplon, a strip-mall lawyer of no repute, would conjure up no miracle to counter it all.

To no one's surprise, Apples announced a defense of temporary insanity, putting forth the notion that Tripp had fallen into a deep, drug-induced sleep in front of the television in the den, a haze from which he'd awakened fully only when he found himself sitting on the floor of the master bedroom, cradling the head of the lifeless Sara. Believing that he'd killed her in a stoned craze, obviously rattled, Tripp had mistakenly called a neighbor, Thomas Chan, before hanging up and calling the police, to scream to come over right away, his fogged mind clutching wildly at dodging responsibility with a hurriedly concocted, wobbly story of a break-in by a short man wearing a long coat and a hat. He'd hid the knife beneath the mattress and her jewelry in the kitchen, and gone room by room, making the house look like it had been ransacked by a robber. And then, under relentless questioning by Detective Slage, Tripp's mind swung wildly back, and he confessed to killing Sara.

Apples Aplon stipulated to all of it, as would any lawyer building an insanity defense. But then he deviated from the expected, and so began the second killing of Sara Jansen – the killing of her character. Martin Tripp had snapped, Apples said, in a drug-induced haze, but not without some justification. Sara had triggered it as surely as if she'd packed poor Martin full of dynamite and then lit the fuse. For months, she'd pushed Martin relentlessly into madness with her reckless spending, demanding that he work more hours to bring home more money to pay her credit card charges for luxurious furnishings, expensive women's clothing, and the pristine Mercedes that only she was allowed to drive.

As evidence of the magnitude of her wild spending, Apples introduced Sara's credit card statements. At the time of her death, Sara had outstanding credit card charges of $105,700, charges that she and Martin could never hope to pay off from their low-wage jobs, charges that it was Martin's responsibility to find a way to pay off. He had to get his oar in the water, she screamed, and row, row, row. She hammered at him relentlessly, daytime, nighttime, even in his dreams.

Apples brought forward witness after witness to testify that Sara had been a shrill, despicable, and demanding woman. Supposed friends, acquaintances, shop clerks, restaurant waiters and waitresses testified in a steady, damning stream that nothing poor Martin did – not his working long hours, not his acquiescence to her every whim, not his yielding to her incessant tirades – and by God, there were plenty of those – seemed to satisfy the hellish fury that was Sara Jansen. In desperation, Apples said, almost weeping though with dry eyes, Martin even took to gambling, so anxious was he to prove worthy to the ever-demanding Sara Jansen. And he failed at that, too, the doomed sap. He racked up more debt at ruinous interest rates that he could never hope to repay. No wonder he turned to find respite in drugs.

Martin Tripp, Apples pronounced again and again, was a bomb built bigger and bigger by the vicious Sara, primed to explode.

And explode he did, Apples railed, on the evening of the unfortunate but understandable passing of Sara Jansen. Fatigue had overcome Martin Tripp; he'd sought relief that night, as he had so often, in the marijuana and oxy that were found in his bloodstream. That last night, her last night, Martin Tripp had collapsed in front of a television, hushed so that it would not bring forth yet another attack from Sara.

Close to midnight, Martin Tripp jerked partially awake from another drug and fatigue-distorted nightmare of Sara's verbal lashing. Horribly muddled and fearful, he staggered into the kitchen, to the seven-hundred-dollar knives, and then to the master bedroom. Martin Tripp, dazed and crazed by drugs, weakened by abuse, finally lifted his oar, the one that Sara found so futile, and so very understandably, smacked her into oblivion with it.

Apples had witnesses to justify Tripp's behavior. He brought forth three paid psychiatrists who testified to the probability of somnambulistic homicide, a kind of sleepwalking, unrealizing murder. The prosecuting attorneys sat back stunned; they'd never heard the term, let alone used in such a preposterous defense. Later, it would be reported that none of the defense psychiatrists had actually encountered such a condition either, nor had they ever found cases of it being documented. They'd only read of its potential likelihood. Neither Apples, nor his shrinks, thought to present that particular nugget to the jury, nor did the stunned prosecution bother to research anything about the unheard-of theory.

And so, Apples thundered in closing, the real victim in this case was not the relentless Sara Jansen but rather the hapless, long-suffering Martin. She took an imperfect man – what man is perfect? Apples asked slyly – and did her own slashing. Not with a knife, but with cutting words, ever so equally lethal. She cut at Martin hour after hour, day after day, demanding this, demanding that, badgering him about that oar in the water. It was he who'd been irrevocably damaged, cut by cut by cut, by the razor-edged tongue of the demanding Sara Jansen until he could no longer tell day from night, real from unreal, dream from reality.

Knowledgeable courtroom watchers gave Apples Aplon's novel defense of somnambulistic homicide a zero chance of success, but as the jury's deliberations went into a second day, their tongues began to cluck. And by the time an exhausted jury filed into the courtroom at the end of a third day, the drawn looks on their faces and their averted eyes froze those watchers' tongues to the roofs of their mouths.

The jury had bought it. Or rather, two of them had. Not just the expected defense of temporary insanity, but the larger notion that a somnambulistic homicide was justified, that Martin Tripp, drug-walking, sleepwalking, had snapped from the abuse heaped upon him by his witch of a girlfriend and, understandably, had lashed back. Tripp was judged not guilty by those two jurors, by reason of temporary insanity, and those two were all that were needed to prevent the unanimity needed to convict Martin Tripp of murder.

Several of the jurors who'd voted to convict were outraged enough to consent to interviews after Tripp walked out a free man. During their deliberations, the two voting not guilty hadn't been bothered why Tripp, unencumbered by legal and marital obligations, hadn't simply walked away from such an obviously toxic relationship. Later, it would come out that one voiced her belief that aliens were occupying two cities nearby, though she couldn't name which two, and that they might have influenced Martin. The other merely believed in forgiveness, and Martin Tripp had clearly suffered enough.

Incredibly, Tripp was not remanded to anything. Some said the judge was so sickened by the trial that he broke tradition and did not order him up for psychiatric treatment of any kind. Martin Tripp, admitted killer, walked out of the courtroom a completely free man.

The outrage at the verdict broke big, coast to coast. It was universal. Editorial writers everywhere raged at the outcome. But another day passed, and another, and other outrages replaced Martin Tripp in the news.

And Sara Jansen – prickly, difficult Sara Jansen – was soon forgotten, too.

FOUR

Martin Tripp returned at eight the next morning.

He sat on the bench, as if content to look at the ducks paddling between the fresh plastic debris set free during the night. Martin Tripp was debris, too. I let him sit for an hour, hoping he'd leave. When he didn't, I walked down to the river.

He wore the same filthy tan trench coat and weed-stained jeans. The only thing fresh about him was another day's growth of whiskers on his unshaved face.

He didn't stand. I didn't sit.

'Have you cooled down since yesterday?' he said.

'I refreshed my memory of your trial. You should die.'

He opened his mouth a little, perhaps to speak, perhaps to smirk.

I swatted at the air in front of it. 'Your jury was crazy, but sane people know you killed her.'

He bent over, as if searching for the little tube of money he'd dropped onto my lap the afternoon before. It wasn't there. I'd come down an hour after I'd walked away from him, to pick it up before some prowling cat hunter spotted it.

Straightening up, he smiled faintly, smug in thinking I'd taken his money and accepted his contract. That little tube of money was in my pocket now, waiting to be jammed down Tripp's throat.

'You're reconsidering?' he asked.

'I don't think you were crazy,' I said. 'I think it was premeditated. That business of ransacking the house, leaving your fingerprints on your own knife, choosing an obvious hiding place for the bag of jewelry in the kitchen? It was all to make people think you'd lost your marbles. But crazy? You weren't crazy.'

Oddly, he nodded. 'You are right about one thing. Some said it was the jury that was crazy. Still, her acquaintances and our neighbors testified that Sara was horrible to me. She never let up.'

'One news picture I can't force out of my mind is of you, holding your court clothes in a hanger bag, dressed fashionably in better jeans than you're now sporting, smirking exactly as you are now, strutting out of the courthouse after being acquitted, accompanied by a gorgeous woman. Nothing crazy about you that day, Tripp. You'd just conned a jury. At least now you don't look to be conning anyone. You're spending your nights sleeping under trees or in alleys, and that's a punishment for which I'm delighted.'

I took out his little roll of twenties and dropped it on the ground in front of him.

He nodded almost absent-mindedly and let it lie. He turned to look down the river. 'I'm not sure I did it,' he said, after a moment.

'Maybe you are crazy after all.' I stepped closer, to loom and block his vision. 'You confessed. Your whole defense was based on justifying why you did what you admitted doing. And then you walked, free and clear. Now you're thinking you didn't do it?'

He looked down at the two hundred dollars. 'I don't remember much,' he said.

'The marijuana? The oxy? The pent-up abuse? Con's over, Tripp.'

He met my eyes. 'I wasn't in the den, watching television. The TV was on, but I'd left it on for show in case Sara woke up and was listening. I was a couple of blocks away. I'd gone for a walk—'

I held up my hand to stop his words. 'Why are you here?'

'I came home,' he said, ignoring me. 'At some point, afterward, I went into the master bedroom, saw Sara. I sat on the floor with her, held her. I called a neighbor for help but hung up quickly because I got frantic – I was going to die because of something I didn't remember doing. And so I went room to room, making the place look like it had been ransacked. Only after that did I call the police. All throughout, it was like I was seeing everything through a fog.'

'Did anyone see you when you were out for this supposed walk?'

He looked down at the water, saying nothing.

'I'll take that for a no,' I said, 'but at the very least, why not feed this baloney to the police after they caught your other lies? Why not admit you panicked and set your house to make it look robbed and then say you were out walking? Why confess?'

'I didn't trust my memory. Still don't. Maybe more happened when I returned that I don't remember.'

'Crap.'

'I told you: I was a couple of blocks away.'

'Out for a walk? C'mon, Tripp.'

'Visiting a neighbor.'

'At midnight?'

'That woman you saw in the courthouse photo. Look, Sara always went to bed early; I used to sneak out, OK? A couple of blocks away. That night, afterward at her place, I fell asleep. When I woke up, I was alone in her bedroom. I got dressed, walked around the neighborhood to try to clear my head, went home, and found Sara . . . I think.'

'You're not sure?'

'Take the two hundred dollars at least.'

'Where was this woman, this alibi, when you were asleep in her bed?'

'Somewhere else in her house. I didn't look for her to tell her I was leaving. Too much dope, too much . . . I just wanted to get away.'

'Why not introduce this woman you visited at trial?'

'My lawyer said I still could have killed Sara after I got home. He said the woman wouldn't be believable. The jury would think she was lying, giving me an alibi out of love.'

'You never thought your lawyer was just out to make a name for himself with that defense of somnambulistic homicide?'

Tripp shrugged. 'It worked.'

'And now you want me to prove you didn't kill Sara?'

'You're like me, falsely accused.'

'You confessed, got off on crazy. I was exonerated.'

'You knew Sara.'

'In one study hall.'

'She said you were nice, that not many kids were nice,' he said. 'I might be innocent, just like you. Maybe the real killer is still out there. Maybe we owe Sara another look.'

'Based on a few words we exchanged, back in a high-school study hall?' I looked out at the river, but I was really looking for an out. I hadn't known Sara Jansen, not really, and remembered little of her except her caustic personality.

'A quick consideration is all I'm asking,' he nudged.

'A consideration?' I asked, turning back to him.

'She seemed scared.'

'Of what?'

'No idea. If Sara didn't want to tell you something, she didn't.'

'That woman you visited—'

'Will you forget the woman? It was a fling. My lawyer said our best defense was insanity and he was right.'

'Change your name, get a job, move on. This isn't for me, Tripp.'

'The oxy and the weed in my system could account for my paranoia, for my thinking I really did kill her when maybe I didn't.' He held up his hand to show a long white scar running across his palm. 'Who wraps his fingers around the blade part when stabbing someone? But there again, I'm not sure of anything.'

'You yelled out about an intruder, a short man wearing a long coat and a hat.'

He looked out at the river and for a few moments he didn't say anything. 'I was crazy nuts, making up anything I could,' he said finally. 'I didn't know what I was doing.'

'It's over.'

'It's not over. I can't get a job so I can afford a place to live. I sleep in freight yards and under viaducts. This next winter I'll spend in shelters with winos. Talk about drug addicts? There are plenty of those, along with perverts, out in the night. I want my life back.'

He picked up the money tube I'd dropped in his lap, and pulled an envelope out of his trench coat. He held both out to me.

The envelope was from a suburban water district in Iowa, and was addressed to someone else. It had been crumpled and then smoothed. He must have fished it out of the trash or found it on a sidewalk or in a dumpster. Inside were five one-hundred-dollar bills.

'Five hundred,' he said, 'plus the two hundred rolled up. It's all I have.'

'Where'd you get that much money?'

'Best you don't know. Find out what Sara was afraid of.'

'Who's the woman you were with?'

'Forget her.'

'Her name?'

'Julianna Wynton. She moved. She was a renter. She has a wide sales territory. She can live anyplace in it and still service her customers.'

'You don't know where she is now?'

He shook his head.

'She's the woman in the courthouse photo?' I said.

'She's angry that we're going no place.'

'Was she in love with you?'

'It wasn't her that scared Sara.' He looked around like he was being watched.

'You know something,' I said. 'You have an idea who scared Sara.'

'See what you can find out. Ask around Rivertown, see if anyone knows what might have frightened her. Be upfront, tell people you're asking for me. All I want is to find out what scared Sara.'

I handed the five hundred in the envelope back but kept the rolled-up two hundred. 'You're worth two cats to me, no more. I'll take a quick look. What's Sara's mother's name and address?'

He gave them to me and jammed the water bill envelope into his trench coat.

'One more thing,' I said. 'Call your lawyer, tell him it's OK for him to talk to me.'

'That's not necessary,' he said.

'Then no deal,' I said.

He walked away without another word.

FIVE

Although it was still early, the day had turned hot, and I'd turned hotter.

Tripp made me feel dirty for not throwing his two hundred dollars back in his face and walking away. But fighting that was my memory of caustic, lonely Sara Jansen, and how maybe Tripp was right about her deserving someone to take a last look at her death. And so I rationalized a trip to Kutz's clearing, thinking some redemption could be had by using some of the dirty loot to square my tab with Leo. And maybe enjoy a hot dog, some barbecue cheese fries, and a soft drink as long as I was there anyway.

The lunch rush was still sixty minutes away. Two of Ma Brumsky's spry septuagenarian pals were scrubbing down the picnic tables. Both were attired in pink poodle skirts and pink T-shirts imprinted with a rendering of the wienie wagon, and swayed in time with the soft sambas playing through speakers in the trees. Leo did not trifle easily with the traditions of the hot dog trailer he and I had loved since grammar school, but introducing sambas played to Leo's soul, and cleanliness was an innovation he insisted be brought to the pigeon-splattered picnic tables. Leo did that for hygiene, but thought also that scrubbing tables would keep Ma and her elderly, though libidinous, Polish lady friends busy. When left unsupervised, they too often indulged penchants for earthy delights like pornographic movies, pole dancing and skinny dipping. Leo hoped that hard scrubbing outdoors, in the somewhat pure air of Rivertown, would have a cleansing effect on their baser instincts as well.

It was a faint hope. The elderly darlings scrubbed relentlessly, perhaps too relentlessly, because it gave them proximity to murmur lewd suggestions to the young construction men who came for lunch. And rarely did the dears wait for a table to get dirty. Often, I enjoyed seeing one or more of them, rag and Lysol spray in hand, squeeze herself between a couple of muscular young men who'd just sat down, at a table that had just been scrubbed. For me, elderly ladies fighting the good fight against aging was optimism, and it was marvelous.

Leo, resplendent this day in mustard-colored chinos and a tropically colored rayon shirt infested with purple coconuts, pink parrots, and smiling yellow snakes, was behind the order window, along with Ma Brumsky.

I strutted up like I was packing money, and said, 'One tube steak, barbecue cheese fries, one small diet soda, and your counsel at one of the immaculate picnic tables.'

'The hot dogs are cooled,' he said, with his usual pride.

'Like always?' I asked, knowing the answer. Kutz had never believed in hot dogs that were literally, well . . . hot, preferring to cut his propane costs and serve his offerings lukewarm. And so that tradition, among many, would continue after Kutz, an agile lothario in his eighties, moved to cohabit a double-wide with a much younger woman in Florida.

'You betcha,' he said, of the tradition.

I passed five of Martin Tripp's twenties through the order window.

'Whoa!' Leo said, as startled as if I, perpetually impoverished, had slipped through five pythons.

'To square my account,' I said, with pride of my own.

He put the twenties in the cash box and slammed the lid fast, as if he feared they would escape.

'No change at all?' I inquired, knowing it was rhetorical.

'I don't keep track of your charges, which is to your benefit, but I'll apply what I think is appropriate toward your past and future purchases,' he said, picking up my tray and stepping out the end door. We sat at a table almost dried of disinfectant.

I took a bite of the hot dog. Once again, it was blessedly the very same as when Kutz ran the trailer.

'You'd be surprised at how cheap those things are,' he said of my hot dog, like that was supposed to be of comfort.

Lukewarm, chewy, with just the right amount of brownish red food coloring to disguise its unmentionable composition, Kutz never would say where he got his hot dogs, or what they were comprised of. So long as no teeth were cracked by the egregiously large chunks of hooves or other matter that were sometimes found suspended in them, Kutz's hot dogs were fine enough for all who came to the clearing.

'Martin Tripp,' I said through the food.

Leo arched his formidable eyebrows just a little. 'Martin Tripp?'

'He came to see me yesterday afternoon and again this morning.'

His eyebrows stayed up. 'You know Martin Tripp?'

'Never met the man before.'

'Never saw him around town, back in the day?' he asked. 'He ran The Hamburger for a while.'

'He's older than us,' I said, 'and don't forget, I lived in Chicago when I was going to city college and then to open an office.

When Amanda and I married, I moved to her house at Crystal Waters.'

'How about recently? Did you recognize him from seeing him walking around town, the past few days?'

I had to stop talking, to chase something tooth-sized to the front of my mouth. I picked it out. Mercifully, it wasn't a tooth of mine or, for that matter, anyone else's. I flicked it on the ground, preferring to not investigate further.

'I did,' I said, 'but I figured him from the health center or the viaduct.'

'Why did he come to you?'

'He sees us as kindred, both falsely accused. He wants me to see if he's innocent.'

Leo is totally bald and very pale-skinned, but his eyebrows are thick and dark. And while they'd been slightly elevated, now they shot up like they were frantic to escape his face. 'He has doubts that he killed her? He confessed. His lawyer even said he did it.'

'Tripp thinks I should help him, because Sara once said I was nice to her. I told him we only sat next to each other in a study hall. She had a lousy home life; mine was ever-changing, being shuffled from aunt to aunt, so we had that, sort of, in common. She was acerbic, condescending, definitely not one of my favorite people. I never thought of her after graduation, at least not until she got murdered.'

'I'd see them around town, but separately,' he said. 'Like I said, Tripp managed The Hamburger for a few years. She worked part-time as a cashier at the grocery and part-time at the bank here.

'According to the papers during Tripp's trial, she moved away and, soon after, he moved away to join her.'

'Her first, then him. I read that,' I said. 'When, exactly?'

'Early last year. Maybe January or February,' he said. 'That they connected was the talk of the town during the trial. He was good looking; her, not so much. Remember her ridiculous hair?'

'Giant curls, one on each side.'

'Mickey Mouse ears, they called them,' he said.

'I'm sure she hated that,' I said.

'But she never gave in and changed her hair,' he said.

'She was tough.'

'Tripp's really serious about wanting you to find out if he really murdered her, after he already confessed? The jury was right. He's crazy.'

'He thinks something frightened her at the end. He wants me to find out what it was.'

'This makes no sense, Dek.'

'He gave me two hundred bucks,' I said.

'Half of which I now have?' he asked, grinning. 'That part makes sense.'

'I figure it will cover my tab for the next several years.'

'The way you earn, it will have to,' he said. Then added, 'Poor Sara.'

'What do you know about her?'

'I think she lived in the old factory district, the poorest of our poor districts. She worked hard. I'd see her at the food store when Ma would send me for something. Sometimes she'd say hello, sometimes she'd act like we never saw each other in school. She was a gnarled kid.'

'Any friends?'

'I never saw her with anybody, but I never saw her except at the grocery store.'

'Not at the bank?'

'I bank in the city.'

'I bank here,' I said.

'People do, who don't have money,' he said, flashing his huge white teeth.

'I've rationalized giving her a day of my time for Tripp's two hundred.'

'You'll tug at loose ends to see what unravels. It won't be just a day.'

He is my friend. He knows me. And so for a time, we sat quietly and looked out at the plastic containers shimmering in the Willahock, lazing downriver to be collected in wealthier suburbs, until finally I said, 'Speaking of Kowalski the Frenchman . . .?'

'The bagman returns, same as Tripp.'

'And he left Rivertown last year, right?'

'And about the same time, if I remember right. Early last year, January or February, too. It's old-home week in Rivertown.' A smile formed on his narrow face, and expanded into another full-toothed grin. 'Not to mention all the cats that have suddenly appeared,' he said. 'People are swarming city hall with black cats, more than I thought possible.'

'For a C-note, it's no wonder,' I said.

The lunch rush was about to start. He stood up. 'Kowalski's a real life lesson,' he said.

'In what?' I asked the man of occasional riddles.

'Got to be careful in life,' he said. 'Otherwise, you end up tattooed.'

SIX

R ivertown's factory district was death.
It had once hissed and pounded, six days a week, from machines molding plastic and rubber, and presses stamping metal. Then those machines went overseas, where hissing and pounding could be done much cheaper. Nowadays, that part of town didn't make much noise at all, except when the wind got up and rattled the rusted For Sale signs outside the shuttered factories and abandoned bungalows. Sara Jansen's mother's place was there.

I crept the Jeep over a heaved-up rail spur and followed a weed-covered road. Other than kids coming to break windows, few had reason to visit the old factory district.

The brown brick bungalow was identical to its neighbors, right down to the rusted For Sale sign in front, except the windows weren't shattered and the weeds in the right half of the front yard had been cut, a month or so earlier, with the rusty push mower leaned alongside the house.

The woman who came to the screen door was gray-haired, gray-pallored, and drunk. 'Mrs Jansen?' I asked.

'Been called worsh,' she slurred through the torn door screen.

'I'm here about your daughter.'

'Dead.'

'My condolences. I'm wondering how she seemed the days before . . .'

She scrunched up her face, trying to understand. 'Before?'
'Before she died.'

'She up and left me years before she up and left here. Rented a basement room after high school, dunno where. Worked two jobs, I'll shay that. Grocery and bank, bank and grocery. No time for me.'

'Who were her friends?'

'What is it with you people?'

'Who?'

'Somebody else came, just a few days ago. Tol' him same—' She started crying and went back into the darkness of her house.

Food World was the only grocery remaining in Rivertown. The other two folded when the last of the factories closed up. The manager's name was Roman, and I'd see him now and again when I shopped there.

'I'm here about Sara Jansen's insurance,' I lied.

'A little late, isn't it? She's been dead for almost a year.'

'Closing a file,' I said.

'A good worker,' he said. 'She started when she was in high school.'

'You knew her well?'

'As well as anyone, I suppose, which means I didn't know her at all.'

'Kept to herself?'

'She was difficult to like. People avoided her.'

'Like her neighbors out in Weston.'

'What I read in the papers sounded like savagery, them turning on her like that. I always suspected she was insecure, and wanted to keep people away.'

'I just came from her mother's place.'

'Bad?'

'Bad place to grow up. Factory district.'

'She was a good worker. Determined to get ahead.'

'She worked here until she left town?'

'End of January, last year.'

'Do you know where she lived after high school?' I asked.

'Her mother's address was on her application, but she moved after graduation. I don't know where.'

'Anybody ever come looking for her, close to when she got killed?'

'Why do you need to know that for insurance?'

'Closing a file?'

He laughed at my obvious lie, and then his face turned serious. 'Nobody ever came looking for Sara Jansen.'

The First Bank of Rivertown sits in a squat, single-story dirty white stucco building where two crooked roads meet, just off Thompson Avenue. That it is named the First Bank is deceptive because there can be no second or third bank. The lizards that run our corrupt little burg would not permit it.

It is a laundry. It washes the cash the lizards' bagmen collect from the tonks, pinball parlors, pawnshops, and every other enterprise in Rivertown that they don't own, along with the excessive cash fees the city charges for business licenses, building renovation permits, and the like. Supposedly, the cash is then used to purchase hard assets like out-of-town real estate, to be held until it is safe to sell them to other entities controlled by the lizards, to sell again when it is safe to return the cash to city hall. Everyone in town knows it and no one questions it. It is Rivertown.

Because it is a laundry, it seeks no retail depositors. It doesn't want the bother of petty savings and checking accounts, but will provide them because that's what bank examiners expect normal banks to do. I have a savings account there to keep one hundred and four dollars and some odd cents. The First Bank does not send out statements so I do not know how much interest I earn, if any, but I have hope that, should I live long enough, my nest egg will grow to one hundred and five dollars.

Because the First Bank is not a hub of retail activity, it has long been staffed only by a son and his mother. They are distantly related to the people that run the town. I guessed the mother was in her eighties and the son somewhere in his late fifties.

The bank was dimly lit as usual when I walked in. Like city hall and the other municipal enterprises, it was run best in shadows.

I went directly to the president's desk. It is twenty feet from the teller line and it is the only desk in the lobby. The president put down his crossword puzzle in such a way that I could not read its heading, but I knew from a past visit that it came from a magazine entitled *Just for Kids*. It was possible he was still working on the same puzzle.

'Yes?' he said, looking startled. Whether it was from my presence, a fellow he knew to have no money, or the fact that anyone at all had entered the bank, I could not tell.

'Sara Jansen,' I said.

He stiffened noticeably. 'She no longer works here,' he said, but only after a minute.

'She's dead,' I said.

'Like I said, she no longer works here,' he said again. 'What do you want?'

The bank was cool, perhaps even cold, but he'd started sweating. I decided to roll dice against the beads of moisture on his forehead.

'I want to know why she quit,' I said.

'Oh boy,' he said, inappropriately.

'Why?'

'Nothing.' He looked away.

'Wasn't she a good worker?'

He slumped back in his chair like I'd just drained all his blood. 'She worked when Mother couldn't. We're required to have more than one person in the bank so I can go to the bathroom.'

'Things were good?'

'I'm usually fine,' he said. 'It's just that sometimes when I drink coffee—'

'No,' I said, cutting off what was sure to become an unnecessary description of his bladder. 'I meant was she a good employee?'

'She was at the teller counter where Mother is now.'

I looked across the lobby. His mother was perched on her high stool, but her head was down on the marble. She snored softly.

'We don't have many customers,' he said.

'Why did Sara leave?'

'Moving to Weston, she said.'

'January, last year,' I said.

'It was cold.'

I left quietly, to not disturb the dozing mother.

SEVEN

'd gotten nowhere in Rivertown. Sara Jansen had quit her jobs and the town without leaving behind any ripples or friends. I didn't wonder if Martin Tripp had known that. I figured that he had.

Weston was just eleven miles west; close enough, perhaps, to provide answers. Midday traffic on the breezer was thin and I got to its downtown in thirty minutes.

I'd been there several times over the years. Twice to investigate suspicious insurance claims back when I had insurance company clients, and more than twice to visit the Lookout, a local bar that served great microbrews and superb chili.

I'd always been charmed by its historic downtown. I used to like to think it was just like Rivertown's, minus the peeling architecture, thrumming tonks, winking hookers, and drunks dozing on the sidewalks. But Weston was changing. What purports to be progress was rubbing some of Weston's quaintness away. Half of the centuries-old brick and wood storefronts had been replaced by modern abominations of sleek stone, shiny metal, and dark glass. Gone were the hardware, paint, and a dozen other mom-and-pops that had stood adequately for decades. They'd been replaced by nonsense including at least three cosmetics stores, a day spa, and two olive-oil emporia, though why folks would want to squeeze olives for oil instead of tossing them in the air and catching them in their mouths has always been a puzzle to me. Mercifully, the Lookout still stood, beckoning as ever. Having had a hot dog for breakfast, I showed restraint and did not stop.

Sara and Martin's subdivision was three miles south of the downtown. It was an enormous development of modest single-story homes that had sprung up from farmland several decades before. Their former residence, a red-brick and cedar, ranch-style, was on Kentbridge Circle, a cul-de-sac four blocks in.

The cedar siding had gone chalky from lack of staining, and the lawn was a beige blight, dead from summer heat and no watering. A For Sale sign listing a foreclosure outfit, as weatherworn as any in the factory district of Rivertown, was stuck in bare dirt ten feet from the front door. Murder sites were not grabbers in any real estate market.

Two plumbing service vans were parked on the cracked asphalt drive at the right. Their rear doors were open, as was the front door to the house. I walked in.

The living room was to the right, furnished with two pale blue settees, a pair of dark end tables, and an ornate, carved white-and-gold oval table. The furniture was dulled with dust. There were no vases, framed pictures, or the sorts of small tchotchkes that clutter most houses. Sticky-fingered workmen, repairmen, and perhaps just outright thieves had found something worth snatching in the murder house.

The sound of voices came down a hall. I followed it into the kitchen.

Two plumbers stood in front of a wall that had been cut open. One looked at me and shrugged. 'You'd best take this place off the market for a while,' he said, mistaking me for the planter of the foreclosure sign.

'Burst pipe?' I asked. The small bookshelf, where the jewelry must have been found behind cookbooks, was barren. A roll of paper towels, yellowed now, still rested in a holder above the counter next to the sink. The doors on the oak cabinets were closed, but I imagined that they were empty. Like the living room, nothing small enough to steal easily would have remained.

'Burst pipe,' he said.

I trotted out one of my most usable, and most used, lies. 'I'm from insurance,' I said.

'Don't know who you can blame for the pipes,' the first plumber said. 'Water's shut off now but whenever it was, it was too late. Nobody drained the pipes. No heat, pipes freeze and break. Real estate company told us to fix. If you ask me, there's too much work to be done here to bring it back up to snuff, and even then, there's the ghosts.'

'Nobody wants to buy a murder house,' I said, and told him I had to look around.

'Help yourself, but be careful. The water from the pipes rotted parts of the floor.'

'This whole place is rotten,' the second plumber said. 'Rotten with dead.'

As if to prove his point, the floor beneath the carpet in the hall was spongy as I walked into the den and opened the door to the garage. It was empty except for one rake with bent tines that hung on a hook.

Like the other rooms, the den was dusty and smelled of being closed up too long. Two plaid chairs faced a mahogany wall-shelving unit. A cable dangled in the space in the center, empty now of the television Tripp switched on to make his wife think he was home. As with the living room and the kitchen, nothing small enough to be a grisly memento remained.

The first two doors past the living and dining rooms opened to spare bedrooms. The drawers that Tripp had dumped onto the carpets had been put back but their contents and the clothing that had been in the closets was gone.

The master bedroom was large, and had windows that faced the end and back of the house. The bed had been taken apart, and the dark Queen Anne headboard and brown metal frame leaned against the wall. The forensics team would have taken the mattress and box spring, between which Martin had attempted to hide the murder knife, for further examination and possible introduction at trial.

One long, low dresser was set against the wall opposite the entry. Its drawers were stacked beside it, empty. Another dresser stood at a right angle to it, its drawers stacked empty as well.

There were two closets, side by side. Empty now, I imagined both of them chock full of her clothes, leaving little room for his shirts and slacks. It was her house; she'd paid for it, she'd told one and all according to the trial reporting, but I saw those empty closets as he must have seen them: all for her, little for him. The thought shocked me, and I thought I ought to feel ashamed. He'd killed her. He'd confessed. Yet the image of a doped-up man, later cornered in a courtroom by testimony after testimony of how compliant and hapless he'd been, was strong. I pushed the image away. The man had confessed. It trumped everything.

They'd not torn up the carpet. I'm no expert on body blood volumes, but the stain spreading from where the bed legs marked the carpet was dark and enormous and spoke to the severity of the cut. The newspapers reported she'd been stabbed once in the center of the chest, severing her aorta, but they'd said nothing about how long she lived after being cut. The heart stops pumping at death, and that large stain might have signified that she'd sat slumped back against the mattress, alive, for some long time. Or the stain could have signified that the blood loss had been sudden and massive. I could only hope that she'd died quickly and not sat there, watching the life ebb out of her.

I stood stock-still, trying to divine what had happened in that bedroom the night Sara Jansen had been killed. It was a fool's game. Nothing could be learned from emptied dressers and stained carpeting.

I probably didn't stand there for more than a minute or two, but I began to shiver. The room was cold and full of death, and the plaster on the walls and the stain on the floor seemed like they wanted to scream.

I hurried out the front door and into the welcoming heat.

EIGHT

Neighbors know, more often than not.

I went door to door, just as if I were peddling things people didn't want, working outward from Sara's house at the end of the cul-de-sac. No one answered my knock at the first house to the left, but a frazzled young woman with sweat-dampened hair came to the door at the second. Screaming kids were in her background, and a green, thick fluid, perhaps upchucked peas from one of her darlings, was creeping, lava-like, down the top of her white knit shirt.

'Maybe not a good time to ask about Sara Jansen?' I asked, perceptively.

She slammed the door.

A man in his late sixties was scraping the underside of a lawnmower in the open garage of the next house. 'Sara Jansen, I didn't know. Hearing her scream at that Martin Tripp was enough.' He glanced at my card. 'I saw you spent a bit of time inside her place. Insurance matter?' He grinned. 'Uh huh, no doubt.'

I couldn't think of any new lie that would work better than the old, so I just waited him out, hoping he'd talk. People hate silences, and often they try to fill them.

He gave the silence a minute and gave up waiting for truth. 'Damn shame about her, though. Martin seemed like a nice guy, though we didn't get to know him after he moved in.'

'Later?' I said.

'She moved in first of last year, then he came along, not that long after. Never did understand that story, but they were here less than a year. They were younger. She was a screamer, like I said. We could hear her giving him holy hell. That's when he was home, which usually he wasn't. According to the newspapers after the stabbing, he was working long hours at some fast-food place.' He shrugged. 'And I read that he gambled, though I don't know when he had the time.'

I thanked him and went on. Nobody was home at the next two homes on that side so I went back to Sara's house to work the other side.

A middle-aged woman in a yellow house dress answered the door next to Sara's house.

'I knew Sara too well, actually,' she said.

'You didn't like her?'

'Couldn't stand her. She was brutal to Martin, just brutal, actually. Screamed at him every waking minute he was home. I could hear her even with my windows closed. I'm surprised he didn't go homicidal long before, actually.'

'Did you talk to her much?'

'Any minute with that woman was a minute lost to no good, actually,' she said. 'Sara didn't have friends, and I testified to that in court. I'm glad Martin got off. No one deserves to die like she did, but she did bring it on herself, actually.'

'Did she appear agitated in the days before her murder?'

'Well, Sara was always agitated, actually.'

I thanked her and turned to leave.

'What's this really about?' she asked, holding up my card.

'Insurance, actually,' I said.

The next house was the address I'd found for the woman who'd been up late, hemming curtains, on the night of the murder. I knocked on the door but no one answered.

Next up was the house three doors from Sara's. A woman dressed in a beige slack suit answered the door. I handed her a card and told the same lie about being there on an insurance matter.

'I hardly knew either, which was fine by me,' she said.

'Not nice people?'

'He might have been all right, going by what others around here say, but there was something wrong with her.'

'Demanding, I heard.'

'Deceitful might be more like it. Something strange about her, for sure.'

'Any idea why he moved in later than her?'

'That's not so strange with young un-marrieds, nowadays. I'll tell you what was strange: a guy came by in the afternoon, the day Sara was killed. Sort of skinny guy, short. I only saw him from a distance and his face was always turned away. Wore a long black coat and a hat pulled down low, though the day was hot for October. After he left, she came over, which was strange because we weren't well acquainted. She was shaking. She said it was a local realtor, that she was thinking about selling, but I wasn't so sure. She knew I'd seen him and seemed too anxious to tell me a lie about who that man was, was more like it.'

'Local realtor?'

'Maple Realty, I suppose, if he was a realtor at all. She was awfully nervous.'

'She was home during the day?'

'Only on her days off. She was a cashier at the Weston Food Rite.'

'You tell the cops about the guy?'

'Told them what I just told you. They asked if I could identify him. I said no, he was too far away. All I knew was that Sara said it was a realtor, so they weren't interested.'

'You're sure, though, that you saw a skinny guy wearing a hat?'

She nodded.

'I read in the papers that's what Tripp said about the intruder he made up when the cops first came. A guy wearing a hat.'

I know,' she said, 'but then he retracted it, said it was a lie or something. I thought that was odd. Like he knew there really was such an intruder.'

'Do you remember the guy's car?'

'No car,' she said. 'He left on the other side of the street. I figured he parked in front of another appointment close by. But one more thing?'

'Sure.'

'Jim, across the street? The night Sara died, he'd been out for one of his cigarettes, had a smoke or two before he saw all the lights being switched on. Thought he saw something, the shadow of a man in a hat and flapping coat against the bricks of that house. It sort of spooked him, but then it disappeared. It was real windy that night, and that's what he decided it was, that and his imagination. But I'm not so sure, after me seeing that man that made Sara so nervous the very same day.'

'I don't suppose he mentioned that to the cops?'

'No, but he mentions it now and again to us around here, still wondering if he saw something.'

I walked the two blocks over to where Google said Julianna Wynton had lived.

A young man in his mid-twenties was in the driveway a couple of doors down, waxing a fire-engine red, mid-Sixties Pontiac GTO that might have represented his entire net worth and certainly exceeded mine. I walked over and asked if he knew Julianna.

'Julianna Wynton?' He grinned, and pointed to a yellow house with green shutters. 'That was hers, though I didn't really know her.'

I gave him one of my insurance investigator cards. 'Who did?'

'Probably every guy on the block wanted to, but I don't think any of them did, except one. She was gone a lot – traveling job.'

'Who was the man who knew her?'

'How's that important to an insurance man?' The guy was young, but he was smart.

I shrugged because I was getting tired of lying.

'I'd be coming home from a date,' he said, 'and sometimes I'd see this guy walking by Julianna's. And once I saw him coming out from alongside her house, like he was sneaking out her back door. The guy had no car, so I believed he must have been a neighbor, out for a little nooky. Julianna was a fine-looking woman.'

His mother had come out the front door in time to hear the last part of our conversation. 'This wasn't her kind of neighborhood. Families with kids live here, or older, retired folks. Giftware sales rep, I heard she was. I imagine she did real well, at least with male buyers.' She sighed, maybe from wistfulness. 'A single like her belonged in a high-rise downtown, close to the nightlife, which is probably what she figured out. Up and moved out, and that's the last we saw of her.'

'Do you remember when that was?'

'Later last year, I think.'

'Around the time of the killing, two blocks over?'

'A few weeks afterward, I'd guess. No mystery to it. She was living alone. I would imagine that shook her up, even though the boyfriend did it. It shook all of us up.'

'Any idea how I could locate her?'

'Julianna's house is a furnished rental. Maple Realty in town put up the For Rent sign when she moved. They could tell you.'

I went on to the next house. 'Insurance about Julianna?' The woman next door to Julianna's former house looked up from my business card to peer over her reading glasses at me.

I nodded at my lie.

'I really didn't know Julianna,' she said. 'She traveled for work, wasn't around very much.'

'No idea where she moved?'

'I just heard she got scared after the killing, and left.'

'Did she have friends here?'

'Why would you ask that?'

'Maybe they could tell me where she moved.'

Her mouth turned down. 'This is a family neighborhood. She didn't fit in here.'

I tried just one more door. No one was home at the house on the other side of Julianna's, but another woman of reading glasses age answered the door at the place next to that.

'Oh, Julianna moved, quite some time ago.'

'Leave it to our records department,' I said. 'When they fall behind, they really fall behind.'

'No change of address information?'

I shook my head. 'People don't always think to notify their insurance companies.'

'Well, she travels a lot for work,' she said. 'She's a sales representative of a giftware company, calls on department stores, pharmacies, card shops, and the like.'

'You lost touch with her after she moved?'

'We weren't good friends,' she said. 'Casual neighbor acquaintances; she wasn't even here a year. And she was a single woman; I have two teenagers. There was the business traveling, like I said, and she did have that second home.'

'Second home?'

'Quite a place, from what she said. Up in Wisconsin, right on a lake, though the taxes were cheap enough.'

'Taxes were cheap?' I asked, because I couldn't think of anything else to ask next.

'Once I got her mail forwarded by the post office up there. I accidentally opened a tax bill that was misdelivered to me. Six hundred a year. Now, that's cheap for taxes.'

'Where in Wisconsin?'

'Verona. I'd never heard of it.'

I said I'd never heard of Verona, either.

The only available parking spot close to Maple Realty was in front of a candle shop. I took it, despite my concern that the proximity of fragrant waxes would kill the smell of the Burger King wrappers stuffed behind the Jeep's passenger seat. Fortunately, precautions were convenient; the Lookout was only two blocks away. I hoofed down there for a quart of chili to leave in the Jeep. It would counteract any candle scents that might stick to my upholstery.

The realty was in one of the historic structures that had so far been spared, a tiny white frame building with lace curtains in the windows. It, too, smelled of scented candles, though none were in evidence on the dozen fake walnut desks that lined the narrow interior, six to a side. All were empty but an attractive gray-haired woman sat in a glass-walled office at the rear. She smiled, perhaps mistaking me for someone who could afford something more than an inherited stone cylinder.

'I'm looking for one of your agents, someone who was pursuing a listing at the Sara Jansen place,' I said.

'The murder house?' she asked.

'The murder house,' I agreed.

'I thought it was in foreclosure,' she said.

'This was before the killing,' I said. 'A short guy that likes a hat and coat, even in warm weather?'

'We have two males here and both are tall. They wear hats and coats in the winter but not when it's warm.'

I gave her a card. 'I'm also looking for one of your tenants.'

'Which is it? Are you looking for a real-estate agent, or a tenant?'

'Julianna Wynton,' I said.

Her face turned rigid. 'Miss Wynton is no longer a tenant.'

'It's an insurance matter. I need to get in touch with her.'

'She's owed?' she asked.

I nodded, lying with a gesture instead of words.

'Well, good luck finding her,' she said. 'She quit her lease suddenly.'

'Moved out?'

'Skipped out. We were holding two months' security deposit, but she was a month and a half in arrears before we realized she'd left. Houses don't rent as quickly as apartments, especially in January. It took us almost six months to find a new tenant.'

'Moved out, lock, stock, and barrel?'

'No lock, no stock, no barrel. We rented the place furnished so she had nothing like that to take. She didn't even trouble herself to clean. She left behind her cosmetics – cheap stuff – and some food in the refrigerator that went bad.'

'Took her clothes?'

'The closets, at least, were empty.'

'Didn't leaving personal stuff, even just cheap cosmetics, behind make you wonder if something happened to her?'

'The jars and tubes were half-full. We tried to find her through her employer. He said to not bother him. She skipped, pure and simple, and there was nothing we could do about it.'

'Can I have the name of her employer?'

'We don't give out confidential information. Why does her employer matter to someone who's trying to give her insurance money?'

'I'm worried there will be liens against an insurance payout.'

It was such a handy falsehood, the vague promise of having to pay off liens, and one, to my small shame, that I used often.

'Liens against a payout? I could file my own—?'

I put my index finger to my lips like the idea of her collecting on money owed to a skipped tenant was a high secret.

Her fingers raced against each other, tapping the keyboard on the laptop in front of her. 'Abbott Gifts,' she read, writing down their address and phone number.

'And the date she took off?'

'December, last year, but it's only a guess, like I said. She didn't notify us.'

That was four or five weeks after Sara Jansen had been killed and months before Martin Tripp, her supposed love, would be acquitted. I tried to find meaning in either of those dates, and could not, but I wrote them down anyway.

I told her I'd be in touch, my last lie of the day, and left.

NINE

The chili and I were halfway back to Rivertown when Amanda called.

'I'm thinking dinner tonight,' she said. That was unusual. Nights were work times for her. She'd set up a small, store-front operation at the outskirts of one of Chicago's roughest neighborhoods to employ at-risk kids to assemble small electrical components, plastic connectors and wires, at good wages after school.

'I'll come downtown, late?' I hadn't seen her in a week, due to her schedule, not mine. Until Tripp came along, I'd had no schedule in the past week, other than to look for a cat.

'I'm thinking more than dinner. Maybe like a night safe in the turret . . .' Her voice sounded a touch tentative and far away.

'Safe?' It was a word she rarely used.

'I'll explain later,' she said.

'I have a fresh quart of Lookout chili.'

'Ooh, that seals it,' she said, jettisoning the tentative and sounding now like her usual self.

Lookout chili was always a slam-dunk. We used to go to the Weston bar when we were dating. Before we got married. Before I crumpled us into divorce.

'I'll see you later,' she said. 'Don't be down a quart.'

I laughed, reveling. The prospect of an evening with Amanda would be a perfect counterpoint to getting nowhere that day, and I drove the rest of the way home anticipating calm, chili, and much more.

Pulling up to the turret, I remembered Leo's mention of people with black cats swarming city hall, and glanced across the broad lawn. Sure enough, at least thirty people were lined up outside the side door, holding black, furry creatures. Their number surprised me. Rivertown is a small town, and while it housed at least a hundred corrupt officials and their relatives, I wouldn't have guessed it was home to so many black cats.

None of those I was now seeing necessarily belonged to the mayor's mother, and so, optimistic, I walked down toward the Willahock to see if the black cat I'd spotted now and again might be lurking next to the saucer of milk I'd set out.

The saucer was empty and there was no cat but there was Martin Tripp, sitting on the bench.

'I meant to ask before – how do you rate such a nice bench?' he asked, by way of beginning a sociable conversation.

'The mayor's niece's husband's brother-in-law manufactures them for the city at triple normal retail,' I said. 'They're everywhere.'

'I've noticed,' he said.

'I made the obvious rounds,' I said, sitting down, but careful to put myself between him and the chili. 'I visited Sara's mother and the places she worked here in Rivertown. None of them saw her after she left town. So, I went out to Weston to earn down the last of your two hundred dollars, so we can be done.'

'Kentbridge Circle?'

'Your old place is in disrepair.'

'I've not been back,' he said. 'Too many memories.'

'Your house has not been disposed of yet. You were found not guilty, by reason of being nuts, and though you weren't married, you might be entitled to some common-law money from the foreclosure. You might get enough for a new trench coat and jeans, and some months, perhaps years, of sleeping indoors.'

A faint smile formed on his mouth. 'As you noted, we weren't married.'

'Did you intend marriage when you followed her out there?'

'What did you learn in Weston?' he said, instead of answering.

'According to a neighbor, a short man came by the day she was killed. Sara came over afterward, acted nervous.'

He nodded, said nothing.

'Sara didn't tell you about it?'

Still, he said nothing.

'Sara told the neighbor the visitor was a real-estate agent, and that she was thinking of selling her house. The neighbor thought she was lying.'

'Was it Maple Realty?' he said. 'They've been in town for forever.'

'I went there. It wasn't one of their two men. Sara never talked about selling, or asking for an appraisal?'

'No.'

'She didn't tell you about the visitor she had that day?'

'My lawyer told me what the neighbor said.'

'He never checked it out?'

'He said it would prove nothing. The only witness, that neighbor woman, didn't get a good look at the guy. My lawyer said it could have been some real estate agent cold-calling.'

'Another of your neighbors thought he saw someone in a hat and a flapping coat lurking by your place around midnight. Did you know about that?'

'I heard that from my lawyer, too. It was Jim Simmons, out for a smoke, but he told Mr Aplon it was the wind playing tricks.'

'Here's what's bothering me, Tripp,' I said. 'You described an intruder, to the first officers to arrive, as being a skinny guy, wearing a hat. An hour later, you recanted, said you'd made it up. You told me you made it up, too. But a woman neighbor described a man, fitting that same description, who might have frightened Sara that afternoon. And another neighbor, Jim Simmons, thought he saw a guy dressed the same way on your property, around midnight. And remember, you hired me to find out what scared Sara the day she was killed.'

'Coincidence is all it was. Sara never told me about a visitor that day, and yes, I made up the story of the intruder.'

'I want to know about the guy who visited Sara that afternoon. I think you can help me do that.'

He stared across the water, and said, 'You're thinking what?'

'Could Sara have been doing what you were doing?'

He laughed then, a high, shrill sound bordering on hysteria. 'An affair? Her?'

'You sound awfully dismissive.'

'It had to have been some guy, cold-calling,' he said.

'Let's go back to Julianna Wynton. You said she saw a future for you.'

'No!' The denial shot hard out of his mouth. 'Leave her out of this.'

'You're sure, or not sure, about her?'

'Absolutely sure we don't have a future.'

'Julianna Wynton left the neighborhood a few weeks after the killing.'

'She got spooked.'

'But not spooked by you, at least not in that picture, taken later, of you walking out of the courthouse together.'

'She believes I'm innocent,' he said. 'She wants us to have a life together.'

'What do you want?'

'To be found innocent.'

'You're no longer with Julianna,' I said, pointing to the hem of his filthy trench coat. 'You're not even living indoors.'

'So?'

'Did you know Julianna had a cottage in Wisconsin? You could stay there.'

'What's all this with Julianna?' he snapped, jerking forward on the bench to look directly at me.

'Giving you full investigative value for your two hundred bucks.'

He slumped back. 'No, she never mentioned any cottage.' He gave me a lewd smile. 'Of course, our time was limited. We didn't talk much.'

'I'll say it again. Regaining your innocence might start with her. Tell the cops she can alibi you. It might not mean anything, but they'll note it for the file. And tell them about the neighbor that said a visitor upset Sara the day she was killed, and that another neighbor might have seen a man lurking in front of your house at night.'

I'd said that mouthful not because I believed him to be an innocent man, but because he had avenues to follow that needn't involve me. I'd done what I could. I wanted him gone.

He gestured at his torn trench coat. 'I can't go to the cops.'

'There's no dress requirement to walk in. Or, take that five hundred you've still got, toss the trench, buy new jeans and a shirt. Take the train or hitchhike out to Weston. Insist that the cops ask around your old neighborhood, too. Maybe someone has security footage.'

Out came the water bill envelope.

'No,' I said. 'It's too much. Go to the cops. You can do that for free.'

'I'm going to work things around here, ask people I still know.'

'One last thing bothers me,' I said. 'Sara moved out to Weston first. You didn't show up until later.'

'I had to give notice.'

'I presume Sara had discussed moving out to Weston before she did, so it was no surprise.'

'It was, actually. She didn't come to The Hamburger much until she went out there. Then she drove in lots of times.'

'To see you?'

'That's one explanation.'

'Where did you work once you moved out to Weston?'

'Why?'

'Just checking all the boxes,' I said.

'The Hot Dog Palace,' he said. 'Day shift.'

It was a dead-end answer to a dead-end question, so I let it go, unsure why I even asked it. Desperation to learn something, I supposed.

He held out the envelope with the five hundred dollars and said, 'What's in the bag?'

'Go the cops, Tripp.'

I left the tarnished five hundred in his hand, and gave him the chili.

TEN

Amanda.

My former wife came at dusk. Dark-haired, dark-eyed, and elegant, even in faded Walmart jeans and a blue chambray work shirt, she carried an enticingly tiny overnight bag.

Before I could kiss her, I saw something low, black, and furred moving beneath the light where my street dead-ended into the short stretch that led to the gamy delights of Thompson Avenue. Quick as a flash, I grabbed the pole net leaning inside the door and ran past her, intent on a better look and maybe a hundred bucks. It was a futile endeavor. Nothing low, black, and furred moved anywhere in the dim of the streetlight when I got to the corner.

Amanda was laughing, almost in tears, when I lumbered back up. 'What's going on?' she managed.

'I'm hunting a fugitive.'

'With a net?'

'I'll explain over pizza.'

'Chili,' she corrected.

'I'll explain that, too.'

She frowned at that, then swept her hand toward the street. 'For one who investigates, you notice nothing?'

'Your ancient rusted white Toyota is parked at the curb,' I said observantly.

'It's not merely a car,' she said. 'It's what it represents.'

For sure, her heap of a Toyota was not merely a car to her. She'd had it since she was a grad student, and kept it along with the cheap garage-sale painted furniture that, along with millions of dollars of art, adorned her luxury Lake Shore Drive condominium.

'Once again, you are not accompanied by guards,' I said.

'Yes!' she said, still beaming and radiant at the newness of it.

The business about the guards was a ritual we'd been playing for some weeks but it still felt strange. Since inheriting her tycoon father's controlling stock in Chicago's largest electric utility, the lady who'd simply been rich became one of the wealthiest women in Chicago, as well as the utility's nominal CEO and chairman of the board. And that made her one of the city's ripest targets for abduction, something she'd actually experienced once before. Her fellow directors insisted she be driven everywhere by two armed guards in an armored Chevy Suburban. The directors maintained it was from concern for her safety. Amanda saw it as understandable fiscal prudence: guards might save millions in ransom.

She chafed under more than just the guards. Being named CEO and board chairman was recognition of her overwhelming stock control, but they were positions for which she was not qualified. And she fought the stuffiness and conservatism of her fellow directors in denying her attempts to improve the utility's social image by increasing its philanthropic efforts. Believing that she could do more for Chicago, and the utility's image, she resigned as CEO, kept the board chairmanship, and pitched the idea of the small after-school assembly operation, where kids could earn reasonable wages and, more important, the self-respect that would come from transcending the hopelessness inherent in the worst of Chicago's neighborhoods. And, she added pointedly, the utility could earn enormous respect as well from doing something that might directly diminish the growing cases of gun violence in the neighborhood where she proposed setting up shop. Hers would be a pilot program, she said; one that, if successful, might spread to many of the worst areas in Chicago.

A majority of the board balked at her proposal, saying it would be seen as the action of a dilettante but privately fearing it would alienate Chicago's more socially entrenched organizations to which some of those directors belonged. She opened the shop anyway, funding the small enterprise with her own money.

She also lobbied for something else, and more successfully. The directors acquiesced and dropped the constant surveillance the guards brought. Guards now were used only sporadically.

'You're not assembling tonight,' I said, closing the large timbered door behind her.

'No . . .' she said. There was more.

'You sounded tentative on the phone this afternoon.'

'Someone threw a brick through our factory window, and followed up with a muffled phone call. Bomb threat.'

The factory was her euphemism for the storefronts where the assembling took place, a mostly deserted strip of buildings south of the expressway, well into the deterioration that was Chicago's no-man's-land of gang violence. I hadn't worried about her setting up shop in such a marginal neighborhood when she was accompanied by guards. Now she was no longer protected.

'You called the cops,' I said.

'I called a board-up service. You've seen our factory. It's just folding tables, plastic chairs, a coat rack, and tubs of small plastic and metal parts. No place to hide a bomb anywhere.'

'But not too small to throw in a bomb attached to another brick.'

'There never will be a bomb.'

'How can you be sure?'

'Why did you race down to the corner?'

'You're changing the subject.'

'Mmmm, I don't smell chili,' she said, heading for the curved wrought-iron staircase. 'Encouraging, which means you've not eaten all of it.'

'I gave it away.'

She started to laugh a little but then she turned and saw the look on my face. 'I can see you giving away a kidney, or a lung, or hundreds of thousands of dollars as you've done in the past, but a quart of the world's finest chili?'

'To a confessed killer.'

'Pizza then, and a confession that better be good,' she said, and started up the stairs.

The wrought iron rang and then, from above, came the sound of something popping loud, like a gunshot. She froze on the fourth step. 'Dek?'

'It's safe,' I said. 'The whole staircase is wedged in place. It doesn't need bolts to secure it.'

'By that wiggly little board?' she said.

'Efficient engineering,' I said.

She went up, because she trusted me. I wanted to trust me, too, but I waited until she got to the top before going up, to avoid loading the staircase too unevenly. I vowed to take a good hard look at it the next morning.

She sat at the plywood I use as a kitchen table while I phoned in an order for vegetarian thick crust, because such are Amanda's sensibilities, and we descended down the wrought iron prudently, one at a time, and Jeeped to get the pizza.

'Now,' she said, opening the box when we were back up in the kitchen, 'tell me first about your recent sprint to the corner.'

'It's a complicated story,' I began.

'All your stories are complicated,' she said. 'The pizza is large; we have time. Start at the very beginning.'

I began with the mayor's mother's black cat and segued, as smoothly as possible, to Sara Jansen's murder, Martin Tripp's visits, and my trip to Weston.

She nodded when I was done. 'I remember that case, of course, because of the preposterous line of defense and the shock that the strategy worked. I remember you saying you knew the victim.'

'She was a prickly thing, without friends. And then, after death, she had to suffer that verdict.'

'A last confirmation?'

I nodded. 'A final judgement that she was too unpleasant to live. That's what nags.'

'Killed twice,' she said. 'And now?'

'It feels even worse. There's something wrong about my doing anything for her confessed killer, and yet . . .'

'And yet you're buying into his wondering if he killed her?'

'Only into the wondering,' I said, to the person who so often knows me better than I do. 'And so, maybe you should re-engage the guards.'

She managed a laugh at the abruptness of my transition, but I thought I saw worry behind it. 'There will be no bomb. I just have to figure out who my little operation has threatened the most.'

'And for that you will need me,' I said.

'For the next pizza?' she asked, smiling down at what little we'd left.

'Oh, for much more than that,' I said.

She stood up and held out her hand.

ELEVEN

We slept in, and then compounded the laziness with a late morning breakfast of leftover pizza.

We talked some of Sara Jansen and Martin Tripp, and more of her nascent assembly operation. She'd started with only four wary kids who distrusted everything she told them about the hiring sign she'd taped in the front window. But then first paychecks came, twelve hours at minimum wage, and it was as if those kids had been given millions. Their eyes, seeming so distrustful just a week before, positively sparkled, she said. As did her eyes now, telling the story again, I said. A girl who'd become a millionaire at birth, studied art history in college, taught for peanuts at the Art Institute and acquired a multimillion-dollar art collection for her otherwise poorly furnished condominium had become a factory foreman, a raging capitalist, of sorts.

After breakfast, she squeezed my hand and thanked me for understanding – apparently for knowing to not intrude on her need to handle the problem of the thrown brick by herself.

And then she rang the wrought-iron staircase going down and left, and I risked jarring my very pleasant morning by looking out the window that overlooked the Willahock.

Tripp wasn't perched on the bench.

I hoped that meant we were quits. I'd given him two hundred bucks' worth of wasted time and pointed to the best path to follow, service enough to a confessed killer. I took a fresh cup of coffee, cold now but acceptable, down to the river, to watch the new morning's ballet of fresh debris float by before I turned to the weighty matters of chasing a cat.

The day's show was colorful. Three clear plastic milk jugs pirouetted around two empty yellow antifreeze gallons, a brown drain cleaner bottle, and an orange jug that had once held Gojo hand scrubber. It was still August and the day was going to be another hot one, but the refuse bobbing on the Willahock presaged the colors of the cooler autumn to come. They were what passed for lovely in Rivertown.

I was barely into my coffee when Leo called. 'Where are you?' he demanded, sounding out of breath.

'By the river.'

'Just hunting that cat?'

'No need to be derisive. I'm enjoying morning coffee.'

'Your coffee?' He snorted, or attempted to. Leo's attempts at snorting sounded more like sneezing. 'You're free?'

'Almost always,' I answered, because it was almost always true. 'What's wrong?'

'I had to fly to New York City last night. Last-minute work on that Rockefeller collection that's being auctioned.'

'*New York, New York*,' I warbled, singing off-key to Leo but in perfect time with the debris bumping and bobbing downstream.

It elicited no laugh. 'I need you to go to the trailer for the lunch rush.'

'Ma's there, right?'

'Unsupervised, for the first time. That's the problem: Ma's there alone, with her friends.'

'But along with preserving Kutz's operation, wasn't that part of your objective when you leased the place? You wanted to put Ma and her friends to work instead of pole-stripping, watching porn movies, and—'

'Skinny dipping; jeez, the skinny dipping at the health center,' he said, butting in before I could remind him of Ma and her friends, buck naked, circling one lone gent who'd had multiple bypass surgeries. 'Yeah, I know what I intended. But I didn't carefully consider the kind of lunch crowd that comes to Kutz's.'

'What's to worry? They're the usual well-behaved kids, business-types, and construction—' I stopped before saying what didn't need to be said.

'Construction guys, as you well know,' he finished for me. 'Young hard-bodies. You've seen the old ladies. They're hitting on them like rockets. I've been getting complaints.'

'From whom?'

'From some of the construction supervisors, darn it.' His voice had risen an octave. 'Their crews have got tight time schedules and the girls are throwing up delays.'

'I thought they were just supposed to be bussing the tables.'

'You've seen the way they work, rubbing backs as hard as they rub the tables, even following the guys to their trucks, whispering about the kind of excitement that can only come from maturity.'

'Not Ma, surely.'

'So far, she's been staying behind the window, but I can see the fire in her eyes. She wants a sip from the fountain of youth.'

'Please don't share more,' I said.

'That's not what's got me worried,' he said. 'Ma keeps saying we need to change the menu. With me gone, she might start overcooking the hot dogs, or worse, serve up pierogies. For Pete's sake, she's almost in her eighties and she wants to become a restaurateur.'

'What's wrong with that?' I said. 'It's a safer sip at the fountain of youth. And if it's just putting the "hot" in hot dogs or cooking up a few pierogies? Harmless.'

'Go over there. Give her the fish-eye. Let her know you're watching for me.'

'You think I can control her?' I laughed. No matter how hard Leo tried to control his mother, Ma Brumsky and her cadre of lusty elderlies stayed a step ahead in finding new ways to indulge their fantasies. I certainly couldn't do it, even over a menu. 'What about Endora?'

'She's stuck at the library.'

Endora was Leo's girlfriend. A woman of great beauty – she'd earned college money modeling for two of the top New York agencies – she quit using her looks to use her brain as a researcher at Chicago's Newberry Library. Ma Brumsky often listened to Endora, in part, Leo believed, because nobody gave a better fish-eye than Endora.

'Hurry with the Rockefeller residue,' I said. 'Handle your mother yourself.'

'Just swing over there. Be visible, hang around. Give the fish-eye to the gals. Let the clientele see that they, and the menu, and the ambience, are being protected.'

It was no joke to him. Kutz's menu and traditions were as sacrosanct as scripture chiseled on stone.

I told him I'd go. Not just because he is my friend, but because I didn't want to deal with Tripp if he showed up. Proving innocence was Tripp's responsibility; giving Ma Brumsky the fish-eye was mine.

And I was hungry.

I glanced across the broad lawn as I headed to the Jeep. Fifty people were lined up alongside city hall, clutching cats. Rivertown was being turned upside down by the hunt for one politically connected cat.

I laughed at the craziness of that, and thought about Leo going crazy, too, over the fear that Kutz's clearing would be turned upside down by people lined up for pierogies.

It was the wonder of the world in which I lived. And that day, it was the only appropriate place to be.

TWELVE

I heard him booming. Even above the clatter of the Jeep's engine, I heard him, as soon as I turned off Thompson Avenue and onto the river road. Crooning, his way, loud.

Down in the clearing, it was deafening. Gone was the hush, where traditionally only the muted 'oohs' and 'ahs' of true gourmands savoring semi-warm hot dogs and semi-fizzed colas broke into the soft rippling of the Willahock as it carried away the plastic debris the mayor's cousin had tossed in upstream. Leo had added to that soft blend with caressing Brazilian sambas, played barely audibly through speakers he hung in the trees. They'd been his only change when he took over Kutz's operation, but they were soft, and unobtrusive, and respectful.

Not Sinatra. He was belting 'My Way' over the loudspeakers, and his way, that day, was real loud.

The usual line stretched ten deep toward the trailer's order window. Ma herself was busy inside. At first glance, it looked to be business as normal, and I anticipated making a phone call to Leo as soothing as the sambas that were sure to be reinstated upon his return.

Movement beyond the trailer caught my eye. A gray-haired lady, who looked to be at least ninety, was squeeze-dancing with an equally spry old gent on top of the picnic table closest to the river. Both his hands were wrapped around the woman's bottom as they swayed, eyes closed, in time with Sinatra's way. They weren't there, not really. They were decades back in time. It was a surefire worry for toppling.

And it was beautiful.

A greater concern was playing out by the goat-racing track that Leo had constructed in an earlier period of lunacy. Ma's least-inhibited friend, Mrs Roshiska, had pressed a young construction worker in a sleeveless white T-shirt against his truck with her aluminum walker. He was holding his brown bag high with his left hand, protecting his lunch, while his right arm, trapped between his chest and the forward-leaning Mrs Roshiska's torso, was simply trying to protect his sanity. Even from a hundred feet away, I could hear the wheels of her walker squeak as she rocked forth and back against the helpless young man.

It was feral hunger. I hurried to approach her from behind, tapped her on the shoulder, and loomed over her gray head. I flashed the flinty fish-eye as Leo had instructed. It broke her momentum. She wheeled back just enough for the young man to jump in the cab of his pickup. He twisted the key, fired the engine, and was gone in a flash.

Mrs Roshiska glared. I laughed. She laughed. She is my favorite of Ma's friends, a septuagenarian of great lust, but also of great humor.

'Why don't you assault men your own age?' I asked.

'They're all dead, or at least their parts are,' she said, with a wonderful wink.

I left her to find new prey. As I walked over to the order line, I sensed a change in the air. Literally. The air in front of the trailer smelled now like a babushka's overheated kitchen, but not just any babushka's kitchen. It smelled like Ma Brumsky's kitchen, back when I was a kid and I'd escaped whichever of my aunt's homes I'd been temporarily assigned to, to hang out with Leo and always, always, to get invited to stay for dinner.

New, hand-lettered sheets were duct-taped below the peeling

plywood menu that had served Kutz, his father before him, and
now Leo, well for over three-quarters of a century. The new
sheets advertised ethnic delights: spicy or regular Polish sausage
with onions or sauerkraut or both; foot-long kielbasas; czernina;
golonka. I pulled out my phone to check the internet.
Czernina was duck-blood soup; golonka was stewed pork knuckles.
Leo's fear of Hell had come, Polishly, to Kutz's clearing.

It was not my place to storm the side door of the trailer and
demand that Ma Brumsky stop the sacrilege. Ma had been the
closest thing to a mother I'd had, certainly more than any of
the sisters who'd taken over, grudgingly, after my own mother
took off after I was born. I could only wait in front, in line, until
at last, it was my turn.

'Hot Polish, Dekkie?' Ma Brumsky asked, with a wink. She
might have been referring to one of the new menu items or, I
realized with horror, she might have witnessed my encounter
with Mrs Roshiska, who was now maneuvering her walker toward
a young man enjoying a hot dog by the bank of the river, oblivious
to what was wheeling toward him.

I gave her the fish-eye too, as Leo instructed.

She laughed. 'Or pierogi?'

I laughed, too. 'Only hot dogs here, Ma,' I said, and laughed
again.

'Not no more. You see.'

'Kielbasa then,' I said, caving like a cliff of soft sand. I was
violating Leo's trust but then, kielbasa was kielbasa, and such
sacrilege demanded the closest possible examination.

'You'll love, Dekkie,' she said, handing out a hot kielbasa on
a warm roll, slathered with brown mustard and sauerkraut. Having
never before experienced anything hot coming out of that window,
I almost dropped it.

'I'm running a balance,' I said, mindful of the five twenties
Leo had impounded.

'Not with me, Tootsie,' she said, holding out an open palm.

'How much?'

'Ten-spot, with tax and tip.'

'Tip?'

She nodded. 'Hot chicks not free.'

'But ten bucks?' Kutz's hot dogs weren't cheap, four bucks,

seven with fries and a decarbonated soft drink, but a tenner for the kielbasa alone was an affront.

'Authentic Polish,' she said, waving the palm up and down, waiting for the green.

I had to laugh, so I had to pay. The ten on her wrinkled palm disappeared back into the window quicker than Mrs Roshiska's restraint.

I hoped my disloyalty wouldn't be spotted by the other regulars who knew of my lifelong friendship with Leo, so I snuck the kielbasa around to the back of the trailer, where Leo kept his freezer. Like with the trailer itself, and the initials carved on the back of it, I had history with that freezer. I'd once used it to hold a corpse. But that was in the past, and the freezer had long since been restored to the purpose its manufacturer had intended.

I bit into the kielbasa. To my shame, I finished it in five splendid bites, and still chewing, beat it around to the front of the trailer. This time, I was in line immediately in front of the mayor's personal cabbie, Horace Gertz.

'Menu's changed,' he opined, oblivious to the tendril of sauerkraut stuck to his lower lip. 'Probably not for the better.'

'The kielbasa is particularly disgusting,' I said, wiping at my mouth to be sure my face offered no such evidence. But Ma Brumsky's smile betrayed me anyway.

'Another, Dekkie?' She smiled the smile of corruptors immortal when I sidled up to the order window.

I slapped a new ten-spot on the counter. 'I need to be sure of the crime you're committing,' I offered up.

'Into the old, for what will be new,' she said, looking past me as she slid another kielbasa out the window. I thought she'd misquoted an old axiom of something old giving way to something new until I turned and spotted another of her ancient crones following too closely behind a young guy heading toward a black Dodge Charger.

I could not be the world's policeman, not even in one clearing, so I grabbed the kielbasa and hurried round back where I hoped the only bobbing I'd see was plastic in the river.

'Sometimes change is for the better,' a voice said.

Standing at the other end was Kowalski the Frenchman,

sporting his usual black beret. Instead of holding anything from the trailer, he was cradling a black cat.

I walked over, chewing. 'That's not . . .?'

'The mayor's mother's?' He laughed, stroking the cat's thick fur.

'Are you going to city hall?' I asked.

'No,' he said with a grin.

'Seems like everybody's got a black cat,' I said.

'Seems you're working for Martin Tripp.'

Tripp had understood, even encouraged, that I might mention he was back in town. But Kowalski was looking at me too intently, seeming to be too hungry for what I was about to say.

'Just a minor matter,' I said.

'Really? What's minor about him?'

'Back in Rivertown to stay?' I asked, instead of answering.

'I hope not.' He pointed to two cops poking into bushes a hundred yards downriver, and set his cat down. It scampered off, and he laughed and walked away.

The second kielbasa went down as swiftly as the first. Afterward, I watched the river flush the town's recyclables down toward wealthier suburbs for a time, until hearing 'My Way' over and over became a drone strike, and I headed around the trailer toward the Jeep. As I passed the goat corral, empty of racing goats since Leo's chaotic grand opening, I spotted movement deep in the woods. Someone wearing a tan trench coat was lurking fifty yards into the trees.

A coat like that, even on such a hot day, didn't need to mean anything. The woods were cool, deeper inside. And lots of folks suffered chills, no matter the weather, due to bad circulation or fever. Still, I knew a man who wore just such a coat on hot days, a man who'd confessed to stabbing his wife.

I walked closer to the edge of the trees while keeping my head turned away, as if I was merely meandering, watching the road out of the clearing and not the woods.

He turned and hurried deeper into the woods. I followed into the trees, tracking the occasional flashes of tan cloth. Five minutes later, he got to where the trees ended up the river road and disappeared. I ran to catch up.

By the time I got to the road, I could only see the back of an old brown Chrysler LeBaron speeding away. I didn't recall seeing it parked along the road or in the clearing when I pulled in.

My Jeep was back in the clearing but luck was closer. Horace Gertz, the mayor's cabbie, came driving up on his way out. He smiled when I jumped in back of his white-topped, green private cab. 'Boy, these things are good,' he said, holding up the last bite of what was surely either his second or third kielbasa. I knew he savored good food as much as I did.

'I need you to tail someone, right now,' I said.

He stuffed the last bite into his mouth and gunned the car up the river road. 'Who we after?'

'Old LeBaron, brown, shouldn't be too hard to find,' I said. 'Just pulled out.'

'Which way?' he asked, when we got to Thompson Avenue.

I could only guess. 'Left, toward the city.'

Turning fast, he sped east. 'I heard Tripp hired you,' he said.

'Kowalski just asked me about that,' I said.

'What did you tell him?' His eyes in the rearview were direct on mine.

I told Gertz the truth, which was next to nothing.

'He's saying he's back to get a lead on whoever killed his wife?' he asked. 'That's why he's been wandering around town?'

'So he says.'

'You got doubts?'

'I've got nothing,' I said, which was true enough.

I'd guessed right about the direction the LeBaron took. We caught sight of it a mile farther on and tailed it straight through the outskirts of Chicago, where it pulled off to the side of a huge public park. We stayed back alongside the road as the driver shifted around on the front seat for a couple of minutes. And then he started up but this time only drove another mile before he pulled into the parking lot of the Afforda-Rest, a small budget motel known for its hourly clientele.

The man that got out of the LeBaron wore no jeans or filthy tan trench or dirty running shoes. He wore a blue blazer, gray slacks, and polished black loafers.

But the three-day beard stubble was the same, only now the

change of duds made it look hip and fashionable. Martin Tripp had transformed.

He walked up an outside staircase to the open-air balcony, and followed it to Room 15. He took a key from his pants pocket and went in.

We sat, engine idling, my mind idling too, unable to kick into a functioning gear. Martin Tripp was a mystery in a mystery in a mystery, like one of those sets of nesting Russian dolls, where one figure hides inside another, inside another.

'I've seen enough,' I said, after a few minutes, but I'd seen nothing I understood.

Gertz turned us around and we headed back toward Rivertown. 'So, Kowalski the Frenchman?' he asked.

'He had a black cat,' I said.

'Did he tell you why he'd come back?'

'No, nor did he say what's under the beret.'

'All kinds of theories,' he said.

'About what's under his beret?'

'That, too,' he said.

THIRTEEN

The most extensive news coverage of Sara Jansen's killing and Martin Tripp's trial was Greg Theodore's in the *Chicago Tribune*. His reporting was meticulous and unbiased, with no trace of the fury he must have felt, like everyone, when Martin Tripp skated on the charge against him.

I emailed Theodore at his *Tribune* address, asking if we might talk about the Tripp case. It was a desperation move; I had nowhere else to turn to learn what might be behind Tripp's charade at homelessness.

Theodore called twenty minutes later. 'How can I help?' he asked cheerfully, but he was really asking: 'What do you know?'

'I'm wondering how much follow-up you did after the verdict,' I said.

'Your interest?'

'Strictly personal,' I said. 'I went to high school with Sara Jansen.'

'Knew her well?'

'Hardly at all. One study hall, second semester senior year.'

'And Tripp? He's from Rivertown, too.'

'He's older. I might have seen him around but I don't remember.'

'So, you're wondering about Tripp's life after the verdict just because of a brief study hall acquaintanceship with Sara?'

'Tripp got no institutionalization, no direction to see a shrink, no nothing. What did he do right after the verdict?'

'Give me a call when you want to lay your cards face-up,' he said, and hung up.

I called right back. 'I can't tell you much, but I'm in contact with him,' I said.

'I'm interested, but I'm late on a piece. And I'm on deadline to finish another.'

'I'll just need fifteen minutes.'

He told me he was downtown, but would be in a coffee shop on the outskirts of Chicago, not far from Rivertown, in ninety minutes.

The coffee shop was along the tracks, one of the old ones that manages to survive by selling morning coffee to rail commuters. The wood tables inside were scratched from decades of better times, the wood chairs were mismatched, and the woman behind the counter was overweight, gray-haired, and beautifully unlike the baristas in trendier places.

Only one customer was inside, working at an open laptop. A tall fellow with a closely shaved head, he wore clay-colored jeans, a muted blue plaid shirt, orange socks, and red suede running shoes – colors so in conflict they might have caused even Leo Brumsky to wince. Barely looking up, he said, 'Get a coffee. I'm almost done.'

I walked to the counter, got coffee, and returned to his table. He kept typing for another couple of minutes, punched a last button, and closed the laptop.

'I was done with Tripp after his acquittal,' he said, 'but a month later, he called to tell me he couldn't find work anywhere, playing it like he was the victim. That wasn't the punishment

anyone wanted, but it was a form of justice and I told him I
hoped he would starve. I quit hearing from him after that. Story
over. And then . . .?' He stopped.

'And then,' I said, 'a few weeks after that, he drifted back to
Rivertown, walked around for a week, and came to see me.'

Theodore sat back and waited, prompting for more by
silence.

'He said he was unsure whether he really killed her,' I said.
'He wanted me to nose around to see why Sara was upset shortly
before she died. A neighbor told me Sara had a visitor the day
she was killed. Sara passed him off as a real-estate agent,
but she acted nervous, real scared.'

'I heard that,' he said.

'Tripp claims Sara never told him about the visitor. I checked
with the largest local realty. They have nobody matching the
neighbor's description. Something else: the neighbor who stepped
out for a smoke and saw the lights being switched on also thought
he saw something earlier. A guy in a coat and hat lurking in the
dark in front of the house.'

'Did he go to the cops?'

'He thought it was a trick of the wind,' I said, 'but here's the
kicker: the neighbor woman described Sara's afternoon visitor
as a small, skinny guy wearing a hat and coat, despite the heat.
Sound familiar?'

'Same guy, especially about that hat part,' Theodore said.
'That's how Tripp first described his fictitious intruder.'

'What if it wasn't a lie?'

'Then Tripp's denying it makes no sense,' he said, 'because
it would have been one of the legs of a defense.'

'Tripp said it didn't matter because he got off anyway,' I said.

'Risky,' he said.

'Do you suppose Tripp's got money?'

Theodore's eyes didn't widen; he was too experienced a
reporter for that. 'Why do you ask that?'

'When he first showed up in Rivertown, he wandered around
for a week, unshaven, wearing a filthy tan trench and grass-stained
jeans. He looked that way when he came to see me. He told me
he slept in viaducts.'

'And . . .?'

'I tailed Tripp. He's got better clothes, and he's living in a cheap motel. He also bought an old car.'

'It's an act?' He leaned forward across the table. 'He's playing a game with his purported homelessness?'

'And perhaps even his hunt for a real killer,' I said.

He got up. 'You've got to find out more. And me? Deadlines.'

'Dead lines, indeed,' I said, making it into two words and one different meaning.

Dead lines ahead.

I swung by the Afforda-Rest on my way back to Rivertown, hoping to confront Tripp about the game he was playing. His LeBaron was parked in the lot. I went up to his room and knocked. There was no answer.

Heading home, I waltzed my mind around any scenarios that made sense. It was a lonely dance to discordant music. Nothing about Martin Tripp made sense, other than the certainty he was pulling a con on me.

On the spur of the moment, I swung into the parking lot of The Hamburger. It is just inside Rivertown's eastern border with Chicago. It has been known as The Hamburger for decades, though the menu offerings changed every couple of years as owners went bankrupt and new optimists emerged. The neon sign on the roof always remained because it was large and too expensive to replace.

The last time I visited, it had been struggling as a seafood restaurant because word was spreading that they snagged their seafood, whiskered, floating among the debris on the Willahock. The guy I'd arranged to meet there, that last time, followed me back to the turret to kill me, though not because I'd recommended The Hamburger as a meeting place. He died shortly thereafter, though not of food poisoning, and the restaurant died from a lack of appetites, shortly after that.

A clean-cut young man waited behind the counter. A clean-cut young woman waited behind the clean-cut young man. Both smiled hugely when I walked in. There were no diners. They were alone.

The menu was Italian, lots of pasta, lots of sausage and peppers and onion dishes.

'New, huh?' I asked.

'Opened three months ago,' the young woman said. They both wore shiny wedding rings.

I didn't ask how business was. Both of their aprons were spotless.

I studied the menu hanging above the back counter. Three twenties remained of Tripp's two hundred dollars. I ordered forty bucks' worth of lasagna.

The young woman blinked several times, as if to ward off tears. 'We prepare fresh,' she said. 'It'll be a few minutes.'

While she went back to cook the food, I asked the young man, 'Martin Tripp been around?'

'Who?' he asked.

It was a long shot. The Hamburger had gone through one previous operator – a guy selling sushi, a gutsy choice given the building's whiskered reputation – since Tripp quit there, early the previous year. Since the young man didn't know of Tripp, we talked sports, of which I know nothing and of which he knew even less. There were gaps in our conversation long enough to perform whole operas. Finally, I asked him if he knew who owned the restaurant at the beginning of the year before.

'A guy named Dennis O'Byrne. I saw his name on an old insurance bill.'

The lasagna came out and they both thanked me profusely for ordering so much food.

I took the bags and left. It was the only decent thing I got done that day.

FOURTEEN

The next morning, after lasagna and garlic toast, I went to see Dennis O'Byrne.

He still lived in Rivertown, in a tidy white frame colonial well away from the sins of Thompson Avenue. He said he'd be in his back yard when I called to ask if I could stop by.

He put down his newspaper and gestured to the webbed lawn chair beside him.

'Of course I remember Martin,' he said. 'He started as an order filler, not that there were many orders – we were selling Chicago beefs – and he took over management of the place when I smartened up and became more of an absentee owner.'

'The place was a struggle?'

'Always, though things picked up when I pulled Martin out from behind the grill window and made him manager.'

'I don't understand.'

'He was a good-looking guy and high-school girls came in after school to moon and giggle at him. They only ordered Cokes and fries but still, it was an improvement. We might even have made it, but for the street taxes.'

'I hear they are expensive.'

'If you're not related to the people who run things in Rivertown, the more you make, the more they want. Their collector would come around once a month, accuse me of lying about what I said I was making. He was a nasty little rat. I had to show him my books just to avoid special assessments.'

'Kowalski?'

'Odd duck. Wore a hat, even in the summer when everybody else was sweating.'

'A hat?' I said, but it was said only in my head, at the memory of a neighbor lady who saw the visitor that upset Sara Jansen.

'Yeah, a . . . a foreign sort of . . .' He stopped, stuck for the word.

'A beret,' I said.

'A French hat!' he said, nodding. 'Martin helped me there, too. He got along with him. They were friends, Martin said, drinking buddies, and he got the amounts reduced. Fine by me. I was nearing the end of a four-year lease, and the walk-away would be too expensive, so I decided to stay open with just Martin and a grill cook. I went back to retail, managing a hardware store in Chicago, to make enough to keep The Hamburger afloat until the lease expired.'

'Tripp got your street taxes reduced with his friend?'

'Not a lot, but it helped.'

'So you had no problem trusting Tripp to manage your place?'

'He seemed honest, and like I said, he packed the place with high-school girls.'

'Did Sara Jansen ever come around?'

'The woman he killed? Yeah. I wasn't in there much after I put Martin in charge, but I recognized her from her newspaper photos. Saw her once at one of the tables farthest from the counter, having a beef and nursing a Coke. She looked so lonely. He never mentioned that he knew her, let alone that he was going out to live with her, when he quit. What a tragedy. I still can't believe it was him the newspapers talked about.'

'He gave notice when he quit?'

'Two weeks; he was good about that. Wouldn't say where he was going, but by then I didn't care. I had six months to go on the building lease. I closed the place rather than hire another manager, paid the rent for the remaining months, and kissed off the experience as stupidity.'

'But still paying street taxes?'

'Nothing to pay since I was no longer operating.'

'Kowalski didn't try to get something out of you, even though you'd closed?'

'He'd quit coming around before Martin quit, but not by much. Two, three weeks, no more.'

'Before Martin quit?' I asked, to make sure.

'Not much before, but yes,' O'Byrne said. 'It was Martin who told me Kowalski was out of the picture, and then Martin quit. I kept expecting someone new to show up, because the town's too crooked to do without any greenbacks, but nobody came.'

'And you closed up with six months left on the lease.'

'Yes, like I said. Why is that important?'

'Can you tell me exactly when Martin quit?'

He counted backward with his fingers. 'A year ago, last February, toward the end of the month.'

I left. I'd asked every question I could think of, even if I didn't understand why the answers mattered. What was for sure was I'd satisfied my obligation to Tripp by tugging two thick threads out of a skein that he could take to the cops. Julianna Wynton should be used to alibi him. Even if the timeline couldn't be used conclusively to prove he wasn't at home when Sara was killed, it might be enough to force a re-investigation.

But it was the second thread that nagged – the identity of the mysterious visitor that had upset Sara in the afternoon. A visitor that might have returned at midnight to kill her.

O'Byrne had seen Kowalski as a rat, a rat in a hat.

Sara's neighbor had described her visitor as a man in a hat.

Sara would have known Kowalski from when he brought street taxes into the bank, the same man Tripp might well have told her was his drinking buddy. If Kowalski was the man the neighbor saw at Sara's house, the last afternoon of her life, there was no chance Sara didn't tell Martin Tripp about it.

On top of Tripp lying about being homeless, it might have been another lie he told me, and that was one more reason to be done with him, to push the gnarled skein away. I drove to the Afforda-Rest to tell him the best odds still pointed to him as Sara's killer, and that I hoped he'd suffer a very hot afterlife.

Tripp's LeBaron was where I'd last seen it, but it had changed from a four-wheeler to a three. A cinder block had replaced the right rear wheel.

My phone rang as I pulled into the parking lot. 'What's happening?' Leo asked.

'Your operation is embracing evolution. You're no longer needed at the clearing.'

'Please tell me you're kidding,' he said.

'How's the Rockefeller collection?' I asked, to change the subject.

'He didn't take it with him. What's Ma doing?' he asked, to change it back.

'Her energies remain moral and behind the order window,' I said. 'It's her friends who are pressing.'

'Pressing?'

'Themselves onto the customers.'

He groaned. 'The construction boys.'

'They're agile, they're young, and some of them are laughing. It's harmless comedy, livens up the clearing.'

'The clearing doesn't need livening up. Ma's behaving with the menu?'

'Serving up new delights,' I said. 'Kielbasa, pierogies, new tastes. The place has gone Polish.'

'Blood soup?' His voice rose an octave. 'Please tell me no blood soup.'

'I don't think that'll last on the menu.'

'She's not slaughtering anything, is she?'

'No blood-letting where anyone can see,' I said.

'I can't leave here. You've got to stop her.'

'Me? She's your mother and you've never been able to control—' I stopped, midsentence. A housekeeper had wheeled her cart, and opportunity, in front of Tripp's room. 'Gotta go,' I said and clicked him away.

I beat it up the stairs. The maid had gone inside but Tripp hadn't come out.

'Hi, Marty,' I called out, stepping inside.

The maid came out of the bathroom, shaking her head.

My phone buzzed.

'I'm Jake,' I said, ignoring it. 'Marty told me to meet him here.'

She shook her head but said nothing. English was not part of her repertoire. She motioned around the room with her hand and shook her head again.

The bed was made, but she hadn't been inside long enough to make it. Tripp's belongings had already been neatened, perhaps from a day earlier, perhaps before that. The tan trench coat hung on the clothes rod, the grass-stained jeans folded on the chrome shelf above. An open suitcase held underwear, neatly folded, too, and a dozen rolled-up pairs of socks, some white, some dark, and his dirty sneakers were under the bed. But the blue blazer, neat gray slacks, and polished loafers he'd worn when I last saw him were nowhere in sight.

My phone buzzed again. I clicked it away without looking and stepped past her, and into the bathroom. A shaving kit was open on the counter but the bathroom was clean.

Martin Tripp hadn't spent the previous night in that room and he hadn't driven himself elsewhere.

I went down to the motel office. A woman in her sixties, a month past coloring the gray closest to her scalp to match the bright red of the hair that had grown out, sat at a metal desk behind the counter.

My phone buzzed. I let it go.

'Martin Tripp?' I said, from the door.

'You come to settle his bill?'

'He's gone?'

'He owes for the past two nights. It's pay as you go, here,' she said.

'Took his stuff?' I asked, like I hadn't just been snooping in his room.

'Nothing, not even his car.'

'Leaving his car means he's coming back.'

'He's gotta see me first,' she said, pointing to a bald tire on a wheel leaning against the wall.

My phone buzzed again.

'Ain't you going to answer your phone?' she asked.

I stepped outside. Leo. I knew it was him that kept calling. He is my friend. Friends, even preoccupied friends, don't make their friends worry when their worlds are threatened, their recipes imperiled. I answered the phone.

'You've got to get over there—' he shouted.

'They aren't bad changes,' I said.

'Kielbasa?' His voice had risen a couple of octaves.

'They're superb,' I said.

'You're my friend,' he screamed, accusing.

'And one other change that's insignificant, too,' I said, because he'd find out as soon as he returned.

'Like what?'

'Like turning up your burners.'

'Hot?' he screamed. 'She's serving hot dogs hot?'

'I don't know about the hot dogs,' I said, hoping he'd appreciate honesty at least.

'You're eating the Polish? Traitor! You gotta get over there, stop this!'

There was nothing more to be learned at the Afforda-Rest. I told Leo I was on my way and would report again that there was nothing to fear from small changes.

But there was. When I got there, the changes I'd touted as small were growing, literally. A construction crane, fitted with the sort of steel basket used to raise workers on multistory projects, had been trucked to Kutz's clearing. That day, it had elevated a deeply tanned, muscular young man to the top of the tallest oak in the clearing, to band a large pulley to the trunk of the tree. He was bare-chested and he was not alone. Strapped tightly by a wide web belt to his muscular young back was Mrs Roshiska, a woman arguably more ancient than the old oak. Both were laughing at something she was whispering with lips pressed to his flesh as tightly as a lamprey's. Four of Ma's friends had gathered below to watch reverently, their lips working in silent harmony with Mrs Roshiska's, their thoughts undoubtedly hotter than anything Ma Brumsky could heat with propane.

I looked away, fearing I'd see something I'd never be able to erase from my mind. Down by the river, another of Ma's septuagenarians was stringing colored lights along the bushes, and two more were stepping portable spotlights into the ground. Fifty feet from them, a young blond man, wearing a shirt and not yet targeted by any of the elderlies, was fitting odd, curved pieces of metal together.

I went to the order window and tried giving Ma Brumsky the fish-eye again. 'Leo's not pleased with the menu changes, Ma,' I said. 'And now you're defacing the clearing at great expense.'

'Disco *Polski*,' she said.

'What?'

'Never mind. You'll rat me out, huh, Dekkie?'

'As soon as I finish a kielbasa,' I said, and then realized I'd dropped almost the last of Tripp's money at The Hamburger the night before. 'Nope,' I said, like I'd changed my mind. 'No kielbasa for me. Just a Coke.'

She gave me her own fish-eye, the same fish-eye she used to give me when I was a kid and, stopping by Leo's to walk to school with him, I'd deny I was being sent to school with no lunch. Every time, she hurried to make me a sandwich as good as Leo's. And so it was that day, in the clearing. I should have known not to try lying about being short of funds to Ma Brumsky.

'What if two kielbasa with extra grilled onions, plus free soft drink and barbecue cheese fries?'

'I'd have to taste them first,' I said. One didn't sell out a best friend's concerns too cheaply, especially not to Ma Brumsky.

She nodded. 'Extra for quiet, Dekkie,' she said, and passed through not two but three kielbasas heaped with grilled onions; one of the colas that Leo, like Kutz, served up from barrels gotten cheap because they'd lost their fizz; and the barbecue cheese fries.

'By the way, Mister Fish-eye, all this work don't cost nothing,' she said.

I slid the feast untouchably off to the side before I dared to disagree. 'Nothing? That crane alone rents for several thousand dollars.'

'On the house, like the kielbasas, Dekkie,' she said. 'Free crane, like I say. On the house from nice Polish man. Labor I pay with kielbasa, like I pay you to keep quiet.'

The crane started whining, lowering the basket. I did not want to witness the arrival of the youthfully blooming Mrs Roshiska, sporting a pink T-shirt damp at the chest with the young worker's sweat. And the kielbasas were piping hot, steaming, and demanding. I hurried around to the back of the trailer.

Horace Gertz, the mayor's cabbie, came around less than a minute later. He was clutching a cardboard tray of pierogies.

'I've always liked this place, God knows,' he said, 'but this Polish stuff is so wonderful.'

'Leo's not so sure,' I said.

'He's paying a pretty penny to rent that crane.'

'Ma conned someone into footing the bill.'

He stiffened. 'Who?'

He asked it casually, but I doubted the mayor's driver, one of his many eyes and ears, ever asked anything that was casual. Likely enough, he heard more confidential conversations than anyone else in Rivertown.

'I didn't ask.'

I realized, then, that he'd never asked why I'd wanted to tail Martin Tripp, though surely he'd recognized him getting out of the LeBaron at the Afforda-Rest. It was something that he should have asked about.

'Sometimes it's best not to ask about things,' he said and carried his pierogies away untouched.

'Especially when you already know the answer,' I almost said, but didn't, to his disappearing back.

FIFTEEN

I knew more than I knew.

But I didn't know that until after I changed course, heading home. The kielbasas, grilled onions, and barbecue cheese fries I'd ingested in great quantity had gone to three-sided civil war, requiring a speedy detour to the Discount Den for antacids.

The Den wasn't a pharmacy. The proprietor dealt in stolen or stale-dated goods and poor knockoffs. He didn't much care about what came in his back door, quality or not, hot or not, so long as he could push it out the front at a cool quadruple of his cost. The lookalikes I bought lacked labeling but were colored close to the proper pastels. More important, they were a quarter the price of normal antacids and the proprietor assured me they'd be good enough in an emergency. I clawed off the cap as I went outside.

Nothing came out. Most of the tablets were stuck together so tight it was like they'd been molded in a couple of multicolored pieces. Desperate, I smashed the plastic bottle against the bricks, cracking the plastic enough to pry out the largest clump and pop it into my mouth. I leaned against the bricks and waited for it to dissolve.

A minute passed, and then another, and then the clump began to swell in my mouth, triggering the fear that I was hosting one of those 1950s movie creature blob-things that slithered out of swamps and grew exponentially as it devoured whole towns. Certainly, the image of the tablet-clump swelling into the back of my throat and up into my brain took hold. I wanted to spit it out but was afraid it was now too large to be ejected, even with tools. But then a small piece of it broke off and then another and at long last the acid fireball in my stomach began to ease. I thought then how much – how so very much – time sometimes matters.

And that got me thinking, between diminishing spasms, about the gap between Sara's quitting her Rivertown grocery and bank jobs to buy a house in Weston and the time that Martin followed.

And I wondered if, in that interval, something got Martin Tripp to thinking, too.

I still had the woman's card from Maple Realty.

'Are you all right, Mr Elstrom? You're gasping and sounding like you're gagging at the same time.'

'Mild indigestion and inefficient antacids,' I said. 'Do you know who handled the sale of the house to Sara Jansen?'

'I do,' she said. 'If only they all went that smoothly.'

'What do you mean?'

'She paid cash.'

'Cash like in a check, for the entire price?'

'Cash like in real cash, if you can believe it, but only for the down payment. Twenty-two thousand dollars in hundred-dollar bills. It was a private sale. The place was empty, the sellers had inherited it, but it had come to them with a mortgage. The sellers assumed that mortgage and, in turn, agreed to carry Sara's mortgage, to fund the mortgage they inherited. We had her sign an affidavit stating she'd gotten the cash money for the down payment from an inheritance because cash transactions are subject to government scrutiny.'

'For drug-money laundering,' I said.

'Exactly.' She sighed. 'Now, it's a murder house. Since the original sellers had been using Sara's payments to fund their own mortgage, the property, without income, has now gone into foreclosure. With burst plumbing and a murder history, it's unsaleable. It will be bulldozed. The original sellers will lose everything they inherited.'

'When did Sara Jansen buy the place?'

I heard her tapping keys. 'February 9, last year.'

I thanked her and hung up.

Sara Jansen had quit her minimum wage jobs at the bank and the grocery in Rivertown, to close on a house, on February 9, in Weston with a twenty-two-thousand-dollar cash down payment. She'd then started to return to Rivertown to make moon-eyes at Martin Tripp. Sometime later in February, he quit his job at The Hamburger to move into her house.

I supposed Tripp could have fallen in love with Sara. I supposed it was more likely he'd been as cunning with her as he was being with me.

What I couldn't quite suppose was whether Kowalski's leaving town had nothing to do with Sara and then Martin's leaving, or that he wasn't the guy in the hat who showed up on Sara's doorstep the day she was killed.

The antacid had finally shrunk to golf-ball size but even better, what had broken off was forcing the kielbasas, onions, and barbecue cheese fries into détente. I risked straightening up slowly from the bricks of the storefront. No spasms. All was fine, except that I was furious about another civil war – the one that raged inside my head over my need to be done with Tripp versus my need to know what more could be tugged from his skein.

I scratched out a note telling Tripp to kiss off for playing me for a chump, telling myself that confrontation no longer mattered. Only closure did. I could slip the note in his car and leave, a master of my own conflicted will.

The mostly red-haired woman was out in front, arguing with a man who was gesturing at Tripp's LeBaron. Both combatants were red-faced, but the red-haired woman looked madder, and freed from behind her desk, more substantial than I'd suspected. She was at least six feet tall, and strong enough to clutch the LeBaron's wheel and tire the man must have grabbed out of her office to put back on the car. A wheel and tire are not light, but she hugged it to her chest as fiercely as Mrs Roshiska had hugged the shirtless young man, up in the construction basket.

The manager's antagonist was not cowed. Although the woman had a height and weight advantage, he stood with his chin not two feet from hers, and looked angry enough to grab the wheel from her.

I parked next to the three-legged subject of their dispute. The lot was almost totally empty. The motel's clientele – managers, clerks, secretaries, co-workers – looking to exchange moisture before heading home to exchange not much at all, were not due until after business hours.

I walked up to the combatants.

'It's a stolen car, lady,' he – likely a repo man – yelled.

'I ain't sayin' it ain't,' she yelled back. 'Go ahead and take it, if it'll move on three wheels, but first you got to settle his back charges.'

It was too much for the man. He turned, got in a dented Ford Taurus, and drove away.

She set the wheel down with visible relief. 'These things are heavy,' she said, contorting her face to remember who I was.

'Holding out to get Tripp's room charges?'

Her face brightened in recognition. 'Did you find him?'

'Not yet, but I'm getting optimistic.'

Her face brightened even more. 'You really got ideas?' she asked.

'I do, indeed. I suppose Tripp paid for his room in cash?' I asked it simply to mark off another box. No one left paper trails from checking accounts or credit cards at the Afforda-Rest.

'Might have been,' she said.

'I'll be back,' I said, hoping I was wrong and could give up on Martin Tripp. I dropped the note I'd written on the passenger's seat. I hadn't signed it. He'd know who'd written it, when he came back.

If he ever came back.

I had to allow there was a chance that Tripp had been abducted. That thought was a long shot from being probable, and I'd been forcing it away whenever it started tingling the back of my brain, but it was a thought.

I had another thought. I snapped a picture of the LeBaron and swung into Archie Midlan's car lot on my way home.

Midlan was a third cousin of Rivertown's mayor, and dealt questionably in questionable automobiles, as had his father and grandfather. From Rivertown, of Rivertown, the Midlans sold used cars on the town's eastern border with Chicago.

It was Archie's father who came up with the pricing dots. Instead of haggling over prices on each car in their lot, a practice he found uncomfortable in the blurred hours after lunch, he slapped little round colored dots on each car's bumper, denoting a non-negotiable selling price. Blue meant $1,000, green meant $1,500, and so on up in five-hundred-dollar increments.

There was a special, high risk category. Red dots, much smaller than the other colored dots, denoted cars with special pedigrees, or rather the lack of them. Red Dot cars, no matter their condi-tion, sold for a flat $400 because no car title was offered during the sale. They were stolen cars, expected to be used for a very short time before being abandoned. I'd spotted one such little red dot on the back bumper of Tripp's LeBaron.

Everybody liked Archie Midlan, especially high-school boys. He let them hang out on his car lot and check out cars that they couldn't afford to buy. I used to be one of those boys. Martin Tripp, almost certainly, was another. He would have known where to get a cheap, short-use automobile.

I hadn't seen Archie for years, but clearly, he'd not suffered malnutrition. The belly hanging over his blue jeans looked to be within minutes of launching the bottom button of his white shirt. A yellow necktie, spotted by the residue of more than one trip to someplace that served marinara, completed the ensemble.

He didn't remember me, like he wouldn't have remembered any of the decades of high-school boys that came to ogle his cheap cars. I introduced myself, gave him a business card and showed him my driver's license. Things would go nowhere if he thought I was a non-Rivertown cop.

'I'm here about a car someone bought,' I said.

His eyes narrowed, as if innocent. 'What do you mean?'

'I'm doing you a favor. There's repossession interest in it, though why, I don't know; it's a heap. Chicago cops will become interested soon enough. Right now, they don't know where it came from, other than it's on their hot sheet. It'll stay that way, but I need information.'

Archie was a businessman that wanted to stay a businessman. 'A LeBaron, you say?' he asked, but it was careful. He looked around, probably from habit, because no one seemed to be watching us.

I showed him the picture I'd taken with my phone.

'Martin Tripp,' he said.

'I already know that.'

'There's nothing more to say about it, then.'

'When was he here?'

'I'd have to check my records, but some of my records must have been accidentally thrown out,' he said, like that wasn't a laughable lie.

'Approximately,' I said.

He gave me a date that was about a week before Martin Tripp came to see me for the first time. I had no doubt that Tripp had checked into the Afforda-Rest at the same time.

It made sense. He would have needed a car to get him from the motel to Rivertown, where he could pretend to be homeless.

SIXTEEN

The nags didn't stop.

The dismissive note I'd slipped in Tripp's three-wheeled LeBaron didn't stop the loose threads of the skein from taunting. I woke the next morning bothered by the same questions I brought to bed the night before. Tripp wanted answers but he didn't want me to find them. He didn't want me to find his lover, Julianna Wynton, and he didn't want me to contact his lawyer, the clever Apples Aplon. It was one reason enough to do both. The other reason was that I didn't know what else to do, except go hunting for a cat.

I'd googled Julianna Wynton once before, to find her address in Weston. There'd been few other listings, and those only on career networking sites, so the only next play was to call Abbott Gifts. Her district manager answered the phone himself. He was angry. She'd quit calling in months earlier. He knew she'd moved, but he didn't know where. Exasperation at losing a high-performing sales representative was clear in his voice, and he pleaded with me to tell him what was going on. I told him I could only guess that she'd been traumatized by a murder in her neighborhood. I supposed it was the truth, and I supposed there was a lot more to it.

Apples Aplon was next. His office was in a storefront in the middle of a struggling strip mall. Half the units were vacant. Those still twitching were a nail salon, a yogurt shop, an auto parts store, a vitamin store for the recovering health conscious, and, next to Aplon's office, a submarine sandwich shop to counter whatever benefits might be had from the vitamin store.

Another storefront was about to become vacant. Apples was moving. A white van, rented for $19.98 for the day according to the paint on its side, was backed up to his door, and Apples himself, who I recognized from his newspaper photo, was putting cardboard file boxes into it. He was short and portly and wasn't dressed in what one of the reporters covering the trial described as the 'flash' of a shiny sharkskin suit. Today's outfit was more plebeian, though it still flashed. His worn blue jeans sported glittery stitching at the sides and across the back pockets, and his yellow polo shirt was piped red, white, and green at the collar. Oddly, he joined the pairing with scuffed brown wingtip shoes, an indication, I took to mean, that he'd not yet become rich.

'Mr Aplon?' I inquired.

He set the box he was carrying down at the edge of the truck. Pulling a crumpled paper towel from an embroidered pocket, he wiped the brow that ran to the back of his head and smiled. 'If you'd like a consultation—'

'I'm Elstrom. I believe Martin Tripp called you about me?'

He furrowed the lowest three inches of his brow. 'I've not heard from Martin.'

'I'm looking into something, at his request,' I said.

'Martin, Martin,' he said.

'Just ten minutes?' I asked.

'We'll sit at that table,' he said, leading me to a wrought-iron table outside the submarine shop.

We'd just sat down when the door to the sandwich place swung inward and a woman in a white apron stuck her head out. 'Apples!' she said loudly, but not unkindly.

'Ten minutes, Linda,' he said, 'and then I'm gone.'

He smiled, unruffled at her intrusion into his business practice, and said, 'I hit a home run with Martin Tripp.'

'He has me looking into his innocence.'

He laughed. 'His innocence? We won!'

'He says that's not good enough.'

'Why? He's free. He can start a new life.' He frowned. 'He was always so difficult.'

'Resisting somnambulistic homicide?'

'He had no trust.'

'It was a very daring approach,' I said.

'It worked!' he said. 'Martin walked out a free man, obligated to nothing. I can see the day when I'll be in all the law texts.'

'Two of your jurors were nuts,' I said.

'That helped, I don't deny.'

'Sara had a visitor the day she was killed,' I said. 'A man wearing a hat and long coat on a hot day.'

'A realtor, a neighbor said.'

'Not with Maple Realty,' I said.

'Then with another firm,' he said. 'It was a nonstarter.'

'Tripp never intimated he knew who it was?'

'He never intimated he knew Sara had a visitor,' he said, 'until I told him.'

'Did you believe him? The neighbor said the visitor frightened her.'

'A nonstarter, like I said. The neighbor was too far away from the man to identify him.'

'It should have been followed up.'

His face clouded for a moment, then brightened with a plausible answer. 'It would have been the basis for appeal if we lost.'

'Another neighbor thought he saw someone lurking outside the house, shortly before Sara's time of death.'

'That was the wind, I heard,' he said.

'You didn't canvass the neighborhood to see if anyone else saw something?'

'The police would have done that, and made available anything they learned. There was nothing usable.'

'Tripp's description of his supposed intruder, before he recanted, described someone who fit the neighbor woman's description of a small man wearing a hat and long coat.'

'Similar to the neighbor's description of the visitor?' He shook his head. 'Like I said, she was too far away to be precise. And like you just said, Tripp said he made the intruder up.'

'Tripp was with a woman that night,' I said. 'Why not use her as an alibi witness?'

'Ah, the lovely Julianna,' he said. 'Have you seen her?'

'Just the one picture of them walking out of the courthouse after the verdict.'

'I've never seen her in person, either,' he said, 'but that picture only confirmed the wisdom of my decision to keep her out of the courtroom. She packs huge firepower. Martin was in bed with her that night, doing naughty things. If I had introduced her to the jury, they would have compared her to the less-than-gorgeous Sara. My client would have suffered, and his infidelity would have hurt the jury's sympathy for him.'

'Your sole strategy was to be unkind to Sara. You introduced several witnesses who painted her as a shrew.'

'Julianna would have been destructive to Martin. She would be seen as a temptress.'

'But she would have said she was with Martin.'

'At what time?' he said. 'He didn't know what time he woke up, left, or how long he walked. The jury would have seen that he could have come home and killed her afterward. Counter-productive, I'm afraid.'

'It might have caused enough doubt that he had time to kill her.'

'What does it matter?' he said. 'The jury bought somnambu-listic homicide. Case closed.'

'Only two of the jurors bought it, Mr Aplon. Two of twelve.'

'Our system doesn't demand unanimity. All it takes is one juror, and I found two.'

The sandwich shop door opened. 'Apples! Now!'

He stood up. 'I've told you what I can,' he said.

I followed him to the rented truck. 'Bigger office?'

'Phone rings all day long, now.' His face clouded. 'Nut cases, moon beams, but there'll be some good ones soon. In the mean-time, I'll work out of my apartment.' And with that, he walked into the darkness of his empty office.

We had that in common. I was walking in darkness, too.

SEVENTEEN

I called Amanda from the Jeep. 'I have lasagna,' I said, the way some men, even some ex-husbands, would announce candy or flowers.

'What about chili?' she asked, the way some women, even some ex-wives, would question a man's motives after he'd admitted to discarding something precious, like a quart of chili, and to a confessed killer at that.

'Alas, that remains gone. As does, I think, the man I gave it to. He has vanished.'

'Martin Tripp is gone?'

I told her of my visits to Tripp's motel.

'What does this mean to your investigation?'

'I'm done with Tripp. *Finito.*'

'You lie. Tell me about the lasagna.'

'I blew almost the last of Tripp's money on four pounds of the stuff.'

'Four pounds? Why did you buy four pounds?'

'The people now running The Hamburger are going broke. They needed a happy night. The lasagna is good and nobly purchased. Come over and find out how good things can get.'

'After we're done assembling.'

'Your window has been replaced?'

'Yes.'

'And you've found out who tossed the brick?'

'That's in process.'

'How much in process?'

'Sufficient for now.'

'And you remain unfearful?'

'Of course.'

'You lie.'

'I am purposeful, but I have to go now,' she said.

I called the Bohemian.

As always, he said that he would see me immediately. I believe he is immediately accessible to all of his clients, though other than Amanda, I do not know their names. I do know that to be accepted as a client, one must be in the heavy cream of those that move and shake Chicago. If one is rich, one knows of him. If one is rich enough, the Bohemian will agree to know him or her in return.

He is always spoken of reverentially, not as Anton Chernek, but as the Bohemian. Mostly, he is a financial adviser, a portfolio manager for higher-ups in business, politics and even, some say, in organized religion and organized crime.

Less frequently, he advises on matters stickier than finances. The very rich have the very real problems of everyone, but theirs are often magnified exponentially by their wealth. In those instances, the Bohemian becomes the most confidential of fixers.

He makes problems go away, quietly and unobtrusively, often legally, sometimes not.

When Amanda first filed for divorce, the Bohemian feared I would be one of those problems. I was summoned to meet with him. I surprised him by saying I was at fault for everything, and wanted nothing from Amanda except forgiveness. Given Amanda's stupendous wealth and my stupendous lack of same, that surprised him. He gave me paper after paper to sign. I signed them all, without more than cursory glances. Over time, we developed a genial relationship, and occasionally, he advised me without fee.

Chernek and Associates had offices just west of downtown Chicago, at the top of a ten-story yellow-brick former factory in one of the city's first rehab districts. The wire-gated elevator opened directly into the hush of a reception area colored mostly in green. The leather on the wing chairs was the same green as old money. The wallpaper was a muted, though lighter, green, and the glass shades on the lamps were green. The Bohemian's place, not coincidentally, was one of green.

I crossed the oriental rug, which was refreshingly burgundy and beige and not green, and smiled at the young receptionist. She was new. They were always new, whip-smart, recent MBAs from Northwestern's Kellogg School. They came to the Bohemian to be noticed by his visitors, to be hired away for six-figure salaries as financial analysts, or moved inside, to work on the Bohemian's own client portfolios. As always, the receptionist that day was noticeable. She wore a beige silk dress that perfectly highlighted her blonde hair and tanned skin. Nothing about her had likely ever exuded green.

'Dek Elstrom to see Anton Chernek,' I said, like I had enough money to belong there.

She acted like she believed that, touched a button on her telephone console, and murmured my name in a way that it had never been murmured, even in my most fevered dreams in high school.

In a flash, contrast came like grit blowing off a desert. The Bohemian's secretary, a helmet-haired, frowning woman laughingly misnamed Buffy, came for me. As usual, she was attired as if to darken a funeral, in a navy pinstriped suit and a white blouse starched and high-collared enough to repel any invasion.

She offered no greeting, merely turned and led me hurriedly

past rows of cubicles as one might hurry a Saint Bernard about to be overcome with dysentery, to the open door of the small conference room adjacent to the Bohemian's private office.

He sat at the round walnut table and rose from yet another dark green leather chair. 'Vuh-lo-dek!' he pronounced, rolling the two syllables of my given first name into three with the enthusiasm of someone delighted at sharing similar ancestry, though as he often laughingly points out, I am only of half-nobility. My non-Bohemian side is Norwegian.

He wore nothing green. His charcoal gray, pinstriped suit jacket hung on a walnut stand. His shirt was a pale blue with a burgundy tie that only accented the deep tan he got from year-round golf at the lush courses at Pebble Beach, the PGA in Florida, or the Masters links in Augusta. Closer to home, he played with the powerful at Butler in Oak Brook.

'My office is being swept,' he said as we sat, nodding at the closed door leading to his office. It was undergoing one of its routine sweeps for listening devices. 'How can I help?'

'I come with primary and secondary concerns. Primary is Amanda.'

I watched his face but as usual, when discussing clients, it was expressionless.

'Someone threw a brick through her storefront window several days ago,' I said, 'followed by a phone call saying there would be a bomb.'

'Minor vandalism?' he asked, which would have been expected and betrayed nothing of what he already knew.

'Vandalism isn't normally followed by a bomb threat.'

'Bricks are being thrown through windows these days. Looting hooliganism.'

'I'm going to continue talking, as if you know nothing of this,' I said.

He offered a faint smile, but nothing more.

'She wants to handle the matter without my intrusion,' I said. 'By that, I hope she means she's talked to you about this, and asked for any inquiries that might pinpoint who's responsible. She suspects someone well fixed who feels threatened by her neighborhood assembly operation.'

'A board member concerned about diminishing his own social

prominence?' he said. 'Someone who might hire someone to toss a brick, but never to actually toss a bomb?'

I laughed, at the relief of the charade. He knew what she was up to. 'As always, you've chosen the perfect words,' I said.

'You are a wonderful ex-husband, Vlodek. Now, there is another matter?'

I told him of my investigation into Martin Tripp.

'You're saying Tripp became interested in the source of Sara Jansen's down payment.'

'She came up with twenty-two thousand dollars, all in cash, to put down on a house. That's a lot to have been saved by a woman working for minimum wages at a grocery and at a bank.'

'A bank,' he repeated, for emphasis.

'A bank where a bagman comes to deposit street taxes he's collected.'

'A bagman who also became interested in the source of Sara Jansen's down payment?'

'A bagman who might have resembled Sara Jansen's mysterious visitor, the afternoon before she was murdered. And who might have returned that night.' I told him of the neighbor who saw something that could have been a trick of a midnight wind. Or not.

He shrugged. 'Anyone can learn of a house purchase on the internet, if not the details of exactly how much was put down.' he said. 'Any clue to the visitor's identity?'

'According to a neighbor, he was small, wore a long coat. And he wore a hat. The small stature and the hat part sound like the description Tripp made up to describe the fictitious intruder. Later, after the trial and about the same time Tripp showed up in Rivertown, another long-absent fellow returned to town. His name is Kowalski. He is short and likes hats.'

'And he is a bagman?' the Bohemian asked, for he is astute.
'He was.'

'You're basing suppositions on the notion that this fellow likes hats?'

'He left Rivertown suddenly, about the same time as Sara Jansen, perhaps a little before, which was just a little before Martin Tripp left to move in with Sara. The bank where Sara worked serves as a laundry for the cash the bagmen collect.'

'So Kowalski and Sara knew each other,' he said.

'Yes, and Kowalski and Tripp were drinking buddies.'

'No salacious rumors as to why any of them left town?'

'Nothing about her or Tripp, as far as I can tell. There were the usual jokes about a bagman fleeing with a bag of loot, which was to be expected, but Kowalski was trusted. Most people think he left because of a certain tattoo,' I said, and explained about the rumors that half the town had heard about.

'Hence his perpetual hat?'

'Yes.'

'You offer all this simply as deduction?' he asked.

'Tinged with brilliance,' I said.

He laughed, long and loud, and then his face turned serious. 'It doesn't go very far.'

'That's why I'm here. If it was the former bagman, Kowalski, who went knocking on Sara's door just hours before she was murdered, he must have become interested in how she got the money to buy a house. He could have come back late that night.'

'The shadow the neighbor saw?'

'Perhaps, but only as a shadow. The neighbor who saw the visitor that afternoon was too far away. She did tell the cops, but to them, and Tripp's lawyer, the visitor was simply a hat and a coat. They weren't interested in something so vague, and also because Sara said the visitor was a realtor. But what's really interesting is the fact that Tripp and Kowalski were drinking buddies.'

'Sharing speculations of misappropriated money?'

'Perhaps,' I said.

'You want me to find out if any money went missing in Rivertown around the time Sara got rich enough to buy a house?'

'If you find that out for me, I will reward you commensurately.'

'You're chasing the magnificent sum of twenty-two-thousand dollars?'

'All of it unrecoverable,' I said.

'It's chump change, Vlodek. That amount, and more, must be what those lizards shake out of local businesses every day. If Sara Jansen swiped a day's take, your town fathers would be angry, but not apoplectic.'

'They're interested in Tripp,' I said. 'The mayor's driver, a cabbie named Gertz, asked me about him, as did Kowalski himself.'

The Bohemian's face turned serious. 'My ability to learn anything about what goes on in Rivertown is extremely limited.'

I understood. My request was for a Hail Mary pass, a prayerful throw into a murky end zone. The corruption in Rivertown was closely guarded by lizards. Their webbed claws did not extend past their city limits, where the Bohemian might troll for information.

I stood up. 'But more important, let me know if I can help,' I said.

He understood. We weren't talking about the Tripp matter any longer.

EIGHTEEN

'This is wonderful,' Amanda said the next morning. 'Hooky!'

We were rattling northwest through Illinois in the Jeep, toward Wisconsin.

'I can't think of anyplace else to look for Tripp,' I said.

Amanda shifted on the passenger's seat so she could watch my face, the loveliest of smiles on her own. 'Or any reason to let this go?'

'I want to get rid of the nags,' I said. It was true enough. Nothing about Tripp coming to see me made sense.

'Yesterday, you said you were done.'

I said nothing.

'And the day before,' she said.

'Maybe today,' I said, with as much false sincerity as I could muster.

'You really think he's hiding out at that woman's cottage?'

'I'm hoping he got spooked, left his clothes and his car at the Afforda-Rest to make it appear he'd been abducted, and decided to cool things safely in Wisconsin,' I said.

'Or . . .?'

'Or he's up to something, and played me like a harp to get it.'

'Or . . .?'

'He's dead.'

'What will cause you to drop this?'

'I'll know right after this Tripp trip,' I said, evading, but cleverly.

She grinned. 'Uh, huh.'

'You didn't ask me where I went after the Afforda-Rest,' I said, thinking to ease into the real reason why I wanted to be alone with her in the Jeep, where she couldn't hang up a phone.

'Stick to the subject,' she said, which didn't necessarily mean the Bohemian had called her to say I'd stopped by, nosing. The Bohemian respected all confidences, even those of a non-client such as me.

I said nothing, thinking to let my silence talk.

'That means you won't push to learn what I'm doing about my brick-thrower?' she said after a pause.

'Now that you mention it . . .'

'That was what you did after leaving the Afforda-Rest? You went to see the Bohemian?'

'He respects confidences,' I said.

'So I learned when I called to find out whether you'd stopped by,' she said. 'So, here we are, intent on not spoiling a nice hooky. Now, tell me about the nice lady, or not, whose cottage we are about to visit.'

'It's still speculation,' I said, after telling her what little I'd learned. 'Everything surrounding Martin Tripp is always speculation.'

'I keep thinking that it makes no sense for a guilty man to hire you,' she said.

'I don't know what makes sense,' I said. 'Sara Jansen is dead. Tripp has disappeared—'

'If we can't find a lead to Tripp up here, this will be a wasted trip?' She laughed. 'You mean it didn't cross your mind to find out what I'm up to with the brick-thrower?'

'Did I mention I went to see the Bohemian?' I said.

She laughed again.

Verona was south of Madison, and north, east, and west of not much at all. Piney, rural, it was a log cabin mini-mart with two gas pumps at the intersection of two country roads, all of it stuck in the permanent shadow of tall trees.

'We've been here before,' she said.

She was right. We'd been to a similar dark meeting of pine-shadowed, rural roads in the Pacific Northwest. She'd charmed a lot of information out of one of the locals, an elderly gent perched, to watch the time go by, at the top of the steps of an abandoned ice house. I was more of mixed expectations this time around. I wanted to put Martin Tripp out of my mind for forever, and I needed answers to do that.

I gassed the Jeep and went inside. The rail-thin kid behind the counter was cast in shadow himself, there being only a single low-wattage fluorescent fixture dangling unevenly above the counter.

'He'p you?' he asked, setting aside the dog-eared movie magazine he was reading.

'Julianna Wynton,' I said.

It brought no change of expression. 'Sorry?' he asked.

'I'm trying to find the Wynton place,' I said. 'It's on a lake.'

'Which lake? Lots of lakes up here.'

'I don't know the name.'

'Big Tick, Little Tick, Saddle Lake, Round,' he recited in a sing-song voice. 'Crystal Lake, White Lake, Red Lake, too. Lots of lakes and lots of cottages on them.'

'Who might be able to help me?'

'That guy your lady friend is talking to,' he said, pointing out the window.

A white-bearded man in a gray postal service uniform had pulled in to gas a rusted yellow Dodge Dart. Amanda had gotten out of the Jeep to talk to him.

'This gentleman says Julianna Wynton's cottage on Little Tick isn't her primary home,' she said when I walked up.

'She ain't there much,' White Beard said.

'Mail piling up?' I asked.

'No mail comes for Julianna, not for years,' he said.

'Julianna's quite a beauty, though?' Amanda asked, giving him a wink.

'She does have an admirer, now and again,' he said.

'The postman always knows,' Amanda said.

I pulled out my phone, tapped into the internet, and summoned up the news photo I'd so despised, of Tripp, carrying clothes and smirking at trial's end, walking with a woman out of the courthouse.

'That's him, with her,' he said. 'Who is he?'

'A man who lies,' I said.

Little Tick Lake looked superb for the exponential multiplication of little ticks. The surrounding marshes and heavy woods kept the small body of water in deep, dank shade, and a number of tamped-down deer trails in the woods offered ready highways for those ticks seeking to mingle with cousins at the surrounding lakes.

Small white cottages, where people went to scratch, were scattered widely in the woods along the clay road. Some were peeling, some not yet. I didn't suppose people came to those woods to spend much time on home maintenance.

We passed four before we came to one that had the name 'Wynton' painted in faded red on its gray metal mailbox. The mailbox was rusted at the front hinges.

'The postman was right,' Amanda said. 'It doesn't look like anyone's gotten mail here in years.'

Like its neighbors, the cottage was in minor disrepair. Its sides were spotted with thousands of curlicues of white paint anxious to drop, and the roof was missing a few asphalt shingles. I parked tight against the trees.

The door at the back, facing the road, was the same faded shade of red that lettered the name on the rusted mailbox. I knocked, waited, knocked again, then tried the knob. It was locked. We walked around to the front.

A screened porch faced the small lake, offering views of the water and, for those with super-human eyesight, thousands of frolicking little ticks. There was no lock on its flimsy door.

We crossed the porch to the front door. The window next to it had been shattered inward to gain access to the inside lock. 'Thieves?' Amanda asked.

'Or Martin Tripp, looking to hide out,' I said. 'He lied about not knowing that she had a cottage.'

'Something else to throw you off?'

'That's what I'm thinking, but who hires someone to throw them off?'

The knob turned easily and we stepped into a sparsely furnished combination living room and back kitchen. Open doors led into two small bedrooms off to the right.

The place had been tossed. There was no furniture on the braided oval rug. Three red vinyl chairs had been pushed against the wall. A scarred cocktail table was leaned on edge next to them.

Amanda stayed by the door as I walked back to the kitchen area. A dented green Coleman ice chest served for food storage. I raised the lid. The ice inside was melted. Plastic-wrapped cold cuts lay submerged in the water, dated the previous week by a grocery in Antioch, just south of the Wisconsin state line.

A pump handle protruded out of the plywood kitchen counter, pointed into a tin sink. I pumped the handle. After a time, water came out. It was clear and not rusty. By the somewhat fresh cold cuts and clear pump water, it hadn't been long since someone had been there.

Each bedroom held a folded-up camp cot and a single small table with a kerosene lantern. There were no clothes, pillows or bed sheets. That meant nothing. The place could have been plundered by thieves satisfied with a cheap haul. Or it could have been recently occupied by someone who hadn't thought to bring sheets and pillows, like someone on the run from a cheap motel in Chicago.

When I stepped back into the living room, Amanda was kneeling at the edge of the braided rug, holding it up. She pointed to a brownish stain on its underside and on the planks of the wood floor beneath.

We folded the rug farther back. The brownish stain had been absorbed into a full third of the underside of the thick braids and I was almost certain it had started out red before it dried. It also seemed likely that whatever sheets and towels that had been in the cottage were used to wrap whatever had spilled the blood.

We folded the rug back and went out through the porch.

'Not animal blood?' Amanda asked. Her voice was small, as if she was speaking from far away.

'People stick around to scrub away animal blood,' I said.

'And the body?'

I waved my hand vaguely at the dense woods surrounding us. 'The killer wouldn't have taken time to carry it very far.'

She took a breath, and pointed. 'Like along there?'

A three-foot-wide swath had been crushed into the weeds leading away from the cottage, clear as a runway. I told her to wait by the cottage and followed the short trail. It ended at a mound of rotting leaves between two trees, about a hundred yards from the cottage. I kicked the top leaves of the pile aside with my foot, exposing a speck of white the size of a quarter. I knelt to expose a little more, touched it to be sure, and straightened up.

'Dek?'

I hadn't heard her footsteps.

She looked down. 'My God! Is that . . .?'

I brushed the leaves back over the bone and we stood together silently for a time, looking down now at nothing at all. My mind raced over scenarios. The trashed cottage suggested a mad search for something, and it wasn't hard to believe it had to be cash, big cash. And that narrowed the number of owners of the bone to two. I might have found the remains of Julianna Wynton, who'd not been seen in quite some time, killed by Tripp for what she knew about Sara's murder. Or they could belong to Tripp, killed for whatever cash he was suspected of having, or, like Julianna, for what he knew. One thing was for sure: the bone I'd just discovered, and the ones that were surely beneath it, demanded the proper ruckus of a lawful investigation. They needed the respect of identification and the chance to point to a killer.

But then I rationalized. The speck of bone was clean; maybe it was recent or maybe it had suffered several years in the ground, time enough for the clues it, and the bones beneath it, could have offered to be nibbled away by animals and insects. And the bones didn't even need to be Julianna Wynton's, or Martin Tripp's. If I were to call the county sheriff, Amanda and I would be detained while some county forensics team and medical examiner processed the cottage, the woods, the body, and us. We'd be asked what we were doing up there. I'd say I was snooping around on behalf of a client. I'd then be asked who my client was. I'd try to cite client confidentiality, but then I'd be asked if I was a licensed private investigator. I'd say no, I freelanced claims investigations for insurance companies when I was lucky enough to find any work at all, and when – I'd have to admit – I wasn't otherwise occupied chasing cats to make a hundred dollars. They'd check Rivertown and eventually they'd learn I was acting on behalf of someone who'd been found not guilty of murdering his wife, even though his own lawyer freely admitted in court that he'd done it. Maybe worse, if the bones were recent, it was possible that the confessed killer who was now my client was likely on the run after burying the bones I'd just found. All of it would incite the ire of whatever passed for tick-bitten, local law enforcement in Verona, and I, and perhaps Amanda, would be tossed in a cooler until I coughed up information I didn't have, and where I could do no one any justice.

'Dek? What now?' Amanda whispered.

'It's a muddle, and it is not,' I said, because to say anything that actually made sense was beyond me.

I swept back more leaves to cover the bone, and drove us south and away.

NINETEEN

I did not expect Martin Tripp to be sitting on the bench by the Willahock the next morning and he wasn't. I was not disappointed.

I didn't think I had to worry about Kowalski nosing around the turret to find out what I knew, and he was nowhere in sight. That did not disappoint me either.

I did not expect a black cat to be nearby, lapping up the last of the saucer of milk I'd put out the evening before, but one was. I was delighted.

Quick as I could say, 'Hundred dollars,' I scooped it up. It seemed affable and tame enough to be the mayor's mother's pet, and purred agreeably as I hoofed across the broad lawn to city hall.

I was grateful for the diversion. Agonizing over whether to report the discovery of what were likely the long-absent Julianna Wynton's remains had kept me up most of the night. Martin

Tripp, the likely burier of the bones, was my client, and I felt some obligation toward confidentiality. On the other hand, he was a confessed killer, and if he'd killed again, he deserved nothing from me.

To my shame, there were other considerations. I'd suffered horrible notoriety, years before, that led to the self-pickling and self-pity that cost me my marriage and my business, an abyss that I was still struggling to completely break out of. I had no appetite for more.

Those thoughts fought it out, all night long, and escorting a cat to city hall seemed the best way to put it all out of my mind, if only for part of the morning.

Even at nine o'clock, three dozen people holding cats had gotten to city hall before me. So had the heat. It was already close to ninety degrees and most of the people and for all I knew, most of the cats, were perspiring.

'It's chaos,' the woman in line ahead of me said, looking at three women spreading apart the shrubbery down by the river. 'I mean, the whole town's out pokin' at bushes.'

'Heaven help us if there's a fire,' said the women ahead of her, pointing at two Rivertown brown-uniformed firemen who'd crawled under a large evergreen. 'The town would burn to the ground.'

'No worry so long as the cat gets found,' the first one said, and they both laughed.

I looked around and spotted three cops, also reaching into nearby shrubs. It was early for any police to be out and upright, being as the bars had only just closed, and though I imagined that no hiccup in law and order would be noticed, something I couldn't identify nagged about the scene I was witnessing.

I had no real expectations about the cat I was holding. The posters that had been slapped everywhere described no identifying characteristics on the mayor's mother's black cat, reason enough why so many black cats were being brought to city hall. Yet there must have been some readily identifiable mark on the missing feline because the line was moving briskly. Cats were being inspected and dispatched quickly.

I gave my furry friend a thorough going-over, and could find no marks, no discolorations, no identifying marks of any kind. I whispered into the cat's ear that I was afraid it was a loser.

When the two women in front of me finally got to the head of the line, they were sent away within seconds. Like everyone I saw, they set their cats down on the ground to scamper away.

'See you tomorrow,' one said to the other. There was a black smudge on the front of her yellow and green sundress, a catalog item of the sort prized by many of the more stylish ladies of Rivertown. I'd noticed that sort of smudge on the clothing of some of the others leaving the line. I held my cat out and looked down. I, too, was smudged. Chicanery was afoot in ever-crooked Rivertown. Someone was coloring cats.

My cat merited less than a ten-second glance before being handed back.

'How do you know?' I asked.

'We just do,' the boy half of the pair said. He sported a losing battle with acne and his hair was short at the top but long and greased back at the sides, in a style I believed was called a 'Flat top with fenders,' back in the 1950s.

I had to ask, because I'd never seen anyone sport a 'do' like that, save for one. 'Is your name Derbil?'

They both said yes. I turned to the girl. She was younger, and had a silver nose ring big enough to hang her on a wall, if someone was so inclined.

'You're a Derbil, too?' I asked her.

She nodded enthusiastically, and that caused the nose ring to swing up alarmingly. I had the urge to reach to stop it before it wrapped around her nose and smacked her eyes.

Fortunately, she stopped nodding and the ring settled back down. 'Derbil, just like my brother here,' she said.

Derbils were common at city hall, clinging like tree tumors to one of the more stunted branches of the family that ran the town. Elvis Derbil, before he'd been sent to prison for relabeling stale-dated salad dressing, had been Rivertown's zoning czar, and my tormentor, when I first moved into the turret. He fought me relentlessly over replacing the leaking original roof. He claimed a new roof would compromise the turret's authenticity as a town landmark, even after I pointed out that the roof was invisible behind the stone balustrade. I won out but it was an exhausting battle. Derbils were not noted for analytical thinking, so putting two of them in charge of inspecting cats meant that the identifying marks of the right cat were readily discernible.

And so I asked, 'There must be a mark you're looking for?' now that we'd established a relationship.

'We know,' they said in unison, almost as if they shared the same brain. And that meant that city hall didn't want that mark to be known, for fear those that were blackening cats would begin further moderations.

As had the ladies before me, I set my cat loose as I walked away, and there was no sense to that. Cats were being set free after inspection, to be picked up again for re-inspection, again and again. I had to believe that the lizards accepted that the chaos absorbing the town's cops, firemen, and much of its population would go on and on until the right cat was found.

Instead of walking back across the lawn, I detoured to take the street that separates my turret from the overgrown mess of a park that stretched out to Thompson Avenue and stopped to marvel at the hundreds of people that were crawling, literally, all over it, looking for the four-legged creatures. It was thorny work, and I imagined a lot of them would go home bloodied that day.

A number I didn't recognize chirped on my cell phone. I answered because I answer every unrecognized call, such is my desperation for paying work.

'I have very limited news,' the Bohemian said, from one of the burner phones he'd begun using as a caution against eavesdroppers. 'A contact, not at all well connected, said, "watch him because they are."'

'Who is being watched?'

'I don't know, Vlodek. My contact, a man of minor knowledge, said only that. He sounded frightened, hence the cryptic few words. I will endeavor to learn more.'

'Law enforcement is doing the watching?'

'No idea.'

'No word about a money theft?'

'He hung up when I started to ask.'

After he clicked me away, I went in the turret and upstairs to the slit window that best overlooked Thompson Avenue, the pulsing spine of Rivertown. The lizards have controlled it for over five generations, feeding off its strip of sinful delights – mostly tonks, but hock shops, too, and slots parlors, tattoo places, and now a weed emporium, just opened, for those who can't get blurred from alcohol. The lizards don't own all the joints in Rivertown, just the most profitable of them. They let dozens of independents, like dry cleaners, an antique store, the Discount Den, and of course the hookers, operate alongside their own enterprises, so long as they are not troublesome, pay street taxes, and smile whenever some zealous law person comes around – except the hookers, who smile whenever anyone at all comes around.

And come around, the Fed, state, and county cops did, but almost always so blatantly obvious that they leave with nothing. And when they do land something, it's a minor fish – an Elvis Derbil, switching salad-oil labels – and not one of the big tunas that run the town. And Rivertown beats on, impervious.

It occurred to me then that it might not be law enforcement that was doing the watching, that it might be the lizards, and that 'watch him because they are' made the best sense if the 'they' were the lizards, and the 'him' was Tripp or Kowalski. Both were newly returned to town. One was a confessed killer, the other a bagman who'd taken off suddenly and might also be a killer.

It was all too confusing to make more sense of, but I was not too confused to know what I should next. I drove to Kutz's clearing because my friend Leo was counting on my vigilance, and because I was curious about what Ma Brumsky was up to with the heavy equipment, and because I was hungry.

The crane was gone but the large curved pieces of metal I'd seen lying on the ground were now assembled into a gigantic tube. Mrs Roshiska, attired of late, like all of Ma's pals, in a pink poodle skirt and pink T-shirt, was assembled almost as closely to two young men seated at a picnic table, perhaps to scrub the speck of table between them. All three were laughing.

Four other ladies of similar septuagenarian ripening were at work at other tables, and on the young men at them. They were laughing, too, and I realized I'd never heard so much laughter at Kutz's clearing. I took a picture only of the long line of people waiting to order, most of them young men, and texted it to Leo with the message that good business and rejuvenation were happening in the clearing.

'What's with the big metal tube, Ma?' I asked when I got up to the order window.

'Big surprise, Dekkie,' she said.

'No combination today,' I said. 'Just the kielbasa.'

'No Coke?'

I shook my head, mindful once more of my lack of funds, but I must have shaken my head like when I was a kid and had no lunch to take to school. And so it was again. She slid a kielbasa through the window, with a cola, a full order of the lethal barbecue cheese fries, and a shake of her own head as she pushed back the money I put on the counter.

It is good that such good can exist.

Kowalski was leaning against a tree. I walked over. 'No cat today, no pierogies?' I said.

'I already ate,' he said. 'Pierogies, not a cat,' he added, being a wit.

'Things are changing,' I said, taking a casual glance around to see if anyone was watching him. 'Pierogies, and cats.'

He nodded, not laughing, and took a slow gander of his own around.

'Ever think about Sara Jansen?' I asked, between mouthfuls to make it sound casual.

He walked away, which was just as well. I had other questions for him but wasn't quite prepared to ask them yet.

I finished my kielbasa and went to the Jeep, but as I turned onto Thompson, to head back to the turret, I caught sight of a shiny metallic-gray Ford 150 pickup truck slipping in two cars behind me. I remembered either that truck, or one exactly like it, parked in Kutz's clearing.

I am not naturally paranoiac but I took an easy turn left onto another highway and headed south. The gray truck followed, again staying carefully behind two cars. The opportunity of a residential side street came up on the right and I turned into it. He followed, but at a longer distance because there were no intervening cars to hide behind. He remained a consistent gray blur as I continued west through several more blocks. Finally, tiring of being a mouse to his cat, I swung back up to Thompson Avenue. He stayed with me and parked along Thompson when I swung onto the side street that led to the turret.

Getting out, I turned as if to look casually at the people hunting for cats in the bramble across the street. As I'd hoped, the overgrowth partially obscured the truck parked across the spit of land. I turned back, opened the turret's timbered door and, stepping inside, partially closed the door behind me. And then I dropped to my knees, crawled outside, and pulled the door shut. I could only hope that the bramble obscured me from my watcher.

I ran across the street in a crouch, and into the park. Nobody paid me any attention; my bent-over posture was typical of the cat-hunters swarming there. I moved low until I got to a stout tree on the far side, fifteen yards from the truck.

The driver had a cell phone pressed to his ear. He was young, wore a white T-shirt and a blue Chicago Cubs baseball cap, and was turned to keep his eyes on the turret while he talked. After a moment he nodded, set the phone down, and settled back to keep watching the turret.

Fifteen minutes passed, and then another fifteen, and then he reached for the ignition, fired the truck, and drove away.

I had a choice. I could either be the Swiffer, or the Swiffee – the sweeper, or the swept-up.

I ran back through the bramble, to the Jeep.

TWENTY

I couldn't find the gray truck along the blocks of tonks on Thompson Avenue, so I cruised the street behind it, which was slow work because it required waving off the geriatric hookers that specialized in working the geriatric men who came to Rivertown for early-bird specials of the sort that couldn't be found at Denny's.

There was no gray truck back there either, but after a few minutes, and a dozen wave-offs, I noticed a dirty red truck with a dented front grill following me, block by block. I wasn't just a one-truck target. Multiple resources were being employed to find out what I was trying to find out.

I had the strong urge to jump out and run back to ask the red truck guy what it was people thought I knew, but before I could slam on the brakes, my cell phone sounded.

'I'm back,' Leo said.

'The Rockefeller treasures have been disposed of?'

'What are you doing now?'

'Slow cruising, trying to figure out who's tailing me and why.'

'Good,' he said, without expressing alarm.

'Good?'

'I'm at Midway.'

'You never call for a ride from the airport. You always limo.'

'I need to get updated before I talk to Ma.'

'The new menu is wonderful.'

'It is disrespectful. Southwest Airlines.'

I said OK, but he'd clicked me away before he could hear that, such was his tension. I swung back to Thompson and headed toward Midway Airport. The red truck stayed a few cars behind the whole way.

Leo, when normally attired in outrageous shirts of colorful birds, serpents, and palms, paired with fluorescent slacks, is easy to spot, but that day he wore a muted charcoal-gray suit, white shirt, and burgundy tie – almost the same duds the Bohemian favored, though many sizes smaller. One does not Rockafella in New York City while sporting tropical birds, coconuts, and snakes, but I realized that belatedly, spotting him only as I was about to pass him by.

I slammed on the brakes, as did the red truck. Horns honked.

He smiled. His smile is arresting, because it transforms his narrow pale face into something that is all white teeth, enormous and bright, lined up like marble tombstones. He unzipped the clouded rear curtain, threw his two suitcases in back, and climbed in beside me.

'When are you going to drive something respectable?' he asked, by way of greeting.

'I gave all my money to you,' I said, pulling us – meaning Leo, me, and the red truck – away.

'Ah, yes, that hundred,' he said.

I told him I was being tailed by someone in a red truck. He turned around as if to look but it was for show. The rear curtain of the Jeep is so clouded by age that only dinosaur-sized and larger shapes can be distinguished. 'When are you going to get a rear window that you can see through?'

'I gave all my money to you,' I said again, savoring a stock answer that might be applicable to everything, adding, 'He stayed with me all the way from Rivertown,' in response to the next question he didn't ask.

'Who?'

'Not sure but the Bohemian gave me a cryptic heads-up, suggesting that someone was being watched. I think the lizards hope I'll lead them to Tripp, though I have no idea where he is,' I said, and filled him in on everything that had happened, Tripp-wise, while he'd been away.

'Kowalski, a killer?' he asked, shocked, when I was done.

'Short guy wearing a hat and coat on a hot October day, the neighbor said.'

'The hat makes it Kowalski?'

'It's weak, but it fits Kowalski.'

'I can't believe it,' he said. 'No idea whose remains you found?'

'No watertight ideas about anything,' I said.

'I fumed the whole flight,' he said, 'worrying about Ma making an end run around the tradition of Kutz's.' He sighed. 'Hearing what you're up to makes that small potatoes.'

'Ma's not undoing anything. She's trying to improve things, widen your customer base. From what I can see, business is way up.'

'Is the tail still with us?' he asked.

I checked the outside rearview again. The red truck was three cars back. 'Yeah,' I said.

We talked a bit about Rockefellers, and art, and things that took too much money for me to understand until I pulled up in front of Ma's bungalow. It was where he grew up and where he still lived. Leo stayed in Rivertown after high school and college to keep an eye on his ma because she was worth keeping an eye on, but he didn't need me to remind him of that.

'Make peace with Ma,' I said. 'She's done something good.'

'She usually does,' he said, and got out to unzip the curtain, grab his luggage, and confront inventive Polish thinking.

The red truck followed me until I turned onto the street that led to my street. Then, like the gray truck earlier, he stayed on

Thompson Avenue and parked where he could watch the turret. I glanced out from time to time. He stayed put for a half hour and then disappeared.

I called the Bohemian. 'Not to nag, but . . .'

'My contact will say nothing further.'

'You tried him again?'

'Ordinarily a voluble individual, but both times, he was anxious to get me off the phone.'

'Scared?'

'Inordinately so. You want to know how this Sara Jansen, part-time, minimum-wage earner, afforded a modest house. Under most circumstances, learning that would be difficult because the amount needed was so small. She could have borrowed it from a relative, for example. But the question has triggered an inordinate response. My contact should not be scared. If anything, he should just lie, and say he'd have no idea how to find out about such a trivial matter. Instead, he murmurs nonsense about watching the watcher, whatever that means. He's petrified of saying anything.'

'Other than to advise to watch whoever is being watched?'

'Doesn't narrow it down, does it? Could it be your man Tripp?'

'It might have been, if he was still around. But he's disappeared, leaving behind his clothes and his stolen car. Now I've found another target.'

'A new name?'

'Mine. I've been followed twice today by two different men.'

He inhaled sharply. 'What do you know, Vlodek?'

'No idea. Tripp's gone and I don't know where he is,' I said, which wasn't quite true unless, for sure, the bones in Verona weren't his.

'You need protection,' he said. 'Perhaps one of Amanda's corporate security guards—'

'No.'

'If she finds out, she'll insist,' he said. 'I'm told they'll freelance.'

'No.'

'What will you do?'

'Hope to watch whoever's watching me.'

But it was not to be that day. I spotted nothing from the

window, so I went outside. The red truck was gone, and there was no sign of the gray one.

I gave up and went inside for lasagna.

TWENTY-ONE

I woke the next morning sure I'd see a gray truck or a red truck parked across the spit of land, but the hordes of people hunting cats in the park had grabbed all the parking spaces.

That didn't mean I wasn't being watched. I went outside and worked my way through the bramble, this time walking straight up. If one of my truck friends was watching, he'd think I'd joined the hordes on cat patrol.

I stopped at the stout tree that offered me cover the previous day to look up and down Thompson. The gray Ford F-150 was parked two blocks up. That spot offered no view of the turret, but that didn't mean the driver hadn't gotten out to move closer on foot.

I crossed Thompson to the tangle of neon on the other side and started toward the truck, poking along as if I was just out for a stroll. To avoid attracting any notice, I stopped at every third doorway, as if I was merely meandering, though pausing to linger dosed me with the stink of stale beer and the desperate laughter of working ladies out to get a jump, literally and physically, on the competition.

After a few minutes, I got to a pawnshop whose window offered a good reflection of the truck. The driver inside was young, late teens, and wore a green knit shirt. A glimpse of blond hair showed between a black White Sox ballcap and a pair of Ray-Bans. He sat angled to see up the street. That part of Thompson Avenue offered diminished opportunities for commercialized debauchery, and dribbled into a string of deteriorating houses much like those in Rivertown's old factory district. Most important, his perch offered no view of the turret.

We remained – him watching ahead, me pretending to look at the items in the hock-shop window while watching his reflection, for five minutes, then ten. And then his head moved, just a little. The truck's engine started.

I looked up the street. Kowalski the Frenchman had come out of a slot parlor in the next block up, and was headed up Thompson Avenue, away from us. He sauntered like he had no worries, an ordinary jamoke, just out for a stroll.

The truck eased forward in a slow glide and stopped after fifty feet. No doubt, the kid driving was tailing Kowalski. I hung back, watching the two of them as they moved forward, roughly in tandem, into the next block and the one after that. The last doorway I was able to duck into was a vacant storefront that used to sell party favors.

Kowalski disappeared from the sidewalk. The gray truck stopped a block back and cut the engine. We remained frozen, the truck and I, for another fifteen minutes, until Kowalski reappeared on the sidewalk, coming toward me. He was carrying two black cats.

There was no other choice but to head back the way I'd come. I walked as fast as I dared, not turning around for fear I'd be recognized by the Frenchman or the kid. I didn't hear the truck's engine. I hoped that meant I was outpacing both Kowalski and the truck.

I turned into the first cross street and ducked behind a parked panel van. Five minutes later, Kowalski passed by, whistling, all saunter and strut. The truck crept by thirty seconds after him, in slow pursuit.

I stayed two blocks behind them until I got to the bramble. I ran through the park, jumped in the Jeep, and was back on Thompson in a flash. The gray truck rode high, easy to see. When he turned onto the river road that led to Kutz's clearing, it was confirmation. Kowalski was headed for pierogies.

The clearing gave me good cover. I was as regular there as anyone in Rivertown. I eased down the rutted road and parked at the farthest end of the clearing from where the gray truck had stopped. I got out. The driver of the truck had not.

Kowalski stood in line in the wienie wagon. I hurried to get right behind him.

'Doubling your chances of winning?' I said to the beret at the top of his head.

He looked down at the two cats as if seeing them for the first time. 'I'm counting on it,' he said.

'I can carry your lunch to a table for you,' I said, ever helpful.

'No need,' he said.

He got to the order window. Leo was behind it and so was Ma Brumsky. Despite the August heat, I could see that frost was between them, colder than the frozen air between the two Koreas.

Kowalski ordered pierogies. 'Hah,' Ma snorted as she scooped them from a new pot sitting on a new warmer.

Kowalski set down the two cats to run free and fished in his pocket for his wallet.

I was shocked. It made no sense. To lug two cats all the way down Thompson Avenue to Kutz's, only to set them free, was ridiculous.

Kowalski passed through a bill. Ma took it, flashed him a huge smile, said, 'Thank you once again,' and put it in a new cigar box. The two Brumskys were competing. There'd be a tally at the end of the lunch rush and I was betting Ma Brumsky was going to win. Kowalski walked around to the back of the trailer.

I summoned up a smile for my best friend and, seeking to defuse two of my most favorite people, said, 'Kielbasa and a Coke. On the tab.'

'Hah,' Ma snorted.

'Hah,' Leo snorted.

A hot dog and a semi-fizzed were fired out the order window with the speed of a North Korean missile.

'I ordered—'

'Only hot dogs go on the tab for such a Benedict Arnold,' Leo said.

I left the Koreas and walked around to the back of the trailer. Kowalski sat on the freezer casket, eating a pierogi with his fingers.

'I couldn't help noticing you set your cats free,' I said. 'Rejected at city hall?' Lying was more suitable than saying I'd tracked him straight to Kutz's.

'Both winners in their own way,' he said, which made no sense to me.

'I don't know how they tell,' I said.

'Keeps everybody busy,' he said, grinning around the pierogi.

'Did you ever run into Sara Jansen after you left Rivertown?'
I asked.

He stopped in mid-chew. 'That's the second time you brought
up Sara Jansen. Why?'

'You could call it curiosity,' I said.

'No,' he said.

'You two left Rivertown at about the same time,' I said. 'Maybe
her a little after you.'

'Coincidence,' he said, and headed around to the front of the
trailer without finishing his pierogies. I waited a few seconds,
then followed him and was pleased to see that, unlike the day
before, he spit his half-chewed mouthful into the barrel and
dumped the rest of his pierogies in after it.

I'd spoiled his appetite by asking about Sara Jansen but not
his interest in what was going on in the clearing. He walked to
the edge of the woods and stopped, pretending to look around
casually, but it was obvious he was looking intently at the changes
that had been made. The long metal barrel had been moved closer
to the river, and now lay perpendicular to it. Small lights had
been strung in the trees and more of the larger colored floodlights
had been stepped into the ground. And the pulley I'd seen a
workman strap on the old oak tree, with the physical encourage-
ment of the always energetic Mrs Roshiska, now dangled a steel
cable thick enough to hoist a car.

The gray F-150 had remained at the edge of the clearing. The
driver was inside, still not eating, his head turned to look out his
side window. I couldn't tell whether he was watching Kowalski
or me and decided it was probably both of us.

I looked back at the trailer. Leo glared back. The order line
was thirty long and as they left the order window, I saw that
most were carrying kielbasas, Polish sausages, and pierogies. I
pointed to the long line and gave him the thumbs-up of
congratulations.

His hand shot up, perhaps flirting with a hand gesture featuring
another upraised finger, but he quickly dropped it as an elderly
couple stepped up to order.

I turned back to look at Kowalski but he was nowhere in sight.
The gray Ford pickup was still parked and that made me the
target.

I strolled over to the pickup, looking the other way as if uninterested, but then, quick as a man can be, having just knocked back a traditionally lukewarm hot dog and lifeless cola, I tugged open the passenger door and jumped in.

'Hey!' The driver was just a kid, still a teen.

'I'm worried you're getting neck strain,' I said to the lad.

'What's wrong with you?' the kid said.

'You'd have to talk to a number of people to determine that accurately,' I said. 'You'd have to start with my aunts, then my schoolteachers, then my college professors, then my ex-wife—'

'Stop!'

'We've just begun.'

'Begun what?' His voice rose higher than I would have thought possible. And it squeaked.

'Do you know you actually squeak?' I inquired affably.

'Sq—'

'Hush,' I said. 'Not to worry. It'll go away when you mature.'

'Get out of my truck!' He was shouting now, which was good.

'Tell me why you're tailing me.'

'I'm not—'

'I won't say anything if you won't,' I interrupted, 'but if you want me to embarrass you by spreading the word that you've screwed up an easy tail, and also, that you squeak when agitated, I will.'

He said nothing, considering his options.

'Who do you work for?' I asked.

'This is a summer job, man. I'm going back to school in two weeks.'

'Who do you work for?' I said again.

'Screw it,' he said. 'City of Rivertown.'

'Rivertown is paying you to tail me?'

'You gotta not tell,' he said, turning in the seat. His eyes had shifted from shocked to pleading.

'I promise.'

'They pulled me from landscaping. It's just a summer job from college.'

'Who do you report to?'

'My regular landscaping supervisor. I just drop off my timesheet every day with notes on who I followed, you or Mr Kowalski, and where you went.'

'You and the guy with the red truck.'

'Me and him and a third guy, drives a black truck.'

'All of you college kids can afford trucks?'

'They're not our trucks. They belong to the city.'

It was so Rivertown, so cheesy, sending out college kids to tail Kowalski and me. What wasn't at all clear was what we had in common.

Except maybe Tripp.

TWENTY-TWO

The next day was too hot to scramble after cats, and since I didn't know where Tripp was or even if he was still alive, I decided to replay the previous day, and scramble after Kowalski, who moved more sedately than cats, yet faster than Tripp – I had to allow – if Tripp was dead. I lingered at the same hock-shop window and pretended to admire the same things – an ornate gilded clock, a set of rusted golf clubs, a banjo – that others did not. The day's truck, parked one block ahead, was black.

Kowalski came waltzing out at the same time as the day before, just before lunchtime, and like before, he carried two black cats. This time, I paid particular attention to the spot where he emerged. Like yesterday, he whistled as he waltzed and I wished I knew why.

He headed down Thompson and, as before, the truck fired up its engine to follow him. I ducked into the same side street as before, and again I watched them pass by. Almost certainly, their little parade was headed to Kutz's clearing, where I expected that Kowalski would turn loose the two cats, buy pierogies, and then saunter away. The mystery of that wouldn't be solved in Kutz's clearing but up Thompson Avenue, I hoped. Once Kowalski and the truck were spots in the distance, I hurried up the two blocks to the spot I'd fixed in my mind.

He'd come out between two brown brick bungalows. I walked through the narrow gangway between them. A chain-link fence ran behind the property to the left, making it inaccessible from the side. That meant the bungalow to the right was the only possibility. Its back porch door faced the gangway.

The porch door opened readily but the door inside, to the kitchen, was locked. I peeked through the glass. Dishes were stacked up on the counter and in the sink. Kowalski was not threatened by dirty dishes.

I was about to leave, to check out the garage, when I heard faint mewing from inside. There was a window next to the door. Kowalski had not thought to lock it. I raised the sash and slipped into the kitchen.

The mews were coming from the basement and there were a lot of them. The door was on the side wall. I went down the stairs to an increasing crescendo of cat noises.

Fifty or more cats were inside four long homemade chicken-wire cages. Food dishes had been set along both sides of each and the litter at the bottoms looked fresh. Whether Kowalski was a killer, and at that moment I had no idea, he was a careful caretaker of cats. They were not being held in squalor.

Nor were they all black. Some were gray, some pure white, some black-and-white spotted. Only a dozen, isolated in their own cage, were pure black, and they glistened.

Three pairs of yellow rubber gloves and a beige rubber apron lay draped over the washtubs. Several boxes of hair dye were set on the shelf above. Kowalski was manufacturing black cats.

It explained the smudging I'd seen on the people lined up at city hall but the larger sense of what he was up to eluded me. I could understand Kowalski dyeing a cat or two, and then standing in line, hoping to scam the city out of its hundred-dollar reward, but he wasn't doing that. He wasn't standing in line. He was setting loose newly blackened cats, two at a time, for others to find, pick up, and bring to city hall.

I went up the stairs, eased out the kitchen window, and left almost as confused as when I'd arrived, except for one thing: city hall's crack tailing crew might have accurately reported Kowalski's comings and goings, but not what he was carrying. Otherwise, city hall would have shut down his cat-darkening operation.

I walked back to the turret, got the Jeep, and drove to Kutz's clearing.

It was not yet noon, but already the line was long. Already

Leo was scowling; already Ma was smiling. Most were coming away from the window with Polish essentials, sausages, kielbasas, and pierogies.

I stepped up to the side door and poked a smiling face inward. 'You're on to something here, Leo. An ethnic upgrade to your menu.'

'This is nonsense,' he said, taking an order for a Polish sausage. He'd abandoned the notion of only filling hot dog orders. From what I was seeing, there weren't any.

'This might be progress,' I said.

'You betcha, Dekkie,' Ma said, beaming at our conversation. 'Next up, five-piece band.'

Leo's back stiffened but he was too busy taking the next order, this for pierogies, to offer up a protest.

'Real progress,' I said, trolling.

Right away, Ma rewarded me with a kielbasa behind Leo's back. From then on, I vowed to wax enthusiastic about everything new in that clearing.

I followed what was now my rut to the back of the trailer and found Kowalski once again. He was enjoying a Polish sausage, two-handed this time. The day's two cats, natural black or recreated, were gone.

'No cats today?' I asked, in innocence.

'Nah,' he lied. He was eying me warily, ready to bolt at the first mention of Sara Jansen.

'You turned loose the two you had yesterday,' I said.

'They weren't the ones,' he said.

'How do you know?'

'I just know, is all.'

I let it go. To force another man to lie when he's eating, to threaten his digestion even if he's a killer, lacks grace. I decided that I'd hold back, and let him sweat whether I was going to ask about Sara. We watched the plastic bob in the river and ate, two liars, coexisting silently behind Leo's trailer.

He left when he was done and I followed him, because by then it was our ritual, and, per the ritual, he didn't leave the clearing. Like before, he stepped to the side of the clearing and again seemed content to take in the sights of the changes in the clearing – the mysterious long metal tube lying at the edge of the trees, the new lights stepped into the ground and strung in the trees, and the long cable dangling from the winch in the tall oak.

I supposed, though, that the small grin Kowalski was sporting might have come from watching the earthy comedy being performed by Mrs Roshiska and her pals, ever at the ready to rub more than the picnic tables.

The black truck was parked at the edge of the access road where I'd accosted the driver of the gray truck. His windows were clean but I couldn't tell whether the driver's head was pointed at me, or at Kowalski. I stood as Kowalski was standing, though fifty yards away, pretending to take in the sights and sounds of Kutz's clearing, and waited for an answer.

It came ten minutes later. Kowalski started walking up the river road. The black truck started up and followed. And so did I, in the Jeep, well behind them both. I guessed Kowalski was headed back to the brick bungalow to color more cats.

I guessed wrong. Kowalski walked along Thompson Avenue, into town, but then he turned off and headed down one of the crooked streets that led to the First Bank of Rivertown. He didn't go inside, but instead continued, still leisurely, around to the back of the dirty stucco building. The black truck followed, but stopped halfway. I stayed at the head of the crooked road, where I could see.

Kowalski paused like he paused at Kutz's, as if admiring the view. The view didn't offer much to be admired. The back of the bank offered sights of lots overgrown with barky weeds following demolitions of an automobile tire warehouse and a furniture store that had gone belly-up after the factories closed.

Kowalski stayed for five minutes, looking here, looking there, seemingly interested in everything, and nothing. And then he came back up the crooked road to Thompson Avenue and continued on to the bungalow where he kept the cats. All the while, he kept whistling.

I drove back to Kutz's clearing. The lunch line had ended. Leo stepped out of the trailer and sat opposite me at one of the relentlessly cleaned picnic tables. The brightness of the day's garb – lemon yellow trousers, blue striped socks and red tennis shoes, and a pink Hawaiian shirt festooned with green-stemmed purple flowers, orange parrots, and what might have been burgundy dinosaurs breathing red fire, all ordered custom-made from a children's drapery house – did not extend to his face. He looked glum.

'I'm of mixed emotions,' he said.

'She's drawing a bigger crowd,' I said.

'Trifling with tradition.' He gestured toward Ma and her friends, giggling like schoolgirls at a picnic table across the clearing. 'They're having the time of their lives, and I hate to say it, but I'm becoming inclined to let it play out.'

'A five-piece band, Ma said?' I asked.

'She won't tell me anything about it, or when they're going to play. All she will admit is that they exist.'

'What about that long metal tube?' I said, pointing to the side of the clearing.

'She won't say anything about that, or the winch in the tree, either.'

Mysteries surrounded me. Martin Tripp, Julianna Wynton, Kowalski the Frenchman, and now even Ma Brumsky. 'What do you know about what Kowalski's up to?' I asked, after I pondered the winch for a moment.

'Other than I can't imagine he killed Sara?' He grinned. 'He comes every day with two cats, turns them loose, and gets something to eat.'

'He has at least fifty cats in his basement that he's coloring black.'

His formidable dark eyebrows, the only fur to adorn his bald head, rose a half-inch. 'He has a basement?'

'And a bungalow on top of it, on Thompson Avenue. No doubt it's a rental.'

His eyebrows crept higher. 'And how do you know about cats in the man's basement?' A grin spread on his substantial lips. Leo, when thoughts dawn and grow in recognition, is a study in facial transformation.

'We share common tails,' I said, appropriately.

He bit at my cleverness. 'Tails, like in cat tails?'

'Tails, like in human tails.' I told him about the kid I'd accosted in the gray truck.

'The lizards were the ones who put the tail on you?' he said. 'What have you got in common with Kowalski?'

'Martin Tripp. He and Kowalski were friends. I'm guessing he left a little before Sara, and a few weeks before Tripp.'

'All of them at roughly the same time? What do you think that means?' he asked.

'To answer that, I need to know why they left.'

He leaned across the table. 'As I told you, most thought Kowalski left because of the tattoo, but as you know, some made a joke about the bagman leaving with the bag.'

'What if both Tripp and Kowalski thought it was Sara who had the full bag?'

'Twenty-two grand is a full bag?' he said.

I shrugged. 'What if Tripp thought there was more, not tied up in the down payment, and that's why he followed her out to Weston?'

'And Kowalski followed them both, thinking the same thing, to get at the money Tripp was chasing,' he said, because it was the only scenario that made any sense. He thought for a minute and frowned.

'And?' I coaxed, because I wanted him to say what I was thinking.

'And the tails are proof it's more than chump change!' he said, beaming. He leaned forward, tensed with a new thought. 'So, speaking of tails, what's with the cats?'

'Chaos,' was all I could think to say.

TWENTY-THREE

It was a spur of the moment decision.

I jumped on the breezer into the city to see how Amanda's assembly operation was doing, post-brick. She ran it until eight o'clock, so I was thinking I'd get there a little beforehand and we'd find a restaurant that didn't serve lasagna after she closed up.

When I got there, her windows were dark. I got out, hoping she was still inside, closing up. As I walked up, a hand touched the back of my neck.

'Sir?' a voice asked.

I turned around, but the hand stayed with me. A quite tall Black man, perhaps in his late twenties, was behind the voice.

'I know the manager, Amanda Phelps,' I said.

'They're closed, as you can see,' he said.

'You're part of the operation?' I said.

'Special services,' he said.

'Why are you closed?' I asked.

'If you know Miss Phelps, you can call her and she'll explain. For now, you should move along.'

And so I did, not yet alarmed, but real anxiety came in the next minutes, when Amanda didn't answer her phone. Almost always, she answered when she knew it was me. I forced myself to drive deliberately up Lake Shore Drive, not allowing my wheels, or my mind, to race.

'She's home, Mr Elstrom,' the garage attendant said as I pulled in.

'She's not answering her cell, which means she doesn't want to be disturbed,' I said, managing a grin.

'And you're just the man to disturb her?' he said, with his own grin.

'You betcha,' I said, pulling into one of the guest parking slots. I was on her approved list – the only one on her approved list. I gave him my keys and hurried into the lobby.

The concierge gave me a nod. He knew me, too.

'Miss Phelps is in?' I asked.

'I don't recall her going out,' he said, which meant for sure she hadn't left. Recollection had nothing to do with his duties. It was certainty that mattered. And, like the garage attendant, he made sure he was always certain about the whereabouts of the residents of his tower.

There was also a guard in the lobby, standing unobtrusively by the bank of three elevators. He pressed one of the buttons. His blue blazer was open as always, to keep his Glock clearly visible on his belt. The concierge was armed, too, I knew, with both a semi-automatic handgun in a shoulder rig and a shotgun beneath the surface of his custom-made, burled elm desk. I didn't know if Amanda was the wealthiest owner in the building, but she was certainly in the heaviest of the cream of its occupants.

I rode the elevator up and knocked on her door. No answer. I knocked more insistently. Still nothing. I entered her code on the keypad, inserted my copy of her keycard, and turned the lock.

'Amanda?' I called out as I stepped into her foyer. 'Amanda?'

Again, there was no answer.

Her unit was relatively small for her high-rise, and furnished spartanly. A large curved sectional sofa filled the smallish living room, positioned to offer the best view of the tens of millions of dollars in oil paintings that adorn the off-white walls. Most prominent among them was a Manet that was valued at over thirteen million dollars, the last time it was appraised. There were lesser works by Picasso, Monet, and others, along with a small Remington bronze on a side table. Many had been her grand-father's, which she bought from his estate with the inheritance he left her.

Much of her furniture was acquired differently, either through catalogs of ready-to-assemble stuff she put together in college or at garage sales after she graduated. That level of purposeful frugality was one of the many things that enchanted me about her.

I was scared. There was no sound in the apartment, no shower running or music playing. The second bedroom and both bath-rooms were empty as well. My dread rose higher; Amanda had been kidnapped several years before. I hurried into her bedroom. Black slacks and a thin sweatshirt – her at-home clothes – were laid out on the bed, as though she'd expected to put them on again that day. I tried to find something calming in that, but her absence, unnoticed in the lobby or the garage, was too worrisome. Her car was in the garage; she'd been home. Yet she'd disap-peared, unnoticed by men too well trained to make sure no resident disappeared. I saw earmarks of a highly sophisticated kidnapping. I hurried back through the hall.

The front door opened.

'Oh, hi,' she said, clearly startled. She was dressed completely in black, black jeans, black long-sleeved top, black watch cap like the one I'd had for years. Her clothes were filthy with an odd reddish dust.

'Thrilled to see me?' I managed, aiming for a joke to disguise any lingering panic on my face.

'Sure . . .' she said, letting the word trail away. It was tentative and yet, there was a faint smile on her lips and a trace of defiance in the way she met my eyes, almost as if she was challenging me to try to know more.

'Didn't the garage guy tell you I was here? Or the guard? Or the concierge?'

'I need to shower,' she said. And then I noticed something else. There was a slight perspiration on her face.

'Been running?' Running wasn't an everyday thing for her, but she did go out to the lakefront a couple of times each week. But always, absolutely, she was noticed leaving by someone in the lobby or garage.

'Let's go out for dinner,' she said, evading.

'Sounds perfect,' I said.

She went to shower and I went to wait with Manet. Twenty minutes later, we walked to a small trattoria, owned by the same Italian family that managed to stay in business for fifty years, despite the relentless encroachment of big-buck towers and trendy restaurants in that part of lakefront Chicago.

We were greeted warmly. By the familiarity of all the faces inside, I imagined that all the diners were semi-regulars. She ordered a pinot, I ordered club soda with a lime because I almost always avoid alcohol. I'd used it to fuel the destruction of our marriage during the Evangeline Wilts fiasco.

'You're not going to tell me, are you?' I asked.

She smiled over the candle and the wine. 'Nope,' she said.

'You now have security outside your storefront,' I said.

'It's sort of a neighborhood group. They're keeping an eye on things.'

'You're neutralizing that bomb threat,' I said.

When she said nothing, I said, 'There's a glint of self-satisfaction in your lovely brown eyes.'

'Yep,' she said.

I wasn't done. 'Tonight, you found a way of overriding the alarms on the service doors in your building, so you could leave unnoticed,' I said.

She raised her glass. 'To you,' she said.

And so it was that I became done in, by her smile and her loveliness, and we talked about safer things. And after dinner, we walked back to her condominium, and through the lobby, where the concierge and the guard smiled, not knowing they'd been fooled by the loveliest of women, and we rode up to her condo without saying much at all.

And then I stayed over, and there wasn't time to wonder any more what she'd been up to that evening.

TWENTY-FOUR

'I can manage by myself,' I said.

It was ten-thirty the next morning. Leo and I were on the roof of the turret, five stories up, preparing to watch Thompson Avenue. It would be easier than following on foot.

'There comes a time in every son's life when he has to cut the strings and let his mother run free,' he said, kneeling to remove his stargazing telescope from its case.

'Have you forgotten when Ma and her friends ran free at the health center?' I asked. It was one of my favorite memories.

He shuddered as he lifted out the telescope. 'Swam free, you mean? That skinny dipping that continues to fascinate you?'

'It's dropping their towels in protest before going into the police station that fascinates me,' I said, pointing toward the back of city hall, where the protest occurred. 'That was real running free.'

He fitted the telescope to the tripod and adjusted the legs so that the telescope rose just enough above the stone balustrade to see without being visible. 'There's no denying the Polish menu has doubled the number of customers,' he said, focusing across the spit of land.

'I can't wait to see what that winch fitted to the oak tree is going to be used for,' I said.

'Oh, I can wait,' he said, peering through the telescope. 'Today's truck is gray.'

'Parked to watch me?'

'No,' he said. 'I see Kowalski. He's on the move. The truck is following.'

'They're early,' I said. 'Cats?'

'Two,' he said. 'Black, both of them. The truck is following a block behind, like you said.'

'Headed to your clearing,' I said. 'Just like the previous two days.'

'Uh . . .'

'What, Leo?' I asked.

'There's a new participant in the parade,' he said, squinting to adjust the eyepiece. 'A metallic-blue Malibu.'

'Probably just somebody stuck behind the slow-moving pickup.'

'Metallic-blue Malibu,' he said again, probably because he enjoyed the rhyme.

After a minute of silence, he said, 'No, definitely the Malibu is staying in sync with the truck, which is staying in sync with Kowalski.'

He stepped aside so I could use the telescope. There was no missing the metallic-blue paint, sparkling in the morning sun.

I swung the telescope forward and saw the truck. When it sped up slightly, the Malibu did, too. And when the truck slowed, the Malibu did as well. I watched for a full minute. There was no doubt.

'Another lizard, as back-up?' Leo asked.

'Could be,' I said, 'but that's overkill to tail one man on foot, especially when they know where he's going.'

The gray truck disappeared at the turn-off down to Kutz's clearing. A moment later, the metallic-blue Malibu disappeared as well.

I straightened up from the telescope. 'They've gone for pierogies,' I said.

'Kowalski, gray truck, blue Malibu,' he said. 'Quite a parade.'

We took fifteen-minute turns, watching Thompson Avenue for the next hour. Five minutes into my third turn, the gray truck appeared in the telescope, headed back the way it had come. The blue Malibu appeared a few seconds after that.

As agreed, Leo opened the trapdoor and climbed down the ladder; I needed to know who was driving the Malibu. A moment later, a loud pop sounded up through the opening.

'Jeez, Dek; these stairs!'

'I think they're safe,' I yelled back.

The timbered door slammed, his engine fired up, and his white van came into view, racing up the stub of the street to turn right onto Thompson. My cell phone beeped a moment later, displaying Leo's number, but only a faint whispering came through.

'Speak louder,' I said.

'. . . pursuit,' I thought he said.

'Leo! Speak normally. There's no one in the van with you, right?'

'I'm in pursuit,' he said, but only marginally louder, and then he clicked off.

And in pursuit he was, if only slowly. I saw him get stopped by one of the long traffic lights before turning onto Thompson Avenue. 'Nuts,' he said, murmuring into my phone again.

'They're probably following Kowalski to his bungalow,' I said. 'Kowalski's got to dye more cats.'

No words came back. 'Leo?' I said after a minute of silence.

'Ten–four,' he said, which was television cop-show language for something that neither he nor I knew. The light turned green and the congested traffic moved forward. I imagined him white-knuckling the steering wheel, eyes fiercely ahead.

Watching a white van tailing a blue car tailing a gray truck tailing a man on foot, who dyed cats black, was slow-motion craziness, and I wondered if I was obsessing over Kowalski to delay phoning in the discovery of the bone in Verona to the police.

The truck disappeared, then the Malibu, then Leo's white van. Twenty minutes passed and then Leo called. 'Metallic-blue Malibu followed gray truck following Kowalski down to the back of the bank.'

'Seemingly to look at nothing,' I said, having previously been a keen observer of Kowalski's detour down to the back of the bank.

'Why?'

'If I had to guess, I would say it's because of something Kowalski got Sara to say.'

'Or just suspects?'

'Sure,' I said.

He clicked off and stayed silent for a full ten minutes, and then called to say Kowalski had returned to Thompson Avenue, followed by the truck and then by the Malibu.

'Can you see who's driving the Malibu?' I asked. 'Another college kid?'

'Full dark tint on the windows,' he said.

'License plates?'

He whispered the number and clicked off.

Another twenty minutes passed, and Leo called again. 'It's all played out as you expected,' he said, speaking normally. 'After the little detour to the bank, blue Malibu trailed gray truck to Kowalski's bungalow, then they both turned around. Gray truck pulled off onto the side of the road across from the park, presumably to look for you.'

'I've got him in the telescope,' I said. 'Blue Malibu?'

'Headed toward the city . . .'

He paused so I could ask, and so I did. 'You followed, of course?'

'Stayed with it the whole way, almost.'

'Past tense? You lost him?'

'Not . . . not really,' he said. 'I was hanging back so I wouldn't be spotted. He pulled into a Holiday Inn near Midway. I waited a minute and pulled in, too, but stayed at the edge of the lot. He parked in an angled space at the back of the building. I watched, hoping he'd not gotten out yet, but thought, after a few minutes, that he'd already gone into one of the outside passageways because the only people outside were women, one with a group of kids, another woman who I thought might have been with them. That second woman . . .' His voice trailed off.

'What is it, Leo?'

'Never mind,' he said.

'Is there a dot on the Malibu's bumper?' I asked.

'I can't tell. It's filthy, covered with gravel dust,' he said. 'Dek, any idea who might be driving that car?'

'Tripp, because I can't think of anyone else,' I said. 'You're sure you see no dot on the bumper?'

'Archie?'

'That's where Tripp got the LeBaron.'

'I don't want to risk getting out of the car to see if there's a dot. I'm going to stick around for a while to see who comes out.'

I went down to wait in the kitchen, where the lasagna was also waiting. I'd just taken it out of the refrigerator and begun to mull whether to warm it in the leaky microwave or avoid the radiation and eat it cold, when Leo called again.

His motor was running. He was in traffic. 'I am not failing!' he yelled over it.

'At what?'

'I did not lose the tail!'

'You already said you followed him all the way to a Holiday Inn.'

'Almost,' he said. He was playing and so I had to play along.

'Almost?' I obliged.

'That woman I spotted outside the Holiday Inn?'

'Yeah?'

'She's the one driving the Malibu.'

'Yeah?'

'You're going to love it,' he said.

'What?'

'What I'm not going to tell you yet,' he said.

TWENTY-FIVE

The only car in the bank's four-car lot was an old beige Buick that I presumed belonged to the bank president and his mother. I parked next to it and went around to the back of the building. And looked again at what I'd seen earlier. Which was nothing but a wall of filthy stucco facing several weed- and litter-strewn lots.

I went into the bank. As long as I could remember, candlepower was never employed to disturb its restful interior, but that day the place was dimmer than usual. I looked up. One of the two forty-watt light bulbs in the ceiling had burned out. I looked then at the bank president, sitting at the lone desk in the lobby. Long burned out himself, he sat bent over, his nose barely six inches above his desk, squinting at the children's crossword puzzle.

'Your light bulb burned out,' I said quietly, so as to not disturb his mother, whose gray head rested on the white marble teller counter, asleep in the gloom.

'Huh?' he said.

'Your bulb's out,' I said.

He looked around, startled.

I pointed up, at the ceiling. 'Bulb,' I said. 'Out.'

'Ah,' he said. 'Have to call it in.'

'You call someone to change a bulb?'

'Rules,' he whispered.

'Lockboxes,' I whispered back.

He frowned, and set down his jumbo pencil.

'I want to go downstairs to see them,' I said, pointing to the back of the lobby, where the wood staircase was that led to the lockbox vault.

I knew the way; I just had to double-check the vault's orientation. I'd gone down those stairs once before, years earlier, with a key I never wanted to possess. It fit a lock on a box rented by a girl I'd loved in high school, who became a woman I'd never known. In that box, she'd kept a secret, for me.

'Why?'

'I might be interested in renting one.'

He knew me as many in the town knew me. I was the guy who lived in the turret that the lizards zoned a municipal structure so that they could control its use as the town icon, a guy who had the wrong sort of glint in his eyes, someone perpetually at war with the lizards over that zoning. But most worrisomely, he knew me as the guy who asked about Sara Jansen, just a few days before.

'You want a lockbox?' he asked.

'I want to see a lockbox,' I corrected.

He moved his hands about eighteen inches apart. 'They're about—'

I cut him off. 'No. I want to see the vault.'

'Why?'

'To make sure they're safe,' I said, instead of telling him I wanted to look at the back wall.

'Oh, they're—'

'Let's look at the vault,' I said.

He stood, turned the crossword over like he was afraid some semi-functional first-grader would come along and finish it. With a finger to his lips to caution for silence, we walked past his mother cooling her head on the white marble and tiptoed down the steps to the basement.

The vault had a thick steel door secured by a spinner locking mechanism. He dialed in a combination, spun the wheel, and pulled the door open. We stepped inside. Just as I remembered, the vault was small and held about fifty lockboxes in three sizes, lined up against the side wall.

'Was Kowalski in here recently?' I asked.

The bank president shook his head too hard. 'Don't know the name,' he said, his eyes wild.

'You know, the guy who used to make deposits here on behalf of the city?'

'Don't know the name.' He'd regained control of his face, and now it betrayed nothing, almost as if a shade containing a mouth, nose, and two blank eyes had been pulled down from the top of his head.

'Everybody knows Kowalski,' I said, not because I believed Kowalski, former bagman, would have showed up to rent a box, but because I wanted to see the man's face when I mentioned the Frenchman. 'Real short guy, always wears a hat?'

'No!' His face had started to flush. With luck, sweat would come next.

'Not Martin Tripp either?' It was an offhand question, something I asked just because I was there. I expected nothing.

The face-shade shot up, revealing eyes gone wild, and around them, little beads of sweat began glistening.

'Martin Tripp came here to rent a lockbox?'

He jerked his head to look out the open door, as if hoping his mother had heard us and would come to give him direction. But a gentle wheezing came from the staircase. His savior was snoring.

I lobbed another grenade. 'Who do you think killed Sara Jansen?'

The beads on his forehead grew and several mated.

'Sara Jansen?' I said, pressing. 'She used to work here, remember?'

'I don't know anything,' he whispered, and started walking toward the door.

I didn't follow. I knelt to examine the largest boxes, set in two rows at the bottom. They were generous, substantially oversized.

'Are those bigger than usual for banks?' I asked, standing up.

'Double-size,' he said, from the door. I was done. I went out, he followed, pulling the massive door shut and locking it. We tiptoed back up the stairs silently, to not wake the slumbering madame.

I called Leo from the Jeep. 'Metallic-blue, Malibu,' I said, rhythmically. 'What couldn't you tell me before about her?'

'You wouldn't believe me,' he said.

'OK, then tell me what I won't believe?'

There was a long pause, and then he said, so quietly I had to press the phone hard against my ear, 'Inside, buying groceries.' His voice sounded strangely subdued. 'But maybe it's not a woman. The person is wearing a hoodie pulled up, and I wasn't very close, so I could have been wrong when I took it for a scarf.'

'Surely you can tell if it's a man or a woman.'

'Bulky clothes, shape-hiding,' he said, but there was something else in his voice, some hesitation.

'What is it, Leo?'

'When you recall Sara, what do you remember first?'

'Her personality. She was hostile. What's going on, Leo?'

'Her image, I mean. The way she looked.'

'Her hair,' I said immediately. 'That pair of strange, huge curls, one on either side of her head.'

'Exactly.'

'What does her hair have to do with anything?'

For a moment, he said nothing. Then he whispered, 'I wonder if I'm tailing Sara Jansen.'

'Come on, Leo!' I yelled into the phone.

'The hair, Dek. Nobody wears hair like that. Mickey Mouse we used to call her.'

'The woman – excuse me, the person – you're tailing, has hair like that?'

'Could be headphones, or huge curls beneath the hoodie. Nothing's obvious from a distance.'

'Leo—'

'What if she's alive . . .?'

'Why?'

'To throw everyone off her tail,' he said.

'Then why would she risk coming anywhere near Rivertown, where people know her?'

'We're not in Rivertown.'

'No, it's ridiculous.'

'What if—?'

'It'll be easy to get an answer,' I said, not out of concern that he might be right but because he sounded too rattled to ignore.

I sped to the county coroner's office. I'd been there a dozen times when my insurance investigation business was thriving. It was located in the basement of the county courthouse, forty minutes away.

I handed my business card to the woman at the desk just inside the glass door. 'I'd like to see someone about a murder case,' I said.

'We did the examination?'

'I believe so, yes. Sara Jansen.'

She told me she'd have it looked into right away and said Sara's name into her desk phone. I waited on a black vinyl chair for ten minutes and then a young fellow came up, holding a file. The receptionist gave him my card.

'Sara Jansen,' I said.

'Stabbed to death,' he said, sitting down next to me and opening the folder. 'Not much mystery to it. Why are you here?'

'Closing our file, before we pay next of kin.'

'What's your question?' he said.

'Who identified the body?'

He flipped over the first sheet and glanced at the second. 'Says here she came to us identified.' He handed me the file. Inside were the perfunctory autopsy notes. There were only three pages. I handed it back.

'No photos?' I said.

'None needed, I guess. As you can see, our medical examiner did the autopsy himself, but it was simple protocol in order to sign the death certificate. No question about cause of death.'

'Or the identity of the victim?'

He leaned back in his chair. 'What are you saying?'

'Probably just closing the file,' I said.

'No, you're not.'

'No one was called here to identify the body?'

He opened the file again, looked at the notes. 'Our wagon picked her up. The police told us who she was. When we were done, the funeral home took her.'

He gave me the name of the funeral home and I drove there. They told me it was a cremation, paid for by the county because nobody offered otherwise. They never opened the county's pine box.

I called Leo. 'As fantastic as it sounds, I can't prove otherwise.'

'Ah, jeez.'

'Leo, this is preposterous. She's dead.'

'Gotta be,' he said. 'When you tug at a loose end, Dek, you tug hard. Maybe I'm doing it, too.'

'Where are you now?'

'Back at the Holiday Inn.'

'No sign of Tripp?'

'Maybe he's hunkering down in the room, enjoying the groceries.'

'With Sara?' I said, trying for a laugh.

'Wouldn't that be wonderful?' he said.

TWENTY-SIX

I called Greg Theodore at the *Tribune*.

'Your reporting didn't include the names of the Weston cops that first responded to the Sara Jansen call,' I said.

'Hold, Elstrom, while I slip on my headset. Makes it easier to take down exactly what you've learned and then, to ask why you want to know.'

'I can get them from the police department,' I said.

'You're dodging,' he said.

'Off the record, not to be repeated until I give you the go-ahead?'

'Lucas and Rainey,' he said, because it was a minor give and I could have gotten them on my own.

'What if the police got the identity of the victim wrong? When the cops show up, Martin Tripp is standing on the front lawn. He says Sara has been stabbed and an intruder wearing a hat took off out the back door. The cops give chase, find no one because, as is thought almost instantly, Tripp made up the story of the intruder—'

'Or did he?' Theodore interrupted. 'You told me that part of the tale might be true.'

'Put that aside for now. The cops find Sara dead. They call for a meat wagon. Wagon arrives, removes the body. Not much of an autopsy is needed because cause of death is obvious. Body is picked up by the funeral home, cremated, and ashes are buried.'

'And all the while it's someone different?'

'Who would doubt the bereaved husband's identification of his wife, even if he's the murderer?'

'There are protocols, Elstrom. Procedures.'

'Maybe someone dropped the ball,' I said.

'What launched this flight of fancy?'

'Idleness, though I can't see a motive for such a thing.'

He laughed. 'You'll explain this to me first, when the time comes?'

'As agreed.'

I called the Weston police department. Both officers were on duty. I arranged to meet them in the parking lot of the police station in a half hour.

'An insurance matter?' Lucas said.

'A closed insurance matter,' I said. 'Life insurance, to be exact. You identified the body?'

'That wasn't our job,' Lucas said.

'The medical examiner's,' Rainey said.

'Identification is up to others,' Lucas added.

I brought up a newspaper photo of Sara. 'This was her?'

'That's a picture of Sara Jansen,' Lucas said.

'Is this the woman you found dead?'

'Well, of course, but . . .'

'But what?'

'She was slumped forward, head down toward her knees. I felt her neck for a pulse, was all. Like I said, formal identification is for others. What's going on, Mr Elstrom?'

'Just closing the file,' I said.

I left but I didn't leave far. I stopped at the Lookout and put two quarts of chili on my credit card, hoping to stretch them until the bill arrived. But then more urgent thoughts intruded, and I called Amanda before I started the Jeep.

'I'm in Weston,' I said.

'Where in Weston?' she asked.

'Business district.'

'The dining district?'

'You could say that,' I said.

'The Lookout district, to be precise?'

'I bought two quarts this time, in case a killer beats you to the first one. The perfect thing to be served with lasagna.'

'See you about nine,' she said.

'Assembling?'

'Assembling,' she said.

Amanda came at nine that evening and I built a fire from scrap lumber in the huge fireplace in the Whatever Room opposite the kitchen. It is a Whatever Room because it is furnished only with a long bench I'd made of thick planking that faces the fireplace. There is a huge stone fireplace on each of the turret's five floors, large enough to burn whole chunks of trees should one decide to roast livestock. My fires were smaller, but no livestock needed to worry about being led up the wrought-iron stairs, shaky as they were becoming.

We sat on the bench, ate small amounts of chili and the ever-available lasagna, and talked easily of everything except brick-throwers; missing, confessed wife-killers; and potentially murderous bagmen. And, at times, we didn't talk, trying to enjoy the easy silences of the long-committed. That evening, the silences were not easy. The bone I'd discovered in the Verona woods was everywhere in the words we didn't say.

We went to bed, and that returned us to easy, and afterward we slept. Until three in the morning, when the gnarled skein of loose ends that was Martin Tripp and Kowalski the Frenchman jerked me awake.

I padded down the stairs to the second floor, to sit on the low bench and poke at the embers of the fire and the twisted strings of what I didn't know.

Sometime later, Amanda came softly down the stairs, wrapped in our blanket.

'Martin Tripp, that Frenchman, and Verona?' she asked, opening the blanket to warm herself before the fire because, though it was August and it was hot, the turret is made of thick limestone that preserves the cold of past winters.

'Martin Tripp and Kowalski,' I said, 'and Sara Jansen and Julianna Wynton and maybe the whole lizard colony of Rivertown. Do you know I'm still being tailed?' I told her about the teen-aged surveillance squad the lizards had unleashed.

'Why, do you think?'

'They must think I know more about Tripp than I do.'

'And Kowalski?' she said.

'He knows more about something than I do,' I said.

'Perhaps Tripp?'

'Perhaps Tripp,' I said.

I realized, then, that I'd been shivering.

'Whatever will you do?' she murmured, pulling me closer to welcome me to her warmth.

'War on every front,' I said to her when I stopped shaking. 'I will attack every front.'

She did not press me about what I meant. That moment was meant for other things.

And so it was.

TWENTY-SEVEN

The blue Malibu wasn't in the parking lot of the Holiday Inn but that didn't mean anything. A kid, no more than eighteen, was working the desk.

'I must have just missed my friends,' I said. 'Their car isn't in the lot.'

'Name?'

'Tripp.'

The kid checked his screen, then shook his head. 'No Tripp,' he said.

'Try Sara Jansen.'

He nodded without checking the screen. 'Checked out this morning.'

'Then Tripp too, right?' I asked, because it was worth a shot.

'The room's empty,' he said.

'No big deal, I'll catch up with them next time they're in town,' I said. I started to walk away, then did a theatrical pause and raised my hand like an Italian cop did on television reruns. Turning around, I slapped my head with my raised hand, because he did that too, and asked, 'Say, does Sara still wear her hair in huge Mickey Mouse curls on each side of her head?'

The kid laughed. 'Sounds really weird, man, really weird, but I never saw the lady.'

'She paid by credit card, right?' I asked, because the name on it would tell all.

He surprised me by answering. 'Cash, in an envelope, dropped on the counter, can you believe it? I'd only stepped away for a moment and when I came back, the envelope was lying there.'

'I didn't think hotels took cash anymore.'

'The manager approved an exception,' he said, reading from the computer screen. 'When she checked in, she said her purse got stolen. Luckily she had cash in her car.'

'I'll have to wait to catch up with her,' I said. She, or he, must have waited for the kid to step away before tossing the envelope on the counter.

I drove back to Rivertown and parked in the block past Kowalski's rented house. No tailing pickup was parked within seeing distance, which I hoped meant Kowalski was out.

No one answered my knock on the front door. No one had locked it either. I went in, like I'd been invited.

It was a standard, front-to-back bungalow – living room in the front, dining room next, then kitchen, and behind that, the back porch. Two bedrooms lined the side, one off the living room, the second off the kitchen.

Each of the side bedrooms held only a cheap pine dresser and a twin bed. The beds were made. The dressers were empty. No clothes hung in the closets.

The kitchen had been cleared out, too. There was no food in the refrigerator and all the dishes had been washed and put back in cabinets.

I went down to the basement, expecting to see what I saw: no cats, no cages, no dye, no apron, no gloves. Kowalski and what remained of his menagerie was gone, leaving no trace of anything behind.

I went out to the garage. The side door opened easily. He'd left nothing there, either.

As I headed toward the sidewalk, I saw four cats – three white, one gray – scampering at the corner of the back yard.

Perhaps they'd escaped as Kowalski cleared out but more than likely they'd been set free along with what remained of the rest of his herd.

My mind ranged over possibilities. Such as it was, I found only one that made sense. Kowalski hadn't set the caged cats free, two by two, in any act of kindness. Kowalski – he of the tattooed head, suspected of thievery and maybe murder – was up to something far beyond dyeing and loosing cats. And nobody other than Kowalski, save one, knew why. And that one, my gut advised, had to be the vanished Martin Tripp. Tripp must know – or had known, if it got him killed and buried up in Verona – what his old drinking buddy was up to, and why Kowalski returned to Rivertown. Whatever that was, it was the same reason Tripp, under the guise of being homeless and harmless, returned to Rivertown, too.

It didn't take too much imagination to think everything was about the bank. Kowalski was interested in the back of it; Tripp had tried to rent a lockbox inside of it. And Sara Jansen had once worked inside of it, until she'd left town with enough money for a down stroke on a house in Weston, and enough reason for someone to kill her.

That much was clear, but there were still too many gaps. I drove to Kutz's clearing to avail myself of Leo's formidable brain.

The clearing was jumping, almost literally. Leo's soothing sambas were playing softly like always, but the tempo everywhere else had picked up considerably. The giant metal tube that Ma Brumsky was so secretive about was being hoisted to a forty-five-degree angle by two young men like they were aiming a cannon over the Willahock and being supervised by the ever-vigilant Mrs Roshiska. Another three elderlies were singing in Polish, without regard to the sambas, as they dragged empty round plastic kids' pools to various spots in the clearing. Even the folks in line at the order window, a longer line than was normal, were swaying to beats, whether in time with the Polish chorus or the sambas, I could not tell.

Ma Brumsky was overseeing it all from the edge of the clearing. Wearing a yellow construction hardhat, she was supervising a young buff testing the motorized winch that operated the thick cable that led up to the pulley in the highest oak. Her right hand rested low on the shirtless buff's bare back, no doubt to steady him in the event of an earthquake.

Leo was inside the trailer. I stood in line, watching person after person come away with kielbasas or pierogies.

'What's up?' I asked, when I got to the window.

'It's tonight,' he said, sliding through one hot dog and no option for a kielbasa.

I took what I was given and went around to the open side door to talk to his back.

'What's tonight?' I asked, then took a bite. It was lukewarm as in days of old, but it didn't taste quite as good as in days of old. I'd become enamored of the heated meat Ma served up.

'I don't know, but word has spread,' he said, serving up a kielbasa for the person who'd been in line behind me.

'Surely not another splash party?' I said.

'You're not thinking another skinny—?'

I cut that thought off out of mercy. 'I was referring to the plastic kids' pools scattered about.'

'I have no idea,' he said. 'Everything is hush-hush, including that promise of a five-piece band.'

'I didn't hear anything about a party tonight,' I said.

'You don't have friends. You're a hermit.'

'What are you?'

'Your friend? So, what exactly did you come here to order?'

I thought it best not to tell him.

'Bring Amanda,' he said. 'Endora will be here.'

'You're really going to be serving food at sunset? Isn't that sacrilege?'

'I'm not serving anything. I don't know what Ma's up to.'

'Maybe it'll be pierogies on toothpicks?'

'She's not saying, and her friends aren't ratting anything out, either.'

'Who's paying for all this?'

'A secret admirer, she says.'

'And you believe it?'

'I'm staying behind the order window to keep an eye on the cash box. I'm not paying for any foolishness.'

He was too busy to talk further. I finished the hot dog, went to the Jeep, sat, and thought about making one last stab in Weston. I googled with my phone and found what I wanted in an old *Tribune* article. A Walter Kowalski, of Rivertown, Illinois, had been arrested on charges of suspected auto theft twenty years before. Those were the days of thick newspapers and broad coverage. The piece included a picture of a younger, beret-less, Kowalski. It was enough.

I drove to Weston. The neighbor woman who'd talked to a nervous Sara the day she was killed was home.

'I told you, I didn't get a look at his face. He was too far away,' she said, when I showed her Kowalski's picture on my phone.

'How about the hat?' I showed her the picture of a beret I'd also found on the internet.

'That's a French hat,' she said, frowning. 'The man who visited Sara wore an old-fashioned, regular hat.'

'A fedora,' I said.

'Exactly.'

I called Amanda from the car. 'I'm inviting you to a party at Kutz's clearing.'

'When?'

'Tonight.'

'We're assembling.'

'You might find this evening to be really interesting.'

'Why?'

'I have no idea,' I said.

She paused, then said, 'There is one young man I want to try out as a supervisor. Former gang, former high-school student, currently wants to change his life.'

'Is there risk?'

'He's still fragile,' she said. 'Ah, what the heck, I'll do it. But, Dek, a party outside a hot dog trailer?'

'There'll be entertainment. A five-piece band, Ma Brumsky said, and . . .' Now it was my turn to pause.

'And?' she prompted, after a few seconds.

'And maybe more,' I said.

She laughed. 'You have no idea, do you?'

'None,' I said, 'but Kowalski set free the last of his cats.'

And that was the truest thing I could have said.

TWENTY-EIGHT

We had to walk down to the clearing. Parked cars already jammed the river road. The promise of a first ever, nighttime party at Kutz's had drawn a frenzy. Even from the top of the road, we could hear that this was going to be no ordinary night. It wasn't simply that Jobim and Gilberto and their soft sambas had been displaced, or that Frank had also been banished, perhaps his way, perhaps not. It was what had dislodged them. The five-piece band that Ma Brumsky promised was playing at full volume, and even from a distance, we heard trouble in that. For, as we confirmed when we got down to the clearing, all five pieces were accordions, played by three men and two women who apparently had found no time to rehearse. I caught snatches of a polka I'd once heard, but only snatches. The rest were random notes played with gusto and independence.

'Disco Polski!' a banner stretched over the base of the road read, but it didn't tell the half of it. The patch by the river had gone nuts.

The plastic pools Ma's lady friends scattered everywhere glittered now with ice and shiny gold cans of Miller Beer. Empties lay everywhere, some kicked aside, most crushed by the happy feet of a thousand laughing, shouting people looking upward, swaying to whatever beat they managed to find in the competing accordions. The upward-facing multicolored spotlights Ma's elderlies had jammed into the ground fired reds and blues and greens into the night sky like searchlights during a blitzkrieg. A giant multifaceted mirror ball hung in the second tallest oak caught many of them, and fired those reds and blues and greens right back onto the laughing, drunken faces.

But it wasn't the spectacular light show that had upturned most of those faces. It was what had been raised to the top of the tallest oak that commanded the night. Mrs Roshiska, attired in a glittering silver tank top and short skirt, had been hoisted in a construction basket, via winch and pulley, to the top of the tree. Clearly unrestrained by underwear, she shook and shimmied with the abandon of an avenging Greek deity, her glitter blazing reds and blues and greens from the light show all around.

I had to stop, and laugh. And admire. Rivertown had gone mad, at least in Kutz's clearing. Yet somehow, up in that tree, the ageless Mrs Roshiska blessed it all with her irrepressibility. I raised my hand to flash her a thumbs-up, and turned away before she could flash something I would never forget back in return.

'Dek, what is this?' Amanda shouted beside me. Tears of laughter glistened against her cheeks, adding yet more sparkle to the night.

'Want a beer?' I shouted back, because there was nothing else, absolutely nothing else, that I could think to shout. I reached down into the pool at our feet and grabbed two cans. 'Someone spent a fortune on all this beer,' I yelled, handing her one of the cans.

'To give away? That doesn't sound like Ma Brumsky,' she shouted back.

'Or Leo,' I yelled. 'He doesn't have a liquor license. He's going to get busted, even though he didn't pay for the beer.'

Amanda laughed and pointed to a cluster of men across the clearing. A dozen cops, all related to the lizards that ran city hall, stood in a circle, blue shirts untucked, ball caps on backward. Inside the circle, two more were doing some sort of tribal war dance. One was shirtless, the other no longer had pants. Several in the circle were trying to clap, but kept missing the alignment of their hands. A pile of empty cans lay on the ground to the right of them. They'd been there a while.

'So much for law and order,' she yelled.

'Nobody's going to get busted—' I started shouting, and then an image flashed from across the clearing. It was a head, backlit by the bright night. A woman's head with a huge curl at each side. In the next instant it was gone.

My night went silent, the chaos gone. I heard only my breathing, raggedy and short. I started toward the spot in the clearing but a tall, slender figure suddenly materialized, and almost gliding, stepped in front of me. The chaos came crashing back, the lights, the accordions, the drunken shouting. The next light burst, this one blue, revealed Endora, Leo's statuesque girlfriend. She hugged Amanda and then me, but there was fierceness behind it.

'Having fun?' she shouted.

I looked beyond her but the woman I'd seen was gone.

'Leo wanted this?' Amanda asked her, leaning forward to be heard.

'He's so furious he can hardly talk.' Endora swept an arm out at the clearing gone mad. 'They're trashing everything. They're all drunk.'

'Where is he?' I thought to shout back, but I was scanning the shapes of the people in the distance. None were topped with huge curls.

'Down by the river, staring into the water,' she said. 'He was hoping you'd come.'

'I can't believe Ma Brumsky wanted this,' I said.

'Go to him, Dek,' Endora said.

'In a moment,' I said, and took off in the direction of the big-curled woman.

There were enough reds, blues, and greens to see to maneuver through the knots of people, but she wasn't there. I gave it up and headed to the Willahock.

Leo stood at the farthest edge of the clearing, where the woods began. His usual colorful garb – tonight an orange tropical shirt adorned with lavender birds of some sort and purple slacks, now made more outrageous by the dancing blues, greens, and reds swatted down by the disco ball – only whitened the paleness of his face. He looked like he had no blood.

'What the heck, Dek?' he asked when I came up.

'Ma wanted this?'

He pointed toward the center of the throng at the base of Mrs Roshiska's tree. 'Ma's in there, somewhere, clutching a beer, shaking her butt.'

'Better than a nursing home, Leo,' I said, and was about to tell him about the woman with big curls, when a roar rose above the cacophony of accordion music and drunken yelling. Cats came, dozens of them, racing through the clearing like rats.

All thought it was more entertainment, and the crowd

fragmented like it exploded. Drunk or the sober few, they chased
the cats like they were winning, hundred-dollar lottery tickets.
Kowalski hadn't freed all of his cats at his rented house. He'd
brought most of them to Kutz's clearing.

As if to underscore the mad scramble, the big iron tube came
to life. It began to rumble like some giant being, clearing its
throat. The ground shook and a mighty flaming ball shot from
its barrel, rising up to light the sky bright orange.

Leo's lips struggled to move, but he could form no words.
The shock was complete. The clearing – his beloved clearing
– had descended into a laughing, shouting, clapping hell.

Yet it was magnificent – the chaos of the swarming cats; the
yelling, shrieking, stumbling drunks; all lit the colors of
the brightest sunset by the ascending flame ball – and I couldn't
help clapping along with the rest of the crowd. And as the
fireball began to descend, shedding sparks everywhere, another
one rose in the sky. But this was ascending from the center of
town.

The crowd paused their cat chasing to look up, taking it as
spectacular choreography, a twin spectacle. The clapping grew
thunderous. Rivertown had never offered such a display.

I saw then what I'd been unable to see before. Bedlam. Perfect,
purposeful, demanding, distracting bedlam. And one wily
Frenchman.

I ran to tell Amanda I had to leave.

TWENTY-NINE

Amanda refused to be left behind. She ran up the river
road, beside me, to the Jeep. It took only a fast five
minutes, dodging, swerving, running restricting reds, to
shoot through town. There were no cops around. They were at
Kutz's clearing, drunk.

Of course. That was expected. That was the purpose.

The crooked road came up fast. I sped down to the bank. The
four-car parking lot was filled and cars were parked on the grass.

People out on a late summer's evening. I jumped the curb and left the Jeep on the grass.

The pungent residue of explosive, probably dynamite, still hung in the air. We ran around to the back. The rear wall yawned open, ragged and torn, still smoking. Some bits of bricks, chunks of concrete, and pieces of dirty stucco lay scattered out in a fifty-foot radius but most of the debris had been blown inward. Too much debris. The stairwell going down caught the brunt of it like a funnel, and filled.

That, of course, was not expected.

A crowd clustered close to what was left of the wall, oblivious to the potential of a second explosion or the collapse of the weakened wall.

'Kowalski?' Amanda said.

'Had to be,' I said.

'All that rubble, filling the stairway down to where you said the lockboxes are,' she said. 'He killed her for nothing?'

'Allegedly,' I said, because nothing made sense yet.

Sirens sounded in the distance and grew louder. Cops, in whatever shape they were in, had been roused from the play pools at Kutz's clearing. The first squad car jumped the curb a moment later and slammed into a tree, crumpling its front end. Two of Rivertown's finest, or at least its most immediately responsive and less inebriated, pulled themselves out of the car, teetered for a moment until the earth stopped wobbling, and made their careful ways toward the small crowd. One carried a flashlight that his partner was able to turn on.

They surveyed the ruined back of the bank. 'Gas exploshun,' the first cop said.

'Yesh,' his partner agreed.

The flashlight beam wobbled across the rubble and twitched around the jagged edge of the hole.

New sirens grew deafening, closing in on the bank. Neither of the first-arriving officers stepped toward the ragged wall, perhaps in recognition that steadier feet would soon arrive. The second squad car slammed to a stop, silencing its siren. Neither of the new pair of officers wobbled as they ran up.

The new pair cast steady flashlight beams into the hole, and one of them leaned in just enough to see inside. His flashlight beam lingered on the debris filling the stairwell, probing the destruction. Much work would be needed to empty those stairs.

His partner moved outward from the building, searching what little rubble was on the ground. There was little to see.

'Gas exploshun,' the first cop told the new arrivals.

'Yesh,' his partner said.

'Jeez,' one of the newly arrived cops said.

The cop that had gone to lean inside, came over. 'That you, Elstrom?' he said, pointing his flashlight beam directly into my eyes.

'Elstrom?' his partner said. 'The guy they've—?'

'Cuff him,' the cop who'd leaned in said. And quicker than I could say, 'Kowalski,' his partner tugged my arms behind me and handcuffed my wrists.

'What are you doing?' I shouted. 'I just got here!'

I was spun like I was on a turntable and propelled toward their car.

'You can't do this!' Amanda yelled to the cop who was marching me. Already, she had her phone out and pressed to her ear.

'I. Did. Not. Blow. Up. The. Bank,' I said, slowly, reasonably, logically, trying to project calm innocence.

We got to the police car, the back door was opened, and with a palm pressing down on my head, I got shoved into the stench of spilled beer. Two empty cans bumped against my feet as I fell back against the seat.

Amanda stood right next to the car, talking into her cell phone. She was calm and utterly icy. 'I need his car keys,' she said to the cop who'd marched me.

'What for?' the cop asked.

'So I can follow you in his car, you cretin,' she said, holding out her free hand, palm up.

Likely the cop didn't know the meaning of the word 'cretin,' because all he said was, 'It's a Jeep, not a car.'

Her upturned hand remained steady.

'Which pocket?' the cop said, bending down to give me a whiff of the good time he'd had at Kutz's.

'Right side, Officer Cretin,' I said, and shifted so that he could pull the keys from my jeans.

The cop handed them to Amanda.

She stood there, unmoving. 'Now, what's the charge?'

For a moment, the cop stood silent, confused. 'I don't know,' he finally said.

'You don't know why you handcuffed Mr Elstrom?'

'I was ordered.'

'I know that,' she said, still ice, still placid. 'But you must have a charge.'

'Explosion, probably,' he said.

She spoke the word 'bomb' into the phone.

'You can move on now,' the cop said to her.

'I'll be staying with Mr Elstrom until his team of lawyers arrives.'

I allowed to myself that it would have seemed like absurd comedy if it was happening to someone else, but to me, sitting in the back of a Rivertown squad car fouled by spilled beer, there was nothing funny about it. My arms throbbed from being pulled tight behind my back. I was scared. Justice, not to mention reason, was not an everyday commodity in Rivertown.

An ambulance pulled up, two EMTs jumped out, ran to the back of the bank, and then scanned the crowd of onlookers before returning to their ambulance. None of the police officers had thought to radio that there were no injuries. The ambulance drove away.

The cop who'd directed that I be cuffed came to the car. He and his partner got in, and drove me to the police station at the back of city hall. They tugged me out and walked me through the front door, locking it behind them so Amanda, following in the Jeep, could not get in.

No one was inside. The beer had not yet run out at Kutz's clearing. They took me to an interview room and removed my handcuffs. Three and a half of the walls were gray. The fourth wall was half-mirrored, though why two-way glass was needed in Rivertown, where nothing was done transparently, seemed odd. I sat on a gray metal chair at a gray metal table. I felt pretty sure I would become gray, too, if I was kept too long in that room.

There was no clock on the wall. The big mirror on the fourth wall was big enough for folks on the other side to watch me admiring the gray but I doubted that would hold anyone's interest, even if they could see clearly.

An hour passed, or perhaps two, and then the door opened. I

was not surprised to see that Amanda had called the Bohemian. Even at that late hour, he wore one of his custom-made gray suits. He was followed by an equally well dressed, equally gray-haired man who introduced himself as James Randeen. He was also wearing a gray suit. Together, they complemented the gray walls and each other. I was the only one, in blue jeans and a yellow polo shirt, that complemented nothing.

'Amanda?' I asked.

'We sent her to your residence,' the Bohemian said.

'I'm your lawyer,' James Randeen said unnecessarily, smiling despite all the gray surrounding us.

Everyone in Chicago legal circles knew of him, He was a giant in legal defense. His clients didn't get convicted. And that was why the Bohemian brought him.

'Apologies for our tardiness, Vlodek,' the Bohemian said. 'We had to find a booking officer. Turns out, he was down at the festivities by the river. Does that sort of thing happen much around here?'

'It was a first-ever, deliberately staged event to mask other goings-on.'

'We'll discuss that later,' Randeen said quickly, likely for the benefit of whomever was behind the two-way mirror.

'We shared a beer while we advised the booking officer of speedy due process,' the Bohemian went on. 'He was most agreeable, perhaps distracted by all the frivolity. He scribbled a note on the back of a beer box, as best he could focus, authorizing your release on your own recognizance. We tried to give that to someone here, but except for your arresting officers, your police station is empty, and we had to knock on the door to wake them up.'

'Personal recognizance on a bombing charge?' I asked.

The Bohemian shrugged. 'Free beer reigns. No one wanted to leave the party.'

'Especially the lady in the tree,' Randeen said, and started to laugh. Perhaps not laugh, exactly; it was more like a roar to accompany convulsions of mirth.

The Bohemian nodded, visibly struggling to keep his own lips from twitching. 'One could go blind from all that glitter.'

'And all that flesh, going in so many directions,' Randeen managed, almost purple now.

'We'll retire to your abode, Vlodek?' the Bohemian asked. 'It's necessary, despite the late hour. Your constabulary will sober up soon, we're afraid.'

'So many things to see in Rivertown,' Randeen said.

'I still don't get why they picked me up,' I said.

'To your abode, Vlodek,' the Bohemian said, taking hold of my elbow. 'Even deserted, this is not the place for conversation.'

THIRTY

Amanda and I each carried up a plastic lawn chair, one ascent at a time, so we could all sit at the plywood table in the kitchen.

I looked back, not hearing the Bohemian and Randeen follow.

'The stairs, Vlodek?' the Bohemian said, pointing to the wavering two-by-four I'd wedged at the top to prevent the wrought-iron staircase from pulling farther out of the wall.

'I don't think the staircase can fall all the way down.' I pointed to how it was nestled into the curve of the wall. Then, realizing a partial fall would be of no comfort, especially since both were large men, I said, 'Only one of you should come up at a time, like Amanda and I just did.'

The Bohemian nodded, and stepped gingerly onto the first stair and then the second. Bouncing just a little on the balls of his feet, he waited for any metallic groan, but as when Amanda and I had gone up, there was only the slightest sound of the staircase shifting, really only a whimper. All seemed safe. The Bohemian came up the rest of the way. When he got to the top, Randeen followed.

The elderly Mr Coffee hissed, unaccustomed to perform at such a late, or early, hour until finally it voided into the carafe. I poured coffee into mismatched cups and joined the Bohemian, Randeen, and Amanda at the plywood. 'You're sure I'll be arrested again?' I asked, still shocked that I'd been hauled away the first time.

'You're close by, handy as a scapegoat if the press gets wind of the bombing,' Randeen said.

He took a first sip of my coffee, winced, and quickly set the cup down. In recognition of his and the Bohemian's prominence, I'd used fresh grounds, even though the ones in the maker were only a day old.

'Later you'll be exonerated, of course,' the Bohemian said.

I looked at Amanda. She understood.

'He's been down that road,' she said. 'He can't do it again.'

'Ah, the Wilts case,' the Bohemian said.

'Still, we must prepare for a trial,' Randeen said.

'A trial,' I said, and shivered.

Amanda's face was tensed with worry. 'Dek can be identified by many people as being at the clearing when the bomb went off, but they'll still maintain he did it?'

'Mr Elstrom says he's already on their watch list,' Randeen said, 'and they can always magically find a timing device in the rubble, something he could have left back of the bank before going to the clearing.'

'But why?' she said.

'They're sweating me,' I said.

'Vlodek's right,' the Bohemian said. 'What we need to be clear about is why.'

Kowalski's been their obvious target since they learned money was missing, but Tripp's return triggered some reconsideration about Sara,' I said, remembering the bank president's agitation when I brought up her name. 'Wondering whether she stole it, and whether Tripp came back to Rivertown to look for it.'

'How did he know?' Amanda asked.

'She might have shared the fact that she was involved,' I said. 'More likely, he learned it on his own, like when he killed her. Whatever it was, it brought him back, and that, coupled with Kowalski's return, must have excited the lizards into a frenzy. They began tailing Kowalski and they began tailing me, for Tripp had quickly disappeared from his motel.'

'They wanted Vlodek to lead them to Tripp,' the Bohemian said.

'Exactly,' I said. 'Tailing us both meant following all roads to get their money.'

'To be clear, we're not just talking about a missing twenty or thirty grand?' the Bohemian said.

'I think she didn't take much more,' I said.

All three looked at me, looking for an explanation of the gibberish I'd just uttered.

'Both Tripp and Kowalski must have concluded Sara left most of it in a lockbox,' I said. 'That's the only thing that explains Tripp's and Kowalski's behavior once they returned here. Both figured Sara for the grab, and both concluded she didn't have the take in Weston, because she wasn't paying for living large out there. Remember, according to trial testimony, she was racking up big credit card debt.'

'Being cagy?' Randeen asked.

'Biding her time before using what she stole, making no one wonder if she had a lot of cash,' I said.

'So both concluded she left it right where she stole it, in a lockbox,' the Bohemian said.

'Tripp tried to rent a box to get access to the vault,' I said. 'Kowalski tried to blow his way in.'

'Kowalski's motive for the explosion we can introduce in your defense,' Randeen said, writing now in a leather-bound pocket notebook. He looked up. 'If we can show how he knew the money was in a lockbox.'

'Either he killed Sara Jansen to gain the information, or she wouldn't tell him anything and he killed her anyway, or he figured it out, on his own,' I said.

'Figured it out on his own?' Randeen asked.

'He might have learned Martin Tripp returned to Rivertown. No way Tripp would have come back—'

'Slowly!' Randeen interrupted. 'How did Kowalski know Tripp came back?'

'I don't know,' I said, 'but Tripp got here first, looking like he was homeless. Somehow, Kowalski found that out. He beat it back to Rivertown. I went and saw Sara's mother. She said someone came a few days earlier, asking if Sara had seen the mother before she left for Weston.'

'That was Kowalski?' Randeen asked.

'She didn't describe the person, but that's my guess,' I said. 'I also guess that she told the person the same thing she told me, that she hadn't seen Sara for a long time before Sara moved.'

'Process of elimination,' Randeen said. 'That left only one

other place for Kowalski to look: the bank,' He smiled. 'Motive to blow!'

'And Tripp, Vlodek?' the Bohemian asked. 'You said he tried to rent a box?'

'I tossed a question to the bank president, asking whether Tripp came to rent a box. His eyes got wild, which I took to mean Tripp tried to rent a box but was rebuffed. And that's why Tripp was forced to come to me, pretending he wanted help proving he didn't kill Sara. He needed a reason, should anyone be watching, to hang around while he figured out another way of getting into the vault.'

'What good was simply accessing the vault?' the Bohemian asked, but it was rhetorical, to make sure everyone was on the same page.

'He must have found the key to Sara's box, and the master she must have duplicated,' I said. 'That explains Tripp's delay between the stabbing and calling the cops. I'll bet he was going through the house, snapping on lights. He said he was staging a burglary, but he wasn't. He was out of his mind, sure, but he was still functional enough to make one last search for what had eluded him. That night, he finally got lucky when he turned over an end table. One of the first officers on the scene found a ripped away panel that had been glued to its underside. He testified it could have been used to hide documents. I'm betting it wasn't documents that were hidden there, but keys – lockbox keys. With those, Tripp could get inside Sara's box. But first, he had to get inside the vault.'

'Why risk killing her and having to make a frantic, last search?' the Bohemian asked. 'What triggered him, that night? Why not wait, take his time to find the keys? Wasn't that what he'd been doing since he moved in, anyway?'

'I don't have an answer for that,' I said, 'other than to guess that he did snap and stab her and that set off the last, final search.'

'Tripp disappeared before Kowalski blew the bank?' Randeen asked.

'Yes,' I said, knowing where Randeen was going.

'Wouldn't Kowalski have taken that as a sign that Tripp got the money and took off? If so, why risk blowing his way into the bank if Tripp was already gone?'

'Maybe he didn't know Tripp was already gone,' I said. 'I agree: if Tripp had gotten that money, he would have left town immediately, unless . . .'

'Unless; unless?' Randeen said, not bothering to conceal his annoyance at yet another wrinkle in my story.

'Unless Tripp didn't disappear voluntarily, and that trail of clothes and car I found at his motel wasn't a ruse to make us think he was abducted, but the stuff of someone who really was abducted, or worse.'

'Worse?' Randeen asked.

I told him of the bone in the woods, but left out any mention of Amanda being with me. 'Of course, that could have been a ruse, too.'

Randeen put down his pen. 'Please tell me there's no way Kowalski could have known anything about that, otherwise our motive gets blown up like the bank.'

'Kowalski would have had no way of knowing whether Tripp got the money,' I said, complying.

'What you've not told us is how Tripp could have gotten inside the vault, if he was rebuffed,' Randeen said.

'Accomplice,' Amanda said.

'Who?' Randeen said.

I thought of the woman with the large curls that I'd just seen at the clearing, likely the same woman Leo had traced to the Holiday Inn and then to a grocery. And I decided to hold off saying anything about her, for fear they'd all think I was being too fanciful about Tripp being too clever. 'Any woman,' I said, instead, and adding, 'I'll bet the lizards drilled those boxes after the explosion last night. They guessed what Kowalski was looking for. If they recovered the money, they'll let me off the hook for the bombing.'

'Getting back to that bone,' Randeen said. 'Whose could it be?'

'If not Tripp's, then Julianna Wynton's, or the unnamed woman accomplice,' I said.

'He killed her after she got him the money?' Randeen said, ever the adversarial lawyer.

'To eliminate a witness,' I said.

'Here's the bottom line,' Randeen said. 'If your lizards didn't recover their money by drilling the boxes, they'll want to keep their thumbs in Mr Elstrom's eyes, even knowing it was Kowalski and not him who blew the bank.'

'Why?' Amanda said.

'To help find their money,' I said.

'I agree,' the Bohemian said. 'You're the only one that seems to have a world-view on this matter. They'll want to know not just what you know, but what you can find out.'

'Is there anything else we should know?' Randeen asked.

'Sara Jansen,' I said, deciding to go for full candor now. I told them about the midnight-blue Malibu and the woman Leo had thought he'd seen, done up, hair-wise, beneath a hoodie, like Sara Jansen. 'I think I saw her too, though only backlit, at the clearing.'

'Every newspaper in the country reported her dead!' the Bohemian said. 'There is doubt?'

'The identification process on Sara Jansen was poor, to say the least. And the clerk at the Holiday Inn said someone using her name had just checked out when I got there.'

'Credit card receipt?' the Bohemian asked.

'Paid cash for the room, which makes it not credible,' I said.

'For pity's sake, why are we talking about this other stuff?' Randeen said, standing up and turning to me. 'Please don't share your suppositions with anyone. Your fingerprints are all over every bad aspect of this matter. In fact, please don't do anything at all until I can sort through all of what I've just heard. In the meantime, prepare yourself for someone sobering up at the police department and coming to arrest you.'

'Under pretext for the bombing, if the money has not yet been recovered,' I said.

Randeen turned to the Bohemian. 'Anton, your friend here, Mr Elstrom, has dug himself into the universal center of bad fates. We must think outside the box, as they say.'

The Bohemian nodded as he got up. 'You're thinking . . .'

'Proactive emissaries,' Randeen said.

'Emissaries?' I asked.

'You'll allow us to act on your behalf, without slowing to obtain your approval first?' the Bohemian said to me.

'Yes,' I said, understanding none of what was being transmitted between the two men.

'Then we'll almost be delighted,' Randeen said, meaning no such thing.

After a wary glance at the propping two-by-four, Randeen and the Bohemian rang the wrought-iron stairs going down, one at a time. I followed, to close the timbered door, certain that the Bohemian was too much a gentleman to slam it in fury.

'Eat a good breakfast, Vlodek,' the Bohemian called out as he got behind the wheel of his black Mercedes.

'Yes, you might be arrested again soon,' Randeen said, as he got into the front passenger's seat.

'Emissaries!' I thought to shout, without knowing why, as they drove away.

THIRTY-ONE

'You're going to lie low and stay away from everything,' Amanda said, as she stepped out the door the next morning.

'Absolutely,' I said.

'Not even to go out to chase cats,' she said.

'I don't know what to do next, except wait to see if I'll be arrested,' I said.

'No Tripp,' she said. 'No Kowalski, no Julianna Wynton.'

'I don't know where to start looking for any of them.'

'But you'll have an inspiration?' she asked, because she knew I did not suffer idleness well.

'I'm thinking it's you that's had an inspiration,' I said, because she'd been resolute in not telling me how she was dealing with the brick-thrower. 'The Bohemian will not calm me.'

'He's not involved,' she said, 'but I have a new, special friend,' she said. 'Frosty.'

'Frosty?' I said. 'What's his real name?'

'I don't know. He's just Frosty the—' She stopped suddenly.

'Frosty the what?'

'You'll get the wrong idea,' she said, 'or at least one that's not current.'

'I'll try not to.'

'Frosty the Blow Man.'

'Blow, like in wind?'

'Blow, like in cocaine. He used to deal. He's reformed. He does a lot of good and has an enormous number of connections. Sort of like the Bohemian.'

'You have a friend who used to deal in cocaine?'

'He stepped in after the brick. You already met one of his associates, that young guy keeping watch outside the factory. They like what we're doing and want to help us succeed.'

She grinned and headed toward her Toyota but then she stopped. A police car was slowing toward the turret. It stopped and the two Rivertown cops that arrested me got out and walked up, one jangling handcuffs. 'Vlodek Elstrom?' the handcuff jangler asked.

'Officer Cretin!' I said with as much enthusiasm as I could muster, which was none. 'We shared special moments just a few hours ago. You don't remember?'

I looked at Amanda. She already had her cell phone to her ear.

'Phone, then turn around,' Cretin said.

I handed him my phone and turned around. He snapped on the cuffs. We walked to his squad car, he palmed my head, and in I went.

'You could have at least removed the empty beer cans,' I said, by way of an observation.

'Shut up.'

'Or did you drink them on the way over here?'

'Shut up.'

'If you hit the brakes, the cans are going to cut you before me,' I said, adding, 'I hope.'

He slammed the door. The two cops got in the front, and turned the car around to drive the short distance to the station at the back of city hall.

I twisted around to look back. Amanda was following in her car. She was off the phone. The cavalry had been called.

I was taken to the same room I'd been in just hours before. It was still gray. Officer Cretin removed the handcuffs and went to the door.

'My lawyer advised me to have breakfast,' I said.

'What?'

'My lawyer,' I went on, speaking slowly. 'He told me to have breakfast. You came too early. I haven't had breakfast, so I'd like to place an order. I'd like French toast, three strips of crisp bacon, two sausage links, five eggs scrambled with just the lightest dusting of shredded cheddar, hash browns done crisply, and lately, I've been enjoying lasagna—' I stopped. 'Shouldn't you be writing this down?'

He slammed the door as he went out.

There was little to do except to again admire the gray but there's only so much admiration any gray can warrant. And so I allowed myself to imagine that Amanda had connected with the Bohemian, and that he, in turn, had connected with James Randeen, and that Randeen had, well, I had no idea who he would connect with.

They did connect apparently, and fairly promptly. I wasn't sure of precisely how much time I'd been left alone in the gray, but it seemed as though no more than two hours had passed before the door opened and Officer Cretin came to hand me my phone and let me out.

The Bohemian and Randeen were waiting in the hall, wearing the same clothes they'd worn earlier. Likely enough, they'd been up all night on my behalf.

'Emissaries?' I asked.

The Bohemian put his index finger to his lips, signaling for silence. We followed Officer Cretin through an unmarked steel door and into the bowels of city hall. The basement was where the public rooms were, and where I'd gone to argue the lunacy of the turret's zoning back when I'd first moved in.

Officer Cretin opened a door, fitted almost invisibly, into a wall in a small side corridor. We climbed interior stairs to the second floor. Never had I, or as far as I knew, any of Rivertown's non-lizard population, been allowed upstairs in city hall. Rumor had it that was where corruption flourished on a never-ending, fertile bed of green, where the street taxes, after being deposited in the bank, were redistributed, the machinations greased, the cigars lit, and the plots hatched.

The second-floor hall was paneled with dark walnut, and lit

as dim as the First Bank of Rivertown. Things that scuttled in darkness needed but few watts.

The cop stopped at a door lettered MAYOR in gold leaf. He spoke into his cell phone, listened, then opened the door and quickly stepped back. We walked into an anteroom furnished with six hardback chairs and no secretary.

The Bohemian knocked on the inner door. The door buzzed, unlocking. He held the door open for Randeen and myself, for he is a man of great courtesy, and we went in.

I'd seen the man called Mister Mayor in person only a few times – he avoided daylight – and always at a distance. Close up, the man was ominous. His eyes were slits and his skin was wrinkled, grayish, and more than a little reptilian. It was easy to understand why generations of his family had been termed 'lizards.' Barely acknowledging us beyond a slight lick of pink tongue at his lips, he motioned, with one finger, for us to sit on the black leather chairs in front of his desk.

Randeen pulled a folded sheet from his suit jacket pocket and passed it across the massive desk.

The mayor began reading in a whisper, accustomed as he was for others to strain to hear him. 'Standard client engagement letter. City of Rivertown engages Mr Elstrom.' He read the rest silently, and set the paper down.

'This discussion is confidential,' Randeen said, 'between you, Mr Chernek, Mr Elstrom, and myself.'

'I am accustomed to confidences,' Mister Mayor said.

'Per our telephone conversation of an hour ago,' Randeen went on, 'you agree that in return for Mr Elstrom's full cooperation and successful recovery effort—'

'What recovery effort?' I asked, like I hadn't suspected the condition the mayor had extracted.

'We'll get to that,' Randeen said to me. Turning back to the mayor, he continued, 'Upon successful recovery, you will pay him $10,000 and offer him full certification, in perpetuity, stating that his turret meets all municipal codes, no matter their nature. And finally, Mr Elstrom may cancel this agreement at any time. Now, tell us everything.'

Mister Mayor swiveled to look at me. 'You may cancel at any time, should you desire to be homeless.' Nodding to Randeen, he went on. 'Some time ago, and on multiple occasions, sums of money brought to the First Bank of Rivertown were under-reported as deposits, their shortages diverted elsewhere. As near as we can determine, this occurred only when the bank president's mother was absent due to a number of ailments. A part-time teller—'

'Sara—' I started to say.

The mayor flashed me a hard look. 'Never names.'

'Deposit slips?' I asked, even though I knew the answer.

A touch of pink flashed between the thin lips and was gone. 'Deposit slips are not always necessary.' That was no surprise. Potentially incriminating paper trails were avoided in the all-cash world that was municipal Rivertown.

'The bank president,' he continued, 'a family relation, was not always vigilant and our depositor—'

I started to say, 'Kowalski,' but the mayor's slitted eyes cautioned silence, and I kept my mouth shut.

'—was felt to be trustworthy. However, when the bank president – did I mention he was a family relation?'

We nodded.

The mayor sighed and continued. 'When the bank president finally did a comparison, many recent deposits were found to be smaller than in previous, similar time periods. Attention focused on the depositor, quite naturally, and he could offer no acceptable explanation, and in fact stammered and sweated and behaved quite suspiciously. We communicated to the depositor that we were not satisfied with his explanation, and that we were going to be discussing things with him the next morning, once he had a few hours to carefully consider his explanations. But the depositor fled Rivertown, gone without a trace. Naturally, this was taken as evidence of guilt. We tried to locate him but we were unsuccessful. And then, two weeks later, the part-time teller moved away, and eight months later, she was murdered by her boyfriend. We did not link our theft with her murder, and that sad event didn't change our conviction the depositor's sudden departure showed his guilt.'

The mayor paused to look each of us in the eye. 'Now, as you know, the depositor, the man we tried hard but unsuccessfully to find after his sudden disappearance, has returned to Rivertown.

He did so flamboyantly, strolling our streets, talking to our barber, our entertainment proprietors, acting as would any innocent man, almost daring us to invite him to continue the discussions he so abruptly fled earlier. We chose restraint, choosing instead to monitor his activities.'

'Questioning, as well, his potential involvement in the disappearance of your mother's cat?' I asked.

He acknowledged that with a slight nod.

'Please continue,' I said.

'We were also interested in the arrival, a few days before our depositor's return, of the confessed killer of the former part-time teller. We did not accept the return of these two individuals as coincidental. Two of our suspicious former residents, former drinking friends, coming back at roughly the same time?' He shook his head. 'And whereas our depositor did not seek us out to offer an explanation for why he abruptly vanished, or behave in a way that would explain his sudden return, we learned, belatedly, that the confessed murderer immediately tried to rent a lockbox at our bank.'

'Your banker knew to deny his request,' I said, carefully, 'but not to tell you?'

'He rejected the rental only because the man had confessed to murdering his part-time teller,' Mister Mayor said, 'and therefore, this . . . this family relation . . .' The pink tongue protruded only to wet the mayor's lip before retreating. 'This family relation did not think it important to tell us.'

'Until after the explosion—?'

Randeen squeezed my forearm. 'Let's let the mayor continue.'

'After being denied the opportunity to rent a lockbox, the confessed murderer sought out Mr Elstrom, ostensibly to find evidence of his innocence of murder, though by then we knew there was something else behind it.'

'Subterfuge,' I said. 'Distraction to disguise what he was really up to, which was to find a way to access the lockbox vault.'

'That seems obvious now,' he said.

'And then he disappeared.'

'Our last sighting was the same as yours?' he asked.

'When your cabbie tailed him to the Afforda-Rest,' I said. 'And after that, you started tailing me to find out where he was, though at that point, you didn't know about his interest in your lockboxes?'

'As I said, we learned about that belatedly.'

'After the explosion at the bank last night,' I said.

'The explosion brought forth the information.'

'You've since examined the lockboxes?'

'Of course,' he said.

'You're absolutely certain the skim is nowhere in any lockboxes?'

'Yes,' he said.

'How many lockboxes were rented out by your part-time teller?'

'Five, under different names,' he said. 'Clever girl.'

'The money could not have been removed months ago, right after the confessed murderer's acquittal . . .'

'Because then the confessed murderer, widower of our clever part-time teller, finder and keeper of her keys, would not have needed to return to Rivertown and employ an accomplice to go into the vault,' he said.

'He waited to let the uproar over his acquittal die down, hoping to avoid notice when he returned,' I said. 'So, an accomplice?'

'One new box was rented just a few days ago,' Mister Mayor went on. 'The only one since the part-time teller rented those five under assumed names, early last year.'

'What has your bank president told you about the recent renter?'

'He was out of the bank, getting lunch.' His thin lips turned downward. 'It was Taco Tuesday.'

'His mother handled the rental?'

His thin lips turned downward. 'Feebly,' he said, 'while awaiting her taco.'

'Her description of the renter?'

'Blurry,' he said. 'The woman wore a babushka, and a neck scarf pulled up over her mouth, supposedly to guard against infection.'

'Anything else of interest?'

'The renter's hair was done up, under the head scarf, into two huge curls,' he said.

Again my mind flashed back to the woman Leo had followed,

and the chill I'd felt, seeing a woman with big curls backlit at Kutz's clearing, and then farther back, to high school. I pushed the images away.

'The renter brought a huge handbag?' I asked.

'The mother didn't notice. We suppose it had to be a duffel bag or a wheeled suitcase.'

'The mother accompanied the recent renter down to the vault?' I asked, suspecting what the mayor would say next.

He did not disappoint. 'She was tired, and felt too unsteady on her feet to descend the staircase.'

'So she gave the recent renter the master key to use, along with her new box key,' I said.

'The new renter asked for both, though neither was necessary,' he said. 'She only needed access to the vault to use the part-time teller's keys—'

'Each stamped with a box number,' I interrupted.

'And the master key she'd duplicated.'

'How much do you estimate was stolen?' I asked.

Mister Mayor offered me a faint smile. 'About five large lock-boxes' worth,' he said. 'The new renter had all the time in the world to fill up her duffel or suitcase because, even if the mother had descended, she would have left the renter alone in the vault, thinking no renter would have the individual keys for other boxes.'

'The depositor, by blowing a hole in your bank, proves my client's innocent of any complicity,' Randeen said, to focus on a dismissal of the bomb charge.

'Of course, but his residence would still be compromised.' The mayor's little pink tongue emerged for a quick lick at his lips, and retreated. 'In fact, it would be uninhabitable, according to any revised zoning codes we might employ.'

'Just as you threatened, when we talked on the phone,' Randeen said. 'We require ten grand for Mr Elstrom's cooperation in helping you to find your money, and a certificate exempting his turret from any and all of the cumbersome zoning restrictions, existing or new.'

'Twenty grand,' I said, 'exemption from all codes, and the City of Rivertown assumes all liability for the payment of my property taxes. Whatever my property owes to the county is to be borne by the City of Rivertown.'

Randeen looked at me, shocked.

'I'm worth it,' I said, keeping my eyes on the mayor. 'I'll point you toward who has your money.'

'We already know who has it: the confessed killer received it from his accomplice, the recent renter,' the mayor said.

'Then why need me?' I said, but it was rhetorical, and wrong.

'I do not feel that my current personnel are best equipped to recover it. We believe you are, Mr Elstrom. Given sufficient motivation, you will recover our money. We will pay you ten thousand dollars once it is returned to us. Plus, you'll be allowed to continue to live in your residence.'

'I want a certificate, drawn up by Mr Randeen, for you to sign to the effect that my property will never be condemned or rezoned, forcing me to leave.'

'Not possible—'

I cut him off. 'That's my condition, plus twenty thousand, not ten.'

'You're hardly in any position to negotiate, Mr Elstrom.'

'Indeed he is, Mister Mayor,' Randeen said. 'The confessed murderer has disappeared. Elstrom here has a record of solving the unsolvable. If you persist in threatening him, I'll tie you up in court, and expose things, through private sources with excellent media contacts, that you do not want exposed. You will suffer a public spectacle, reported far beyond your city limits. Twenty thousand and perpetual happy times for Elstrom's turret.'

The mayor yawned, unimpressed with Randeen's threat, and reached into his center drawer to pull out a thin stack of currency. 'Two thousand dollars for expenses.'

Randeen swore. He was unused to defeat, but we had no trump cards. The mayor could have me thrown out of the turret on the flimsiest of pretenses.

'I need your police and your banker to be cooperative,' I said.

'I will make calls immediately.'

We stood up, the mayor buzzed his door, and we went into the anteroom and out into the hall.

Outside, Randeen said, 'I'm going home to shower and change clothes, and then conduct the rest of my day in a more rational universe.'

As we watched him drive away, in a black Mercedes identical

to the Bohemian's, I envied his ability to do that, to just drive away.

The Bohemian spoke beside me. 'We've not done well, Vlodek.'

'Did you have a choice?'

'Your mayor is desperate. It must be a lot of money.'

'Let's walk across to the turret, make coffee—'

'Not like last night's, one hopes?' he said, smiling to ease the tension.

'Same grounds, new water,' I said.

He laughed and shook his head. 'I already have a bad taste in my mouth.'

THIRTY-TWO

Amanda's ancient Toyota was parked back at the turret, and another vehicle was parked directly behind hers. It was even older and rustier. A dark blue Ford Explorer with dark-tinted windows, it was the sort that used to be favored by suburbanites to drive while illegally texting, before even bigger and more lethal vehicles came along.

She sat on the bench by the Willahock. A cup of capped coffee sat on the bench beside her. Beside the coffee was a very tall Black man dressed in a gray T-shirt, khaki pants, and white basketball shoes the size of small window planters. I guessed his age at thirty. They both stood when I walked up.

'All set?' she asked, handing me the coffee.

'I'm screwed,' I said, offering up the best smile I could manage.

'I'm Frosty,' the young Black man said, holding out his hand. He was close to seven feet tall.

I wanted to find humor in the name of the protector of Amanda's fledgling assembly shop because I wanted to find humor in anything at that moment. There was nothing funny about the meeting I'd just had with Mister Mayor and there looked to be nothing funny about the man standing on the bank of the Willahock. Despite the warmth of the day, he wasn't sweating.

Nor was he blinking much. His gaze was unsettlingly direct. I wondered if some of his confidence came from the slight bulge beneath the hem of his oversized T-shirt, untucked and hanging loose and low enough to accommodate a small handgun.

I shook his hand.

'Frosty has become an invaluable ally,' Amanda said. 'He, and his organization, are intent on taking back some of the rougher streets in the city.'

'With what?' I asked him, thinking the piece at his hip played into his modus.

'Support for food distribution, for one thing,' Frosty said. 'Big chain supermarkets don't like excessive risk, and so we have food deserts where, if food is sold at all, it is sold by little pop-ups for outrageous prices. Folks have to travel too long by bus to get basic things, so we encourage economic development by offering safety. We want shoppers to feel safe, and store developers and shopkeepers to feel safe to commit to a neighborhood.'

I resisted the urge to look at Amanda. The man did not talk like a reformed cocaine dealer.

'College?' I asked him.

'Dartmouth, major in economics,' he said, smiling. 'Full ride scholarship. And yes, I played basketball.'

'After the Ivy League, you returned to . . . ah . . .?'

'Opportunities are dictated by environments,' he said. 'I returned to my neighborhood, assessed the job opportunities, saw that they were limited, and began selling drugs. It was nasty work and people die from such endeavors, but it was necessary, for income and to integrate myself into the communities I most wanted to influence.'

'Other drug dealers?' I said.

'I was small enough and they left me alone,' he said. 'When I could, I moved on, to help better our economic activities. Whatever impedes those objectives is of interest to me,' he said.

'Like bricks tossed through a window,' I said.

Frosty looked at Amanda.

'Frosty is here as a favor to me,' Amanda said quickly. 'As to that window incident, let's just say it's resolved. In fact, one of my fellow utility directors committed a million dollars to set up a storefront library not two blocks from our little assembly operation.'

'That wouldn't be the same director that experienced an incident that alarmed his neighbors . . .?' I asked.

I thought she started to shoot a quick glance at Frosty, but in the next fraction of an instant she must have reconsidered. 'What incident?' she asked, keeping her eyes steady on mine, daring me to push.

I pushed. 'Odd thing. I googled. According to the amateurish online news that reports on the North Shore, it seems one of your directors received a couple of hundred bricks dumped right outside his iron gates, after dark, blocking anyone from driving in or driving out.'

'Oh, my,' she said.

'Yes, and some of those bricks were actually tossed in over the gates, to underscore any message the pile was meant to convey. That must have caused quite a dusting of reddish brick dust on the perpetrator's clothing,' I said, and stopped before making any mention of the red dust I'd seen on Amanda's clothes the night I surprised her at her condo.

'The perpetrator must have had to wash his clothing?' she said.

'Or hers,' I said.

'Oh, my,' she said. 'Think of the laundry detergent expense. Twenty-five or fifty cents?'

'Here's the odd thing,' I said. 'Your fellow director didn't report the incident to the Lake Forest police. One of his neighbors called it in. Yet when they arrived, your director said that he ordered the bricks and there was nothing amiss going on.'

'Oh my,' she said, for the third time.

'Crazy, right? A nighttime delivery of bricks blocking the man's driveway, and yet he assured the police it was expected?' I smiled at the woman whose fierceness has enchanted me for years. 'I don't need to ask if your library donor is the same guy who received the bricks because I could find that out on my own.'

She smiled extra-sweetly which conveyed no sweetness at all, and said, 'I asked Frosty to stop by because I think you're in dangerous waters and, knowing you, you're probably going to swim out even deeper. Frosty might help with certain things.'

'Safety,' I said.

'Within reason,' he said.

'Thank you,' I said to them both, then said to Amanda, 'Besides inviting,' I paused, unsure, 'Mister Frosty here—'

'No "Mister,"' he said. 'Just Frosty.'

'Besides inviting Frosty here, your confidence in the Bohemian and Randeen was well placed. They worked quickly, and as effectively as they could.'

'But . . .?'

I outlined the terms of my new employment.

She reached to clasp my hand. 'What if Martin Tripp is dead and there's no knowing who has the money?'

I didn't have time to answer the unanswerable because just then a narrow-faced girl in her early teens walked up to us. Flashing a cardboard identification card that looked like it had been created in less than a minute, she announced she was a building inspector.

'This identification card looks like it was created in less than a minute,' I said, appropriately.

She blushed. 'Oh no,' she said. 'It took me almost five minutes just to get help.'

Amanda and Frosty exchanged glances but said nothing.

'Your name is Derbil?' I asked, because that's what the card said.

'Samantha Derbil,' she said. 'People call me Samantha Derbil.'

'That's your name?' I asked, unsure I'd heard her response correctly.

'Yes. My name is Samantha Derbil. People call me—'

'Got it. And you're a building inspector?'

'Yes.'

'For how long?'

'Today,' she said. 'They pulled me from raking mulch.'

'Related to Elvis Derbil?' I asked. By name and intellect, she appeared to be related to Elvis Derbil, my former zoning nemesis.

'My uncle,' she said. 'People call him Elvis—'

'Got it,' I said. 'And the two Derbils who are inspecting cats?'

'Yes, they are—'

'Got it,' I said, because I didn't, and didn't care. 'How may I help you?'

'Your building inspection.'

'What does that mean, exactly?'

'Huh?' she said.

'What for?'

'To see if you're OK.'

'OK?' I asked.

She wrinkled her forehead, and she scratched her head, as if trying to scratch the right words into it. 'Yeah, if you're OK,' she said, when she was done scratching.

'How are you going to do that?'

She handed me a sheet.

It was the report of a building inspection. It was dated that day, and it was already filled out.

It listed a number of violations, including improper installation of a new roof, which I'd done several years before to replace the leaker that greeted me when I first moved in; improper venting of a furnace, which was the last major improvement I'd made, to thwart freezing to death; unauthentic window glazing, which was preposterous because glass was almost totally unavailable in medieval times; unauthentic caulking compound used to seal around the slit windows, same reason; use of improper hinges on the front door because they appeared to be machine made, even though they'd been in use for over ninety years, and so on. They were trumped up, preposterous charges, written down in official-ese; an underscoring of what Mister Mayor could employ to evict me, should I not recover his money.

'Did this take five minutes, too?' I asked.

'Yes, but by another person. My sister Louise Derbil. People call her—'

'Louise Derbil?' I asked.

'Why, yes,' she said.

I thanked her because it was useless to reason with Derbils. Words thrown at them simply bounced away, like pebbles off steel.

'What just happened?' Frosty asked, watching her walk away.

'I'll explain later,' Amanda said. She knew all about Elvis and his kindred Derbils and the battles I'd fought with them over the years.

She turned to me. 'Where are you going to start?'

'Across town, at the bank,' I said.

'You mean the laundry,' Amanda said.

'I love this town,' Frosty said.

THIRTY-THREE

The bank president sat hunched over his desk in the dank gloom of the First Bank of Rivertown, but not as far over as on my last visit. The proper forms had been submitted. The dimmed bulb – the one above, at least – had been replaced.

Across the black and green tiles, his mother, an ancient not nearly as spry as Ma Brumsky and her band of libidinous friends, rested her head on the white marble teller counter, braced for another day.

The bank president looked up, no doubt startled by the shape darkening his crossword puzzle.

'Mister Mayor called you?' I asked.

'Yes.'

'I understand the barn door has been closed, now that the horses have escaped,' I said.

'What?' Fear was in his eyes, and fatigue. He must have been up all night, explaining why he neglected to report Tripp's attempt to rent a lockbox, and the woman who came to rent a box afterward.

'The lockbox vault is safely sealed up, even though the money is gone?'

'Oh. Yes.'

The sound of hammering came from workmen outside, repairing the back wall. I thought it a wonder the man's mother could sleep at the teller counter, but I supposed sound sleep was a benefit of a liquid breakfast.

'I'd like to see the boxes rented out by Sara Jansen.'

He stiffened. 'There are five,' he said.

'Mister Mayor said there was another rental, very recent, by someone you didn't know?'

'Mother did it,' he said, throwing the old lass under the bus.

'I understand it was lunchtime,' I said.

'Taco Tuesday.'

'Just a quick look at the five boxes will do,' I said, 'to get an idea of volume. And the key to any box that size.'

'I don't know . . .' He remained seated, inert.

'Call Mister Mayor,' I said. 'Displease him further, if you dare.'

He stood up and I followed him to the teller counter where his mother was dozing. Very carefully, he slid open a drawer beside her, extracted a dull old brass key on a red, Woody Woodpecker fob, took another from a blue plastic bowl, and slid the drawer closed. As he did, I caught a strong whiff of gin, coming either from her mouth or the uncapped extra-tall Thermos next to her. She'd been low hanging fruit for the recent renter, indeed.

I followed him down the stairs, stepping beside two workmen plastering the staircase wall. He dialed in the combination on the steel door, spun the massive wheel, and opened the door. We went in.

He looked at the number stamped on the individual box key, bent down, and inserted it into one of the two locks on a large box on the bottom row. He then inserted the master key into the other lock, and pulled the inner box out.

'Do you want to see inside?'

'You already did, this morning, with all the boxes?' I said, because that's what the mayor had said. Problem was, none of the locks looked shiny, as if they'd been replaced after drilling the old ones out.

'Oh yes, first thing this—' He stopped abruptly, sensing the danger in confirming that the crooks that ran Rivertown kept duplicate keys for all the lockboxes, unbeknownst to the box renters. For sure, if Sara Jansen had known that, she would never have thought to leave most of the skim inside the lockbox vault.

He slid the inner box back in, locked the door, and withdrew both keys, and stood up.

'Let's see the rental record for the one the woman rented,' I said, and we went upstairs.

He had to reach around his dozing mother to get the ledger and carried it to his desk. He opened it to the most recent page and pointed to what looked like an ink blot at the bottom of the page.

'That's an ink blot,' I said.

'Mother said the woman used a fountain pen.'

The woman knew how to make it leak, but there was no point in telling him that. I took out my phone and brought up the picture of Tripp with Julianna, the day he was set free. 'Is this her?' I asked, though the mayor had already said the woman was disguised with a babushka and a scarf.

'I don't know! I was gone to get lunch.'

I pointed to the gray head on the teller counter, softly snoring. 'Can you ask her?'

'She's sleep—'

I cut him off. 'Mister Mayor did call you, right?'

He took my phone and went to his mother. She stirred after he bent down to whisper, then held my phone sideways so she could see the screen with the eye highest above the counter. She murmured something I couldn't hear, and he came back to his desk.

'The woman had big curls under a babushka, and a scarf to protect her mouth,' he said, defensively.

Again I thought of the woman I'd seen with two big curls, backlit the night of the chaos at Kutz's clearing, the woman Leo had followed, and the girl I'd known in high school. I pushed the thought away. Murder victims don't come back to life.

I moved on. 'Is your mother subject to blackouts?'

'She gets tired,' he said.

I thought about suggesting he float a cornflake in her breakfast for stamina but decided that would be petty, even from someone whose feet were being held to the fire, so I said instead, 'The renter hadn't been in previously?'

'Mother told Mister Mayor she didn't think so.'

I would have bet the woman had come in at least once before, after the president left to pick up a lunch. She would have only needed an instant to see the old woman so deep in her cups by noon that she wouldn't want to wobble down the stairs to the vaults. And so the plan was hatched. The recent renter would come back at another lunch hour, and offer to spare the old woman the wobble by offering to take the master down herself

– a master she wouldn't need anyway, since she'd brought the one Sara had duplicated already.

But I let all that go and left.

The mayor called before I could start the Jeep. The bank president had wasted no time in reporting back to him.

'It's so pathetically obvious, isn't it?' the mayor said.

'I'm sure, now,' I said. 'Your part-time teller left most of what she stole right under your noses, initially to avoid any chance of getting caught with it. Later, I'm guessing she caught the confessed killer ransacking her house looking for it, and decided to still leave it in the bank where he couldn't get at it. After he killed her, he found the keys – or maybe she caught him when he discovered the keys, and that's why he killed her, though we'll never know what did happen that night. Once he was acquitted, he returned to Rivertown with a plan, but got rebuffed trying to rent a box, and used the recent renter to empty the boxes.'

'And now I'll pay you ten grand to recover it.'

'Twenty,' I said, 'but I'll need that certificate of perpetual occupancy before I do anything.'

'I'll have you thrown out by evening,' he said.

'And you'll have no money. Fax the certificate to Randeen, my lawyer.'

I clicked him away, then, having done something smart.

Or really dumb.

THIRTY-FOUR

The only next step was to find out who was dead, and that required candor, and risk, and Verona, again.

Randeen called forty minutes after I left Rivertown, while I was bouncing north over the potholes on the Illinois toll road. 'What did you do that I couldn't?' he said.

'Nothing,' I said. 'No occupancy certificate will be solid unless I deliver.'

'Well, your mayor faxed one and it looks somewhat good. No

mention of your demand for them paying your property taxes, though.'

'If I deliver, there'll be room for negotiation,' I said, which caused my hands, already trembling on the steering wheel from the vibration coming from the Jeep's misaligned wheels, to shake even more. If I didn't deliver, the vindictive lizard mayor would make sure I was out on the street.

I got to Verona at one in the afternoon. Late August evenings are long; I'd have plenty of daylight for a talk, a walk, and a drive back to Chicago.

The sheriff's office was in a white-frame building. The sheriff himself was in a white office at the rear of the white-frame building. Unlike behavior I'd ever encountered in Illinois, when I called ahead, the desk sergeant told me the sheriff would see me when I arrived, though it must have helped that I said I was driving up to show him a corpse.

The sheriff sat tall behind a yellow metal desk. His name was Redd and his uniform shirt was blue and sharply creased with starch. He was about fifty, and the wrinkling around his eyes showed he'd seen every bad thing the world had to offer, twice.

I recognized the music playing softly on his credenza boombox as Bach, *Violin Concerto in E*. I knew it only because Amanda insists I accompany her to Symphony Center in Chicago. Among the many things that enchant me about her is her hope that I'll become a classy fellow.

The sheriff motioned for me to sit on one of the green vinyl chairs. The entire spectrum of color abounded in that office.

'I enjoy Bach, *Violin Concerto in E*, as well,' I said, hoping he would recognize me as a fellow classy guy. I handed one of my cards across the desk.

'An insurance investigation turned up a body in these parts?' he asked, smiling only with his mouth.

'I'm not here regarding insurance,' I said. 'I'm here to ask you to identify a bone in the woods.'

His smile grew broader but his eyes remained wary. 'A bone; one bone?'

'Many bones will likely require your expertise,' I said.

'That certainly sounds wonderful,' he said, this time smiling with his eyes, too. 'Coffee?'

I nodded as best I could because I had a caffeine-withdrawal headache. I'd only had the one cup Amanda gave me that morning. I'd picked up a second after I'd finished talking on the phone to the mayor, but I'd spilled most of it onto the floor of the Jeep when I hit a pothole breezing on the underfunded, under-repaired tollway south of the state line. In Illinois, road-repair money gets diverted to plump the already fat pensions of the state's politicians, their cousins and, some suspect, their pets.

The sheriff got up. My initial guess was right. He was tall, at least six feet five inches. He poured a cup from a Mr Coffee that, unlike mine, looked like it had been acquired new. He handed me the coffee and sat back down at his desk.

I told him my story. I told it all and I told it straight. When I was done, he swiveled around to summon up a search screen on the laptop on the credenza behind him.

He tapped keys for a couple of minutes, then asked, 'Evangeline Wilts?'

'A crooked mayor in a suburb almost as crooked as my own town. I was handed documents I didn't recognize as doctored and had no business authenticating anyway. I was acquitted on the charge of falsifying evidence but you'll have to hunt hard for those reports.'

'Help yourself to more coffee,' he said, swiveling back to his laptop. 'Looks like this might take a while.'

'Do you have doughnuts?' I asked. I hadn't eaten since a bite of breakfast lasagna.

'Do you believe that because I'm a cop, I'll have doughnuts?'

'I'm OK with stale.'

He said no, and so I sat more, sipped more, and enjoyed my headache fading as he searched for more on me.

'Amanda Phelps? You married the daughter of one of the richest men in Chicago?' he asked, after another few minutes.

'Yes,' I said, 'but she was wise enough to divorce me. We remain in love and together, but we live apart.'

He switched off his laptop and turned back around. 'You're an odd duck, Elstrom. Any character references to prove you're not a liar?'

I gave him James Randeen's cell phone number. He dialed it on his desk phone, introduced himself, and told him that I'd come requesting something preposterous. Then he listened, and listened some more, then hung up and said, 'You seem to be a real handful.'

'More and more with each passing year,' I agreed.

He'd suggested that I drive so we wouldn't attract undue attention by going in a police car, but he immediately expressed reservations as I pulled away. 'Do you have issues?'

'No more than some other people.'

'What's that puddle on the floor?' he asked, of the moisture between us.

'Only coffee.'

He moved his feet to rest high on the slant of the footwell, safe from any coffee waves that might rise up when I turned, and I explained about the unfixed potholes and fixed political pensions in Illinois. He nodded. He knew about the crooks who run Illinois, and why so many Illinoisans moved to Wisconsin, where the politicians share their stolen cheese curds, highway slaughtered deer meat, and other takings more equitably.

After we'd bounced along for a mile or so of rural blacktop, he asked if I'd ever considered shock absorbers.

'I have meager funds,' I said.

'You're an odd duck, Elstrom.'

I found the intersection where Amanda and I had stopped for gas, and from there I drove to Julianna Wynton's cottage.

'You say the cottage shows signs of a struggle?' he asked as we got out.

'Yes. It's what tipped us – I mean me – to have a walk in the woods.'

'Who was with you, Elstrom?'

'A friend.'

'We're neighborly up here. I'll find someone who saw who you were with.'

'I'll tell you later,' I said, knowing I wouldn't but that he could find out for himself if he put resources to it.

He tried the front door and the knob turned easily. Just like before, there was no need to reach in through the broken glass.

'Kids break in,' he said, 'when the vacationers are gone.'

The room had been righted. No furniture was tipped over, no dishes were in the sink.

'A struggle? You're sure?' he asked.

I lifted the edge of the braided rug and pointed to the stain on the floor and then to the underside of the rug. No amount of cleaning would have eradicated the bloodstain Amanda had found.

'Could be old,' he said, 'maybe from dragging in a deer for meat.'

'They do that here: carve up animals in living rooms?'

'When there are no doughnuts,' he said.

He went to check the two bedrooms, and I went to lift the other end of the rug. There were no bloodstains beneath it, just the four seams of a trapdoor that likely led to nothing except the dirt beneath the cottage.

There was a slight indentation to lift it, but before I could, Sheriff Redd stepped out of the last bedroom. 'No signs of struggle, and we're trespassing in someone's private property,' he said, with some irritation. 'Let's get out of here, see your corpse.'

He bent down to attach short elastic cords to the cuffs of his pants. I didn't ask what they were, for fear of showing more ignorance than I'd already exhibited.

I led him to the spot between the two trees where I'd discovered the protruding bone.

The leaves I'd mounded were swept or kicked away, and the depression between the two trees was deeper, but not a whole body's depth deeper.

The sheriff kicked at the few leaves that remained. 'This is the place?'

'Yes, but the body is—'

'Wait; don't tell me. The body is gone?'

'Yes, or at least what there was of it. Are those fresh shovel marks?'

'Could be something's been dug up,' he said. 'You're not blowing smoke at me, are you? I mean, like that business back in my office about Bach's *Violin Concerto in E?*'

I could only shake my head. I had no idea where he was going.

'It was Bach's *Concerto in G Minor,*' he said.

'Ah,' I said, without confessing that all concertos, unless played on a tuba, sound the same to me.

'That bone, you're surer about that? You're sure it was human?'

'Who would bury a large animal?' I pointed to the ground. 'The depression is not deep enough for that. I backed away at the first sight of the one bone. Something human-sized could have been removed. Of course, it could have been in the ground for some years.'

He arched his eyebrows. 'And why is that?'

'The bone was white.'

'Picked clean, you mean?'

'Exactly,' I said. 'By creatures in the woods, big and small.'

'Because they have no doughnuts to eat?'

'Exactly,' I said, accepting his derision.

'Bach's *Violin Concerto in E*,' he said, which made no sense.

I almost corrected him to G Minor, but realized he was probably making a larger point which I did not understand. Instead, I said, 'The body was likely re-buried nearby.'

'Too big to move far?'

'Yes,' I said.

'We can tramp around a little, since we're here,' he said. 'The woods are cool, the days are long in my office, and we so rarely encounter people such as you. But we'll search only for a little while, Elstrom. There might be other nut-jobs waiting for me back at the office.'

We walked through the trees for a few minutes, neither of us saying anything, or finding anything.

'You don't think someone tied it to his car roof so it could collect a political pension in Illinois?' he asked.

There was nothing to say to that, and so we walked more, in silence, in ever-expanding circles, until finally, we got to the water's edge.

'This is where the little ticks must frolic,' I said.

He pointed to the elastic bands securing the cuffs of his pants tight to his legs above his boots, his eyes positively alight with mirth. 'Let's go,' he said. 'I've seen enough of not seeing anything.'

Again we walked in silence, back to the Jeep, and that silence accompanied us all the way back to the sheriff's office. But instead of getting out, perhaps slamming the Jeep's thin door to underscore getting rid of me, he turned to me.

'Even though we found nothing, I'm going to assume you mean well,' he said. 'But there's nothing more to be done about this, Elstrom.'

I allowed as to how he was right, and then I asked, 'What was that business, back in the woods, about reminding me I was wrong about that violin concerto?'

'You were blowing off again, about something you don't know.'

'About the correct concerto?'

'About a bone having to be in the ground a long time to be picked white. It can happen quickly, depending on what's around that's hungry.'

'So that bone could have been in the ground for a short time?'

'Exactly,' he said, getting out.

I bent behind the steering wheel to scratch my leg.

'Cigarettes,' he said. 'You'll need cigarettes.'

It was a strange thing for him to say.

'I don't smoke,' I said.

He laughed and closed my door.

THIRTY-FIVE

The drive back to Rivertown was long and difficult. I'd struck out in Verona – no corpse meant no further sheriff's interest – and I hoped the road miles home would point to what to do next. But the concentration I needed went out the window within minutes of leaving the sheriff. I began to itch.

At first, I simply scratched, but that did no good, so I pulled over and dug something almost unseeable from my ankle. Having just been in the land of little ticks, and being something of a sleuth, I deduced it was a little tick. I tossed it out the window and resumed driving.

Not for long. The ejected tick had brought along family, all of whom were intent on itching me into insanity. I had to keep pulling to the side of the road to dig them out of my skin. It didn't always work. Some had dug in too deep to be easily evicted and after a few unproductive stops, I remembered Sheriff Redd's parting admonition about cigarettes. Obviously, he was a veteran tick man, not just another curd. I stopped and bought a pack of smokes and a lighter and experimented. Embers brought exodus. The ticks emerged. By the time I got back to the turret it was dusk and I had littered a hundred highway miles with dozens of former denizens of Little Tick Lake.

Leo's silver Porsche Carrera was parked at the curb, but it was big-curled Sara Jansen who sat slumped on the bench by the Willahock River, watching the water ripple in the last rays of sunlight. My throat went dry and my knees felt like they were someone else's as I walked up from behind.

It wasn't Sara. It was Leo, dressed in his usual tropical mismatch of colors, topped now with a high-eared Mickey Mouse hat on his head.

'Leo!'

He barely summoned the energy to turn around. 'Sit with me, you idiot,' he said softly.

I sat.

'I spent the whole day picking up litter,' he said. 'And I was not alone. All Ma's friends showed up to help. They were delighted with themselves, chattering and laughing the whole time. They'd had the time of their lives.'

I started to scratch my ankle, then remembered to light a cigarette from the now half-empty second pack I bought at the state line.

'Smoking?' he asked, shocked.

'Ticks,' I said.

'You mean like crabs?'

'No. Ticks,' I said.

'You're infested?' He jumped up and stepped back.

'Somewhat, yes,' I said.

'I want no passengers,' he said from five feet away.

'Behold the technique: tip to the skin, critter emerges.' I held the glowing end of the cigarette close to the spot and the souvenir emerged, orange in the glow of the ember. I grabbed it and sent it airborne.

He jumped back another foot, fearing the astronaut would land on him.

'So, Mrs Roshiska?' I said, remembering James Randeen's almost convulsive laughter as he described Ma Brumsky's most libidinous friend.

He shook his Mickey-topped head in resignation and came back to sit down, though at the precarious, very edge of the bench. 'I've got to admire her, shaking and bopping like she was seventeen. And today, when she came to help pick up, pushing her walker, she was smiling like she won the lotto even though she wrecked her sciatica, jiving in that tree. You should have been there.'

'I was,' I said, aiming the still-lit cigarette. A tip of the tip and the Wisconsinite emerged, which I then launched to join its friend.

'No, I meant you should have been there instead of running away,' he said, continuing the thought he'd been making before he got distracted by my skin zoo. 'Mrs Roshiska got caught up in those fireworks from the bank, and the ones from our ridiculous cannon, and then there was the disco ball, the music, the accordions – Jeez, the accordions! – and the whole ruckus and she . . . and she . . .' He bent over and put his head in his hands, which was quite a feat, considering that he was leveraged so far out from the end of the bench that he risked falling.

'She what, Leo?'

He murmured something between his palms.

'I can't hear you! What did Mrs Roshiska do?' Perhaps I was being unappreciative of his distress, but I loved Mrs Roshiska's fervor in attacking life.

His head shook as he murmured more into his hands.

'Raise your head!'

He raised his head and with that, his ballast, slight though it was, shifted. He fell off the edge of the bench. Flat on his back, swearing under his breath, he scratched at the dirt, rolled over, and clawed at the bench to pull himself up to stand. And then he did a ridiculous little dance designed, I supposed, to shake off any tiny travelers that I'd not flicked far enough.

Beneath the ridiculous Mickey Mouse ears, which I guessed he was no longer aware of, his normally pale face was flushed a deep red, visible even in the dusk. 'She twirled!' he screamed, dropping hard to sit on the bench, as if he'd lost all strength in his legs.

'She twirled around, in that tight construction basket?' It seemed an impossible thing for a woman reliant on a walker, hoisted and confined in a steel cage.

'Her top! She twirled her top!' He buried his head into his hands again.

Mrs Roshiska, the least restrained of Ma's enthusiastic friends, had unrestrained herself even further. She'd taken off her top and twirled it high above the crowd.

I started laughing, hard. 'In New Orleans, they toss beads for that,' I managed.

He saw no mirth. 'I'll never get the sight of that – of them – out of my head, going north, going south, going . . .' He shuddered. 'Neither will anyone else.'

'What did everyone do?'

'They cheered! Can you believe it? They cheered! They were all drunk, of course. The clearing erupted! People started dancing! The accordion players formed a conga line, each of them playing something different, and started weaving through the drunks. Everybody was going every which way, like . . . like . . .' He paused, stuck for the right word.

'Like Mrs Roshiska!' I said. But then a horrible thought me. 'She didn't . . . she couldn't . . . remove . . .'

'Her skirt? Mercifully, the construction basket was too confining for that, what with her walker in there.' He sighed and turned to me. 'You took off so fast. That gas explosion at the bank.'

'That's what the word is?'

'Break in a buried gas pipe, city hall is saying. Heaved up and blew a hole in the back, but no damage to anything inside. By evening, all will be right as rain.'

'Let me tell you about that rain,' I said. And did, going back to my first arrest, at the back of the bank.

'Whoa!' he said. 'You've really been thinking the Frenchman killed Sara, and now he's a bomber, and you were arrested for it?'

'Arrested twice, as I said, but the second time was for leverage.'

'That sent you to Wisconsin?' He reached to scratch the top of his head and became aware of his ridiculous adornment. He snatched off the Mickey hat. Holding it in his hands, he scratched carefully, felt nothing that smacked of Wisconsin, and went on. 'I think this was what you thought were Sara Jansen's curls. I found it when I was picking up.'

'Could that be what you saw, under the scarf, at the Holiday Inn?'

'And later, grocery shopping?' He nodded. 'Sure.'

'It was deliberate. That motel room was rented in Sara Jansen's name.'

'Tripp?' he asked.

I dug at a spot on my shin, but it was from habit. Its tenant had been evicted minutes before.

'He needed a woman accomplice,' I said. 'Either it was Sara, which I don't believe, or it was Julianna Wynton.'

I looked at the Mickey Mouse hat now resting on his lap, and smiled.

He followed my gaze and looked down. 'Maybe we both wanted to see Sara Jansen alive. And really, what adult would wear such a thing?' he asked.

I said nothing. He is my friend.

He put the hat on his head. 'It works with my casual clothes,' he said, gesturing at his purple rayon shirt festooned with orange coconuts and bronze iguanas. 'Kowalski left Ma four thousand cash in an envelope, detailing what he wanted done, and said he'd already called the contractors. All she had to do was pay when the work was done.' He shook his head. 'Big gamble for someone who never took any money from the lizards in the first place.'

'He must have skimmed something,' I said, 'because he didn't come up with that kind of cash wrangling carts at Walmart.'

'He surely spent a fortune.'

'He was expecting a fortune from the free beer, the distracting cats, the madness – a grand finale to divert everyone's attention away, while he blew the bank open.'

'You really think he killed Sara?'

'I don't know what to think,' I said, 'but I've got something I want you to check out.'

'Yes . . .?'

'Remember Archie Midlan?'

'He was at the clearing, sucking up the free beer, having the time of his life.'

'That metallic-blue Malibu?'

'Yes . . .'

'See if that's one of his,' I said.

'Another of Tripp's?'

'Threaten Archie with cops, if you have to,' I said.

'I already looked for a dot on its bumper, remember?'

'Maybe someone pulled it off,' I said.

'You're grasping at straws?'

'I am.'

'You better come up with something,' he said. 'Otherwise, you're moving into my basement.'

After I didn't answer, he said, 'Dek?'

'I'm having another inspiration,' I said.

THIRTY-SIX

Figuring that Frosty was more of a nocturnal operator, I called Greg Theodore at the *Tribune* first, the next morning.

'Be straight and totally forthcoming, Elstrom; straight and totally forthcoming.'

'I don't know that I can be, yet,' I said. 'Here's what I do know, off the record.'

'No. For publication, if I find it interesting.'

'It's not as interesting as it will become, and some of it you can never use, if I'm right.'

'Off the record for a little while, and then maybe never?' He laughed, and told me to go on.

I started with the bank explosion, and he interrupted immediately. 'Someone blew a hole in the back of your bank, and word hasn't gotten out?'

'In terms of transparency, Rivertown is like China, but I need you to report the bombing, and right away,' I said, and went on.

Again he interrupted. 'Someone skimmed money from that same bank, early last year, and that escaped notice?'

'Think Beijing.'

'I can report that, too?'

'Yes,' I said.

'How does this figure in with Martin Tripp?'

'Sara Jansen might have been killed to get keys—'

'Hold up, Elstrom, you are going to tell me what I can use right away?'

'Yes, but not the theory about her being killed for keys. I'm also going to tell you how I want to use you.'

He was a good reporter, inquisitive enough to continue listening. I spoke for almost twenty minutes and he did not interrupt once. He was so silent that I had to pause, several times, to make sure he was still on the line.

And when I was done, I asked the question.

'You want what?' he asked.

I repeated what I needed from him.

'Do you know how many people are taking buyouts around here?' he asked. 'This paper is shrinking, like all newspapers. What you're asking could shrink me right out the door.'

'This kind of story garners new readers,' I said.

'One can only wish,' he said. 'Can I call your Sheriff Redd to verify at least some of this?'

'No. I want the benefit of surprise. Besides, he'll deny, maybe even say I am crazy. All he knows is that I showed up there yesterday saying I could point him to a body. I could not. The body was gone.'

'So, as far as Redd thinks, you're nuts, a goof with a fantastical story.'

'Could be. That's why I need your help, to prove that the story is real.'

'How do I know you're not a goof with a fantastical story?'

'Maybe I am. If you'll help, and we can prove what I'm saying to be true, then you'll have one heck of a follow-up to the Tripp outrage.'

'One that I won't be able to print, because of an agreement with your lizards?'

'Only some of it.'

'I have to talk to my editor, because he's worried about his job, too,' he said, and clicked me away.

I called Frosty next, but all I got was his voice mail. Or at least, I thought all I got was his voice mail. There was no name attached to it, just a woman's voice saying to leave a message if I wanted. I did, and so I did.

Frosty called back five minutes later. 'Just to keep watch, that's all you need?'

'To see who comes knocking,' I said.

'Your message said it would be one of two guys?'

'Tripp or Kowalski, and I'm not sure why either would want to come,' I said.

'Hold on,' he said, and I heard him tapping keys. 'There's only one picture of a Walter Kowalski on the internet, and it's old. Tripp's pictures are everywhere, though. Neither looks tough.'

'One of them is tough enough to stab a woman. And don't overlook that there's big money involved as a motivator.'

'How much?'

'No idea, but enough to kill for.'

He chuckled. 'When do you want us to start?'

'Maybe tonight, maybe tomorrow. I'll let you know.'

He clicked me away and a second later, my phone chirped with an incoming call.

'This is in desperation for a good story, Elstrom,' Greg Theodore said.

'You'll do it?'

'I did it, exactly as you laid it out. It'll be online in thirty minutes, and in print for the evening edition, but there's no guarantee that your person, or persons, will read it or see it.'

'If they're nervous enough, they will.'

'TV, too,' he said.

'TV?'

'My editor knows an editor. Slow news day, and there's word we're about to be acquired by a hedge fund that specializes in gutting newspapers. My editor is hoping to land a gig with the TV station.'

'When's the TV?'

'News at noon, repeated starting at four o'clock this afternoon. Going to get a move on?'

'Yes.'

'Back north?'

'Yes.'

'The sheriff's name, again?' he asked.

'Redd,' I said.

'And he doesn't know about any of this?'

'I told you he probably thinks I'm crazy,' I said.

'He might not be alone,' he said, and hung up.

I called Leo next. 'Any luck with Archie?'

'The Malibu came from his lot,' he said. 'A woman bought it for a grand.'

'A woman wearing a head scarf and a mask to protect from germs?'

'Big curls under the scarf,' he said.

'Stay away from the turret.'

'That inspiration you had?'

'Exactly. I'm having it watched tonight by friends of Amanda's.'

'Things could get uncomfortable?'

'One can only hope,' I said.

I called Frosty, said the deal was on for the evening. He wished me a happy trip.

I packed appropriate Wisconsin eveningwear, which consisted of a black nylon jacket that I thought was tick-proof, a black wool knit hat that I thought was unlikely to be tick-proof but might make me look dangerous, and a couple dozen extra-large rubber bands because I didn't have the more efficient braided cords that Redd had used for the woods.

Before going out to the Jeep, I checked my laptop. Greg Theodore had posted on the *Tribune*'s website six minutes earlier.

WISCONSIN MURDER MYSTERY

Vlodek Elstrom, a Rivertown, Illinois, insurance investigator, reported yesterday that remains he discovered in a wooded area of Verona, Wisconsin, might be connected to three crimes: the murder of Sara Jansen of suburban Weston, Illinois, last year; the unreported theft of a substantial amount of money from an unnamed bank; and most recently, the bombing of the First Bank of Rivertown, west of Chicago. Elstrom theorized that clues still being extracted from the Verona woods might re-energize examination of all three cases. Efforts to obtain official comment are ongoing and will be reported as they become available.

And there it was. My own fuse.

Lit.

THIRTY-SEVEN

Greg Theodore phoned while I was still in Illinois.

'I've been getting calls and emails,' he said. 'Cops, readers, even the hedge fund axe-wielders who are trying to take over the paper. People want to know the story behind the story.'

'I'm getting calls, too, from numbers I don't recognize. I clicked them away.'

'Sheriff Redd called my editor, furious,' Gregory said.

'And . . .?'

'Such is my editor's mood these days, he told Redd to close his eyes and insert earplugs.'

'You were precise in your reporting,' I said. 'You laid your story on me, repeating what I was saying, not vouching for the truth of it.'

'Redd wasn't buying that. He yelled that there was no bone.'

'You never mentioned a bone,' I said. 'Just that I said there was evidence.'

'If nothing results from your plan, either in Verona or Rivertown, we'll have to do a follow-up about your history of getting fooled and fooling others. We'll have to reference the Evangeline Wilts trial.'

'Without mention of the exoneration?'

'Keep me posted,' he said, and clicked me away.

Amanda was even more furious, calling a moment later. 'Are you out of your mind?'

'I—'

'Don't be flippant,' she yelled.

'You didn't give me a chance to be flippant,' I said.

'What are you up to?'

'I've got Frosty watching the turret—'

'He told me. What's your part?'

'Watching the woods to see if someone shows to check whether reburied bones were discovered,' I said.

'Watching who shows with a gun, you mean,' she said. 'You are aware that the *Tribune* inference is that bad people are going to be identified, thanks to you, unless you are stopped? Whoever – the killer of the bones, the robber of the money, the real murderer of Sara Jansen – will know one truth: you know what's going on, and someone, or some *ones*, will come for you. Do you understand this?'

'They'll come to one of two places. Frosty is watching the turret. I'll be safely hidden, watching the woods. Soon, all will be clear.'

'What is clear is that you're putting yourself in danger. Tell your reporter friend you think Tripp faked his own abduction from that motel, and fled to Verona because it was an ideal place to hide while Julianna rented the small lockbox and used the keys Tripp gave her to open the bigger boxes. She brought the money to Tripp in Verona but then they had a falling out, and one of them killed the other, and hid the body, almost, in the woods, maybe leaving the protruding bone inadvertently, maybe leaving it as a teaser. Whoever survived is long gone, or – and here's the scary part – they're waiting in those woods for stupid you to show up so they can silence you.'

She stopped to take a breath, and said, 'Leave it all to that Sheriff Redd.'

'I will, tomorrow,' I said, because I never lie to Amanda.

I gassed up fifty miles south of Verona, for cigarettes more than fuel, should multiples of ticks anxious to see Illinois be waiting in the woods.

An hour later, I eased into a partially grown-over fire lane, cut into the trees, a half-mile from Little Tick Lake. Likely, the fire lane had its own tribe of ticks, big or little, but I'd come prepared. I rubber-banded the cuffs of my pants and jacket sleeves, tightened the collar of my jacket, and got out to lay a few fallen branches across the Jeep to cut the brightness of the red. And then I got back inside and sweated, with the windows closed against any trampolining ticks. At dusk, I set out, moist, through the woods.

There appeared to be no one about and that surprised me. Even angry, I'd expected Redd to assign a deputy to keep an eye on the woods after Theodore's piece broke, to see if anyone showed up. But the woods were dark and silent. I seemed to be alone.

My windbreaker and watch cap were hot, and I was more than a little spooked by the darkness all around me. Someone might already be in those woods, someone as invisible as a tick, someone I'd drawn there, wanting to do me no good. I stepped slowly, trying to make no sound on the thick carpet of years of dry, brittle leaves.

I estimated I was about halfway to where the bones had been when a thud, like heavy wood being dropped, came from somewhere in front of me. I stopped, held my breath, and squinted into the darkness. A large dark shape blotted a big hole in the slightly-lighter woods ahead. It was the Wynton cottage, black against the faint shimmering of the lake a hundred yards beyond. The muffled thud must have come from inside, and that sent my mind back to the trapdoor in the floor that I was about to open when Sheriff Redd hustled us out of there.

Breathing shallowly, I moved forward slowly, straining to see, straining to hear, until I got to within a few yards of the cottage.

No light showed from the back window I remembered. If someone were inside, he, or she did not want to be seen, which meant they'd wait for total darkness to move to where they'd reburied the bones, to see if they'd been discovered. I'd have to wait until then, to see where the person went. And when I got a fix on where that was, I could call Sheriff Redd to hurry to the precise spot, and he could determine whose bones were in those woods, and maybe brace the killer.

I moved up the few yards to the back of the cottage, and pressed against the peeling clapboards right beside the window. The window would show me nothing – only darkness was inside – but the glass would transmit sound.

I sweated for an hour, maybe longer, pressed against the peeling clapboards beside the window. No noises came from inside but outside, all around me, little sounds became big sounds in the darkness. Twigs snapped, leaves rustled, and creatures – I begged the night that they were small – breathed and scurried and dithered and dug. It was a foul place, those dark woods, and every minute that passed, passed slowly.

And then muffled footsteps started up inside, and an instant later, the screen door creaked open. Footsteps, louder now, reverberated across the porch and then got quieter. A gentle whooshing came from around front as the feet stirred leaves, walking away from the cottage and into the woods. I moved up along the side in a low crouch and stopped beside the front porch.

The halo of a flashlight beam, blocked at its center by the black shape of whoever was holding it, was heading toward the lake. It was impossible to tell whether the blur within the halo was tall or short, man or woman, but the blur seemed hunched to the left, as if carrying something heavy.

The flashlight halo grew smaller as it got farther away, and then it turned to the left. The length of the beam was fully exposed now, but it was still too far away to see who was holding the flashlight. The beam swung down to the ground. Several glints of water sparkled just beyond. The person was at the shore.

I moved around to the front of the cottage and looked up onto the porch. There was enough moonlight to see blackness through the torn screen door. The front door had been left open. Whoever was down by the lake was coming back to the cottage.

Through the trees, the flashlight beam was moving slowly back and forth along the ground at the shore, searching to see if whatever was reburied had been found.

The wise play was to leave and then call the sheriff. I knew where the person was searching.

But I would not know who was in those woods and that person might leave before Redd showed up. I moved into the trees, toward the flashlight beam, testing each step for silence before putting my foot down all the way onto the leaves.

I smelled gasoline. A lot of gasoline.

Carrying it had caused the figure in the night to hunch to the left. A lot of it had spilled as it was being carried toward the lake, to destroy, once and for all, the bones in those woods by the shore.

I got to within two hundred yards of the light, and then a hundred. All the while, the flashlight beam kept sweeping the shore of the lake, stopping now and then before moving on.

I stopped fifty yards from the shore. Any closer and I'd be spotted.

The flashlight was set on the ground, and loud whooshing rose from the shore. The shape of whoever was there grew smaller and then larger, and then I realized he, or she, was bending down and straightening up, as if scooping leaves into a pile.

A huge flame erupted, raging up ten feet into the night and out in all directions as it fed on the gasoline and the thick mass of dry leaves that had been mounded on the ground.

I ran away, fumbling in my pockets for my phone. The world was all orange behind me, crackling and snapping as a thousand fallen branches along the shore caught fire. The trees lining the water would soon catch fire and topple, sending up more sparks, more fire.

I had no phone. I'd left it in the Jeep, for fear I would jar it off silent mode as I moved in the dark. All I could do was run.

I slammed into a tree, knocking the breath from my lungs as I fell. My head hit a fallen limb. Blood coursed down the side of my head. I gasped for air; the air was hot. The fire was chasing me through the woods.

I'd burn to death if I stayed down.

I pushed up to my knees, then to my feet, and stumbled on, dazed, unsure, knowing only to run from the heat growing hotter on my back. The cottage appeared ahead, a black blur dancing and changing shape as the superheated air lightened with orange. I started to run around the cottage, and then remembered. The thud, the front door left open.

I had to know.

I ran up the two steps, pounded across the porch, pulled at the screen door, and started in. Everything inside was turning orange from the firelight ranging in through the windows.

I tripped on something just inside the door. I fell onto it. Please, not a body, I begged, rolling off of it and onto my stomach, and onto my knees. Please, not a body.

I reached down.

I ran out, onto the porch, onto the ground and into the trees behind the cottage. The world was bright orange behind me. My lungs heaved in the growing smoke. I ran, encumbered, guided by the clear orange ribbon of road beside me.

The fire lane came up, orange from the glow behind. I pushed away the few branches I'd laid against the Jeep, tossed in, jumped in, twisted the key, and spun the Jeep around. The left side of the lane beside me was on fire now, jagged with flames.

The fire jumped then, right in front of me, igniting the right side into a sudden fury. I shot out to the road, not shifting, gears shrieking, as I pawed the passenger seat for my phone. Finding it, I thumbed the three numbers.

'Nine. One. One,' the woman said, too calmly. 'What is your emergency?'

'Fire!' I shouted, slowing to cut the gear whine. 'Little Tick Lake.'

She started to ask who I was. I clicked her off, shifted up to quiet the engine, and sped away, into the night.

Sirens sounded after long minutes, growing louder, coming toward me as I sped from the fire. An access road came up. I turned into it and cut my lights. Two fire engines roared past, followed by two sheriff's cars. I could only hope the pumpers had enough suction to drain the whole of Little Tick Lake. They'd need all of it.

I looked toward where they'd disappeared. I saw no orange through the trees. The fire was far away.

I closed my eyes, leaned back, and fell into sleep.

THIRTY-EIGHT

I t was daylight in Verona – seven-thirty in the morning – when he called.

'Guess what?' Redd asked, without introducing himself.

I had a choice. I could lie by saying I didn't know what he was talking about, or I could be truthful. I chose truth.

'Crisped ticks,' I said.

'You called it in?'

'Sometime in the middle of the night,' I said.

'How soon can you get here?'

'Ten minutes.'

'Thank you for not lying about your whereabouts.'

'I'm often a teller of truths.'

I parked where Julianna Wynton's cottage had been. Only the stone pillars it had rested on, and some of the floor, remained. All of it was charred from the fire, and still smoking.

I consolidated the scattering of Burger King wrappers behind the passenger's seat. Amanda says I keep them as mementos of good times, but that morning, they offered utility as well.

I got out into a landscape that looked like World War II photos of firebombed countryside. The leaves were burned off most of the trees, leaving the branches that remained twisted like fingers accusing the heavens for what had happened there. The thick carpet of leaves on the ground was now white ash, and smoke rose from it in a hundred little tufts. Four firemen roamed across it, stomping them out.

Sheriff Redd stood in the middle of it, talking to a fireman wearing a white helmet. Redd nodded to me as the chief walked away.

'Wisconsin was better off without you, Elstrom,' he said, by way of a warm greeting.

'I did not start this fire,' I said.

'But you are responsible for it?'

'Most certainly, as an intermediary, but it started with that savagery in Weston.'

'Sara Jansen,' he said.

'Good that you remember.'

I told him everything I'd done since arriving in Verona the previous evening. I skipped nothing except running into the cottage just before the flames engulfed it.

'Our fire chief says there's no way to pinpoint exactly where it started,' he said.

'Let me give you my best guess,' I said. Using the site of the cabin as a reference, I led him to the spot where I'd seen the fire erupt. The ground was mounded highest there with smoking ash, and uncomfortably warm beneath my running shoes.

Redd knelt and, with a stick, brushed away the ash to expose the blackened dirt below. After a minute of probing and finding nothing, he stood up. 'We'll dig but we'll find nothing usable unless the bones were buried real deep. If not, they're goners. Bones are not strong enough to withstand extreme heat.' He looked at my eyes. 'Our fire chief says gasoline was deliberately splashed from the cottage clear down to the lake.'

'I think it was set to destroy down there first and then work back.'

'So it was no accident, then, that the cottage was destroyed as well?'

'Seems likely.'

'Why?'

'To burn any evidence of who was staying there,' I said.

'Julianna Wynton?'

'Martin Tripp, the man who confessed to killing Sara Jansen.' We headed back to the remains of the cottage.

'You're sure you saw nothing identifiable about the arsonist?' he asked.

'The flashlight held in front blurred his, or her, shape into shadow.'

'You weren't afraid the fire would find you?'

'I thought the fire would be localized, down by the shore, and I needed to see more.'

'Neither the person or you went into the cottage?'

'The person might have, before or after setting the fire,' I lied. 'I was only interested in anyone who came to see if evidence had been discovered, as the *Tribune* said, and where it might have been reburied.'

'What's your guess?'

'About the bones, or the arsonist?'

'Both.'

'I'm out of guesses,' I said.

'There'll be an inquest,' he said.

'For a fire?'

'For the bones we better find,' he said.

He let me go, which surprised me. He probably sensed, by the way I'd begun to scratch, that I was full of ticks. Which, despite my precautions, I was. I needed the glow from cigarettes, pronto.

It took me eight hours, two stops for cigarettes, and eighteen visits to roadsides before I got to Rivertown. By then, I was so tired, so sore, and so scratched I didn't think I'd have the strength to shower before crawling into bed.

That was not to be. I'd given Frosty a key to the turret, but he was sitting behind the steering wheel in his battered Explorer when I pulled up. There was another car, an old black Chevy Impala, parked immediately in front of him. The two vehicles were nudged so close that their bumpers almost touched.

Frosty powered down his window when I walked up. The man who'd checked on me when I'd driven up to Amanda's storefront factory was sitting beside him on the passenger's seat.

'Good trip?' Frosty asked, conversationally.

'Good enough, I suppose. There was a fire, and an arsonist, but I couldn't identify the arsonist.'

He nodded at that, and looked ahead through the windshield. 'This is a strange town,' he said.

'How so?'

He pointed across the spit of land toward Thompson Avenue. 'That street there, it goes all night long.'

'Thompson Avenue,' I said. 'Neon, music, and love.'

'Does anyone sleep around here?'

'The walls of my place are really thick,' I said.

'I'm sorry your trip wasn't what you wanted, but you might have better luck here.'

'How so?'

'You had a visitor in the middle of the night,' he said.

'Do you have a description?'

He held a forefinger to his lips for silence.

I strained to hear above the traffic noise coming from Thompson Avenue, and was able to make out muffled thumping and shouting.

I looked around, saw no one, but then I spotted movement. The Impala ahead of us was rocking, ever so slightly. Its trunk lid was slightly ajar, held down by a black rubber bungee cord hooked from the back of the trunk lid down to the back bumper.

'My visitor?' I inquired.

'Man had a set of picks,' Frosty said. 'Old lock like yours, he would have been inside in a flash.'

'He didn't bother to knock?'

'Not so's we could hear,' he said, 'so we asked him to wait.'

THIRTY-NINE

I unhooked the cord and let the trunk lid rise.

The Frenchman peered up at me in panic with eyes as bright as a trapped ferret's. His hands were clasped over the top of his head.

'You'll be killed if you try to run,' I said, which was a necessary exaggeration.

A Rivertown police cruiser slowed, passing by. The two cops took in the half-visible Kowalski, cowering in the trunk with both palms crossed over the top of his head, and me, looking dumbly down at him from the side. The driving cop ignored the two of us and gave Frosty a nod. He nodded back, and the cops sped up, going away.

'I love this town,' Frosty called out through his open side window.

I started to tug Kowalski up by the arm but he pushed my hand away with his elbow. With his hands still clasped across the top of his head, he struggled up to his knees, only to bend down to put the top of his head on the floor of the trunk. I took his cowering to be trauma from spending the night trapped in a car trunk, but then he moved his elbows outward, like some huge, winged insect steadying itself, and with the top of his head still pressed to the bottom of the trunk, began feeling for something in the darkness. His hands found it in an instant. It was his beret. He slid it beneath the top of his head, pulled it down snug, and rose.

He was not ready. When he'd almost straightened up, he teetered, not having quite gained equilibrium with the world, and flopped out the back of the Impala and onto the hood of Frosty's Explorer with a soft grunt. He did not swear; he did not cry out. He merely touched the top of his head to make sure his beret was still on. Satisfied that it remained safely secure, he rolled onto his belly and slid off the hood, feet first, onto the pavement.

'Resilient people, too,' Frosty called out, laughing, having witnessed the whole contortion through his windshield.

His sidekick got out of the Explorer and came forward to get in the Impala. 'You can handle this?' Frosty asked out his side window.

'If he gives me any trouble, I'll ask you to come back and enthuse him,' I said, mostly for Kowalski's benefit.

Frosty nodded and started the Explorer.

'Thanks,' I said, 'and thanks even more for helping Amanda.'

Frosty smiled and said, 'Me, help her?'

'I don't figure her for having the strength to move a load of bricks.'

Frosty leaned back in his seat. 'Man, you were married and you don't know her?' he said, laughing loud enough to be heard clear across to Thompson Avenue.

'What do you mean?'

'I didn't so much help as I had to restrain,' he said and, still laughing, he pulled away and the Impala followed.

'One false move and I'll bring them back,' I said, putting a hand on Kowalski's arm. 'Let's walk down to the river and you can tell me about the difficulty you had breaking into my home.'

He looked across the broad lawn toward city hall, as if contemplating a run.

'Frosty has friends everywhere,' I said, 'as do the lizards.'

'OK,' Kowalski croaked. He must have howled through most of the night but I didn't want to risk going inside to get him something to drink for fear he'd bolt like one of his black, or blackened, cats.

We sat on the bench. I gave him a moment to compose himself, and then asked that he start at the very beginning and omit absolutely nothing.

'What will you do when I'm done?' he asked.

'That depends on your veracity,' I said.

'My what?'

'Your truthfulness,' I said. 'Start at the beginning.'

'They suspected me of skimming,' he began.

'The lizards? Yeah, I know.'

'I didn't, at least not much.'

'I know that, too,' I said. 'How much, exactly?'

'No more than twenty grand, and that was over a few years,' he said, 'just for retirement. How do you know?'

'You needed money for that show at Kutz's clearing. Go on.'

'That last night, a year ago January, they were waiting for me at the bank when I come in for my regular drop. About eight-thirty, like normal. Mister Mayor, a couple of his beefs, the bank president. Even the old lady, the ma, was there, though she likes her gin and was cross-eyed by then. Mister Mayor asks how much I got in the plate. That's what they call the collection, like in church. I say I dunno; I never count, I just carry. He says there's irregularities. I say, huh? He says money irregularities. Missing money. He says to think real hard about what coulda happened the past few weeks, and come to his office tomorrow at two the next afternoon, before my rounds. A quarter of the district each day, work four days each week, is what I did. I'm scared to the moon, not gettin' what coulda happened, how they know money is missing and how they coulda thought it was me that took it. So, after them all bracing me, Mister Mayor and all, I head for the tap, like every night, only that night I'm needin' my pops more than ever. Like always, I'm riding my regular stool next to Marty, him coming in after closing The Hamburger, like always, and I tell him what just went down. Oh, man, big mistake.'

'Telling Tripp?'

'I was havin' pops and needin' to talk. He tells me, you sure you ain't took it? Just a little, I says. Fifteen, twenty tops. They ain't looking for no piddlin' twenty tops, he says. I ain't took it, I says. Who then? he asks. Gotta be that little sweetie, except not so sweet, I tell him. The part-timer they got to cover for the old lady? he asks; the one with the hair? Has to be her, I says; no one else coulda done the skim. He says I see her at the bank and she comes into The Hamburger. Mousy thing, gives him the creeps the way she's moonin' at him with those eyes under that hair, he says. I don't know I ever said more than a few words to her. Me neither, I says, only when I'm making the deposit. He was buyin' me pops, all the time smilin', not keeping up, being careful with his own pops like he was real concerned about me and wantin' to stay clear-eyed and calm me down like a friend, you know?

'Only later did I think I shoulda known what he was thinking. Then he asks me: Who they gonna believe, you or her? You're cooked, he says. You think? I ask him. They're gonna kill you, even if you return the dough, he says. I didn't take nothin', I says again. Maybe you'll be lucky, he goes on, and they'll let you eat a bullet first, before they put the cement blocks on you for the Willahock, but you're gonna die. What am I supposed to do? I ask him. I think I even started cryin', I'm so scared. You gotta run, man, he says, you gotta get out of here, unless you got what spilled from the plate and can give it back to stay alive. I ain't got nothin', I says, except maybe a little I keep every now and then, for expenses and all. You gotta run, man, he keeps sayin', buyin' me drinks like he's feelin' sorry for me and all, but now I know he's already thinkin'. She done it, gotta be, I keep tellin' him. Gotta be her, doin' the skim. Sweeping off the top, nights a week when she's working. They don't check, I tell him; they trust me like they oughta. She's just a mouse, I tell him, just like you say, but she's doin' it. She workin' enough nights for a really big skim? he asks. Plenty, now that I'm thinkin', I tell him. Plenty enough to clean lots of plates. Old lady sicker and sicker, her son says, but she's probably goin' home early to get comfortable with her cocktails. All the time, lately, Sara's there when I come in with the plate. You're fried, Kowalski, Marty says. Fried like a fish. They're not never gonna believe it's her, a tiny part-timer, workin' her butt off at the grocery and at the bank.'

'It was Tripp all the way,' I said.

'He had it figured it was her, and set me runnin'.'

'To get out of his way,' I said.

'So he could put the move on her, Miss Moonin' Eyes, for the plate.'

'So finally you decided you'd had enough running and came back at her.'

'No,' he said. 'I stopped runnin' out in Wyoming, working at a Walmart wranglin' carts, figuring I'd spend the rest of my life out there. I had some money saved—'

'From the skim?'

'Only a little for expenses, like I told you. Anyway, I'm living OK, gettin' by on what I made with the carts. None of them out there was pinchin' at my beret or nothin', so it was OK living out in the middle of nowhere. And then, one day, I'm pushin' a long train of carts up to the store, and I give a glance at the parkin' lot, and there's this guy looks just like one of the cops who was with Mister Mayor that night they done the accusin'. I'm thinkin', man they tailed me all the way out here. I jumped in my car and drove all the way to Sioux City, didn't go back to my room for my clothes or nothin'.'

'I don't think it was anyone from Rivertown,' I said.

'I think that now, but I didn't think it then. I was edgy, always lookin' over my shoulder. Anyway, I hole up in Sioux City, decidin' where to go next and it sure ain't back to Rivertown, so I move on, this time to Albuquerque and do carts at a Walmart there. Then one day, I call my aunt collect, like I do every couple of months, to keep up in case I'm still bein' looked for, only this time I ask you still see that Sara Jansen at the grocery? And my aunt says, nah, she moved over a year before, bought a house in Weston and nobody could figure where she got the dough, workin' for peanuts at the grocery and at the bank. Well, I coulda told my aunt where she got the dough but I didn't. Then she says ya know what? That Martin Tripp from The Hamburger is out there, too, cohabitatin' with her. That's when it all clicked solid. My old pal Tripp sent me runnin', then made the move on mousy Sara so he could grab what she took off the plates. But there ain't nothin' I can do about nothin'. I can't go back to Rivertown, but it's gratin' on me, see? Gratin' bad.'

'So you went to see Sara,' I said.

'No chance.'

'You braced her at her house.'

'Thought about it, plenty. Thought about scaring the crap out of her, when she saw who was standin' on the stoop. Tellin' her I came for half.'

'You were seen that day,' I said.

'What day?'

'The day you cut her.'

His shock looked genuine. 'You're nuts! No chance. I don't know nothin' about no cuttin' until I see the big news that Tripp's been arrested for killin' her, and he confessed!'

'Your aunt didn't tell you?'

'I only called now and again. She keeps me informed about like whether any of her lady friends hear anything about people still bein' interested in me. But I watched the news every day.'

'Where were you when she was killed, if not in Weston?'

'I told you, man: Albuquerque.'

'Same as when you first heard Tripp was living with Sara?'

He nodded fast, several times.

'And then he got acquitted . . .?' I asked.

'Saw that on the news too. Could have knocked me over with a feather. I called my aunt two or three times after that, thinkin' he's livin' the high life, but then, a couple weeks ago, not even, she says, guess who's just come to town? I says who? She says that killer, Martin Tripp. I ask her why does she think? She says nobody knows why, but he's back in town, lookin' like just another homeless, walkin' around. I didn't say nothin', but I knew why. Sara never coughed up the plate. He cut her but she never coughed it up. He came back to Rivertown because he knew something that tol' him it was here. So me, I'm outa Albuquerque on a train, because my car was stole though why I'll never figure, it was so old. The whole way back, I'm thinkin'.'

'Thinking the money never left the bank.'

'Not then, I wasn't. I was thinkin' she hid it at her ma's, after takin' out enough for the house, but that old gin bag said Sara ain't been around for years before she left for Weston. And then I got to thinkin' where a mouse like Sara put it where no one would think to look, like no one would think to look at her because she's a mouse, and where it would be safe, and that got me thinkin' where else but a bank?'

'You didn't wonder if Tripp was thinking the same thing?'

'Sure but then I heard he was talkin' to you about proving him innocent—'

'Which you believed?'

'I couldn't figure why would he confess if he was innocent?' He shook his head. 'It didn't matter. Maybe he had a different play going on, another con like when he conned me into runnin', maybe he really did want you to prove he didn't do it. Not my worry. I was only thinkin' bank.'

'You didn't think he thought what you thought, and beat you into the bank?'

'I didn't know where he was or what he was up to. He wasn't hangin' around, public, like me.'

'You didn't know he'd already disappeared before you blew the bank?'

'He was still around when I started my play so that meant he hadn't scored it yet, if that's what he was after. And me, I didn't know for sure about the bank either but I couldn't think no place else that was better to try. A quick look-see inside. Dough or no dough, at least I would know, one way or the other.'

'So you put your own play in motion.'

'I rented a place so's people would think I was back to stay. I knew where Mister Mayor's ma lived. I grabbed her black cat, started grabbin' others to dye to look like hers, and turned just a few of them loose to get people used to chasin' cats. I got me some explosives, set up Leo's ma for a big night at the clearing, sent in enough beer to get the cops so sloshed at Kutz's they couldn't see straight enough to respond to the bank so . . . maybe you can figure the rest.'

'The blast blew the wall inward, filling the stairwell,' I said.

'I didn't think of that.'

'How were you figuring to get inside the actual boxes if it hadn't?'

He squirmed, forever clueless. 'I was hopin' the blast would do it.'

'Why try to break into my place?'

'Ain't no other shot left. Somebody said Marty had took off, gone, vamoosed, but he'd been layin' low anyway. If he was gone, he was gone, but I figure since you were workin' for him, you might know somethin' about that, like where he was. Unless . . .'.

'Unless what?'

'Unless you killed him and stole the plate, and dumped him in the Willahock. My time was up here; I figured they had to know I blew the bank, what with me reconnoiterin' there a few times. I hid in the park across the street, watched your place, saw you drive away. Maybe you knew where Marty was, maybe it didn't matter. Your place was worth a look inside. I didn't figure there'd be guys waitin.' He looked out at the water. 'What are you goin' to do to me?'

'Let's go,' I said.

'Where?'

'Mister Mayor,' I said.

He turned and grabbed the back slats of the bench like he was going to fix himself to them. 'I can't.'

'It's the only way for you to stay alive,' I said. 'I'll tell him you're innocent of the theft.'

'And that little damage to the bank?'

'We'll work something out,' I said.

I called the mayor, told him I had news. He said to come in the front way, that he'd have a guard escort me. I marched Kowalski across the broad lawn to city hall, tugging him all the way by the shirt collar like a dog fighting a leash. A cop was waiting by the front door. He walked us down a short hall, through a door I didn't know existed, and up a flight of stairs to the mayor's office. The anteroom door was unlocked. I knocked on the inner door and it immediately clicked open.

Mister Mayor sat implacable behind his desk.

'This is an innocent man,' I said of the quivering Kowalski as I pushed him down onto a chair. I sat beside him, then raised an ankle to evict a passenger I'd missed on the drive home.

'The plate?' the mayor asked, looking at Kowalski. Kowalski jerked a shaking thumb in my direction. I jerked a thumb back at him, and he told it all, just as he'd said it to me, minus any mention of the twenty grand he'd skimmed over the years.

When Kowalski finished, I asked, 'How much was missing?'

Mister Mayor paused, evaluating what he should tell me. 'Plenty,' he said.

'Do you really think a guy like this is capable of stealing much?' I said.

'The capture of our depositor, here,' he said, pointing to Kowalski, 'doesn't square things between you and me, Elstrom. What are you going to do?'

'I still don't know who's dead,' I said.

FORTY

I t was the bones. It was going to be the bones until I could figure them.

I called Sheriff Redd. 'Are you digging?' I asked.

'It's a large area, Elstrom. We're working out from finding

nothing but some dust that might have been bone where you showed me. But now it's afternoon. I can't keep men much longer, and even if more dust or bone fragments are found, the next hurdle would be to find who to test for a DNA comparison.'

'We might never know.'

'There's someone here who'll be as delighted to talk to you as I've been.'

A woman's voice came on. 'You're the Vlodek Elstrom in the paper?'

'Occasionally,' I admitted. 'In the papers, I mean. I'm always Dek Elstrom.'

'The person who said there's evidence in my woods?'

'Who might you be?'

'The person who's responsible for burning down my woods?'

'Who are you, lady?'

'The person responsible for burning down my house?'

'Julianna Wynton?'

'You . . . you, jerk,' she screamed. 'You idiot!'

'I'm pleased you think so,' I said. 'Delighted, in fact, that you're angry.'

'You've ruined—'

I cut her off. 'When did you rent the lockbox? The old lady didn't note the date—'

She clicked me away, which didn't surprise me. But then the same number called again.

'Look, Miss Wynton—'

'It's Redd,' the sheriff said. 'Miss Wynton threw my phone onto the ground and stormed off. You lack people skills, Elstrom.'

'You're right,' I said, employing people skills now, meager though they might be. 'Where did she go?'

'Back to the ruins of her cottage.'

'To poke through the char?'

'There's nothing left,' he said.

'That's my hope,' I said. 'Is she poking beneath where the floor was?'

'Why does the floor matter?'

'It doesn't,' I said, without explaining that the two thuds I'd heard the night of the fire made any search under the floor irrelevant. But Julianna Wynton didn't know that.

He swore.

'What time did she show up today?' I asked.

'An hour ago.'

'How did she find out about the fire?'

'People hear about fires.'

'She didn't hear about it from Martin Tripp,' I said.

'What are you talking about?'

'When she showed up, did she immediately start poking at the floor?'

'Of course. The floor was all that was left, and a lot of that was burned away. She was rooting around for an hour, poking, swearing, and sometimes screaming. We were worried she'd gone mad with rage.'

'That would have been as warming as the fire,' I said.

'What are you saying?'

'Things I'm becoming sure of,' I said.

'I'm going to hang up,' he said.

A tiny window opened in my head. 'What does she drive?'

'We're done—'

'A metallic-blue Malibu,' I said.

'You been stalking her, Elstrom?'

'That's not important,' I said. 'A metallic-blue Malibu, right?'

'No. She drives a white Volkswagen Jetta. Tell me about the Malibu.'

'I don't know enough yet,' I said.

'I saw that Malibu around here a few days ago,' he said. 'I couldn't tell who was driving. The windows were dark-tinted. Whose car is it?'

'She bought it, but Tripp's been driving it,' I said. 'Check around. Maybe someone saw it the night of the fire.'

It had to be Tripp I'd seen, setting the fire. But he hadn't told Julianna. It had taken her most of the next day to learn of it. Only then did she hurry to Verona.

'By the way, Sheriff, you can quit digging.' I was sure of that now, too.

'There are no bones? You're saying there are no bones, after we've been digging in these smoldering woods, this stinking burn pit, for hours?'

'There are bones, all right. Lots of bones, but only one was put in the ground, meant to be found.'

'Found by whom?'

'By me,' I said. 'And that one was moved to the shore, where the mound of ashes was.'

'Where are the rest?'

'Probably in the lake, just off the shoreline.'

'You want divers?' he yelled. 'You want me to spend money to hire divers?'

'Nah,' I said. 'Just put a couple of guys in those rubber waders fishermen wear when they want to splash without getting splashed, and have them look along the shore.'

'Your corpse is there?'

'They're big bones but make no mistake, they're herring bones,' I said, and hung up, fooled no more.

Of course the bone was for me. There'd been only one, one to mislead, one to convince me that it was Tripp's, dead after suddenly disappearing from the Afforda-Rest. One bone to stop me from looking for him any more; one bone to buy him a little more time to ease Julianna into the bank. He'd seen me spot him in the woods at Kutz's clearing, seen Goetz's cab follow him to the Afforda-Rest. He'd known that I would come back to confront him, to demand an explanation. He'd run out of time, he had to disappear, but he had to make it look like he'd been abducted. He knew the only road left to me would lead to Verona. I would come, but he had to make sure I'd see the bone and see a cottage trashed in search of something, or someone, that would convince me that it, and him, was no longer there. I had to believe Tripp was dead and that whatever he had was gone.

I played into it. I followed the scent of his herring. I saw the trashed cottage, the buried bone, and he knew that. Maybe he followed Amanda and me; maybe it was her. Then the bone had to be moved, so that it could never be examined and found to belong to some animal that died at the shore. There needed to be no bone, to neutralize me into a crackpot, convincing anyone I told about Tripp that I got things wrong.

Either Tripp, or Julianna, moved it, though it was moved carelessly. It should have been thrown into the middle of another lake, or better yet, thrown in a dumpster or somebody's trash. But it wasn't. It was reburied hurriedly, probably shallowly at the shore, and too close by. They must have thought that didn't matter.

And at that point, it didn't matter because I had not reported discovering the bone. Tripp must have seen that as just what he'd wanted – my giving up – and they righted the cottage because, after all, Juliana Wynton still lived there and that was certainly an explainable thing for her to do, after discovering someone had broken in.

But still there was Kowalski, and what he might have figured out and could tell the lizards about being certain it was Sara, and not Kowalski, that took from the plate. He, or Julianna, tailed Kowalski in the dark-tinted Malibu a time or two, enough to figure his play with the cats and his interest in the back of the bank, and enough to figure Kowalski was harmless, even if he blew his way into the by-now emptied lockboxes. They even dragged another herring across their trail, by renting a room at a Holiday Inn under Sara's name to further confuse things while they bided their time in Verona, where people expected to see Julianna anyway, until Tripp was sure no one was looking for him anywhere, alive, at least.

But then the *Chicago Tribune* and Chicago television reported that unnamed evidence was being sought in a Verona woods. That brought panic, fear not only that the woods were being searched for something inadvertently dropped or poorly hidden, or the bone itself, but also the likelihood that the cottage would be searched, the bloodstain tested and found to not be human. It might all point to Martin Tripp, and to wondering whether he might not be dead at all, and that he had, in fact, been staying in Verona. Even if he fled, a manhunt would result. Any evidence in the cottage and the woods had to be destroyed.

The best plan required gasoline.

But first, a lifting of the trapdoor, to set the object of it all by the front door, to be grabbed after all else was done. Then a quick walk through the woods, sloshing gasoline to the approximate spot where the bone was buried. It could not be found at that last minute, but that didn't matter. A last slosh, a toss of a match, and fire was unleashed. Tripp would be a mystery, maybe for forever, thanks in some part to a bone that might never be found and to a cottage that could never be examined.

He – for it had to have been him alone; her fury at learning of the fire did not sound faked – hadn't figured on the speed and the spread of the burn. The fire spread too rapidly, too wildly, too fast along the gasoline trail back to the cottage. There'd been no time to get inside.

I could imagine his anguish, seeing it all burn.

And hers, when she realized that it, and he, were likely gone, too.

It pleased me enough to head out for something special for dinner.

FORTY-ONE

R edd called just as I'd stepped inside The Hamburger. He was furious.

'We found a deer in the water close to the shore. You think it was a deer bone you found? You wouldn't do that to me, would you?'

'Certainly not in the beginning and never deliberately,' I said. 'You could be sure by checking to see if the deer is missing a bone.'

'You'd like me to summon the county's medical examiner to do an autopsy? Find cause of death? Do a murder investigation? Contact the deer's next-of—'

'If things are slow enough to permit such effort, that would be great,' I said, 'but most likely, the deer died of natural causes and fell into the lake.'

'Why I, and the taxpayers of my county, had to foot the bill for your foolishness will play hell when news of this gets out.'

'At least you won't have to do a blood analysis of the stain in the Wynton cottage,' I said. 'The fire destroyed all traces of that.'

'Deer blood,' he said.

'Spilled to confuse like the bone.'

'Who's dead, Elstrom? Is anyone dead? Was all this just a colossal waste?'

'Sara Jansen is dead,' I said. 'We must never forget that.'

'Again: who's dead?'

'Sara Jansen,' I said, and clicked him away.

The husband and wife going broke inside The Hamburger gave no indication they'd heard my conversation. Maybe they hadn't. Maybe they were too alone inside, too focused on scrubbing the plastic booths with disinfectant, to leave their disaster spotlessly clean for the next optimist.

'Hello again,' he said.

'Hello again,' she said.

'The lasagna was exceptional,' I said, 'but I'm going to try something different.'

I pretended to look up to study the fluorescent menu board that had once offered hamburgers, whiskered fish, excellent Italian food, and always, the promise of the great American dream. Now, the letters and numbers had been removed, and it offered nothing.

'As you can see—' the young man said.

'I'll have part of it,' I said.

That brought them both over to the counter. 'Sir—' she said.

I counted onto the counter what I'd hurriedly grabbed, leaving the turret. $5,800 in fifties and hundreds. Some were clean, some were greasy. And then I walked out without looking back, and I drove all the way to the turret without smiling at myself in the rearview, either.

I'd opened the timbered door and was clicking his number into my phone to thank him again for his help, when a voice at the back of my neck said, 'Put away the phone!'

I spun around and saw the gun, but it was the garb that held my eyes. She'd dressed definitively, as she had once before, perhaps this time also to confuse anyone watching.

She followed me in, soundless as a panther, and kicked the door shut behind her.

The beautiful woman in the courthouse photograph wasn't beautiful now. What I could see of the lower part of her face was tensed pale, and white, the skin drawn tight across her mouth, cheeks, and chin, as if shrunken. Worse, her gun hand was tensed and white too, aiming the semi-automatic at my gut. The slightest flinch would send a bullet into my stomach.

I dropped my phone hand to my side. 'I was going to call Frosty the Blow Man,' I said loudly, 'to tell him about your gun, Miss Wynton.'

'Cut the crap, Elstrom. The duffel.'

'You know, like Frosty the Snowman?' I said, loudly. 'Only he's different. The Blow Man won't melt from the challenge. He'll always show up, fast, especially when a woman is holding a gun.'

'Stop screaming! The duffel.'

'A duffel?' I tried to fake a hearty laugh but it came out weak. 'What duffel?'

'The duffel,' she said, too calm now and too in control. She took a fast look around my first floor, saw the table, the two plastic chairs, the empty roof tar can I use as supplemental seating, and nothing else. 'Up the stairs!'

'Tripp didn't send you this time, did he?' I shouted. 'He's gone, right? It's just you here?'

The gun flicked up and she fired into the plank ceiling. 'Up the stairs, or I shoot you and go up by myself.'

I turned and hurried across the concrete to the stairs. As always, I stopped on the first step, to be sure the two-by-four I'd wedged at the top still pinned the iron railing against the limestone wall. The two-by wobbled side-to-side like a gently wagging finger, but no more than usual. So long as that wood stayed pinned, there was no danger of the staircase breaking loose from the wall.

'Up!' she shouted.

'Can't you hear the ringing? Staircase is loose.'

'Move!' she shouted.

'You're the one holding the gun,' I yelled, hoping she'd think only that I was partially deaf. I climbed to the third step and stopped to let the staircase absorb the shift in weight. The ringing sounded louder than usual, but the two-by still wobbled normally.

'Keep going!' she shouted, stepping onto the staircase to jam the gun barrel up into my back.

The staircase shrieked like something wounded, from being weighted in two places. I shot a glance up to the top. The two-by still wagged side to side, but now it had loosened, and was also moving up and down, making a dangerously erratic oval.

'Look at that board!' I yelled. 'Wait until I've reached the top!'

It was true, but what I really wanted was to put enough distance between us so I could run across the second floor, up different stairs to the third, and then scramble up the ladder to the fourth floor and pull it up behind me.

I climbed to the fifth step. The wrought iron began shuddering worse than ever – another bolt must have fallen out from the wall – but the two-by, still making its new, dangerous oval, stayed in place.

'What do you think I have?' I yelled over my shoulder, this time at her.

She fired, sparking a round off the limestone to the right of me. 'You were up there during the fire!'

'I was not!' I yelled.

'That's what the sheriff said!'

I cursed my stupidity. She'd already accused me of setting the fire, on the phone from Wisconsin. The sheriff had told her then that I was up there.

'Up!' she shouted again.

'Tripp didn't tell you, did he?' I yelled back, because now I understood. 'He didn't tell you he was going to torch those woods? He didn't tell you and now he's gone?'

I climbed two more steps and froze. The two-by was slipping out slowly, as if being squeezed from a tube.

'Move, or I'll shoot!'

'Of course he didn't!' I screamed. 'He wouldn't tell you he was going to burn down your house and take off with the precious duffel!'

'Move!'

'Look at the board!' I yelled.

She fired, pinging another bullet off the limestone. 'Next one's in you.'

I went up the eighth step and stopped on the ninth. The two-by had slipped out another inch.

'Hurry!'

'You had to find out for yourself, right?' I said, conversational now, hoping to calm her, but not moving. There were seven steps to go and I had to be sure of my next moves. 'You had to hear about the fire from somewhere else?'

'Up!' she shouted a third time, pounding up three stairs in a fury. The staircase shuddered; a bolt broke away and fell to the concrete below. The two-by wavered, but it stayed where it had slipped.

I climbed up two more steps. Only five remained. 'Confronting Sara that afternoon, to demand she set your Martin free, must

have been your idea.' I shook my head. 'I can almost hear Tripp
reassuring you that night, telling you it was fine, that you did
great.'

'Shut up!'

'Saying you could both be free, if you went back to finish
what you started?'

She pounded up two or three more steps, sending tremors rolling
up from the bottom like an earthquake. I shot a glance up. The
vibrations were shaking the two-by free, inching it out even more.
There couldn't be much wood left pinning the staircase.

'Move!'

I climbed to the twelfth step. Only four remained. I stopped.

'Give it to me and I'll let you live!'

'What can't you understand? He wouldn't have let it burn up.'

Enraged, she charged up again, shaking the staircase with such
force that I had to grab at both handrails to keep from falling.
My phone fell from my hand and clattered to the concrete below.

Above, the two-by was waving like a mad arm gone berserk,
side to side, up and down.

'The board!' I yelled.

She stopped. 'The duffel,' she said, sounding too close to
me now.

The staircase settled; the tremors stopped. One more jolt, one
more shift in the weight load, could free the two-by, sending the
staircase into a free fall.

I was four steps from the landing, still too far to jump. I eased
up two more steps, turned around, and sat.

She was only five steps below. 'Get up!'

'He's gone, Julianna. And so's the plate.'

She was too close to miss with her gun. I leaned back carefully until I felt the slightest pressure of the two-by on my back.
'That board at the top?'

She shot a confused glance up to the landing.

'Do you remember how it was almost out?' I asked.

She nodded, sensing.

'You can't see it any more, right?'

'Stand up, get moving,' she said, but her voice was weak. It
was good. She understood.

I stayed seated and said it anyway. 'You can't see it because

I'm leaning against it,' I said. 'I'm like the little Dutch boy with his finger in the dike. Shoot him and everybody gurgles. Except we've got a staircase that weighs a ton or more and a board barely pinning it to the wall. Shoot me, I fall back, the board pops out, and we both go down, broken backs, snapped necks. Dead or paralyzed.'

She fired off to the left, pinging another round off the limestone, and pointed the gun back at me. 'Get up nice and easy.'

Her finger tightened inside the trigger guard.

Only two steps remained to the second floor landing.

I gave a shrug of acceptance and made to push my legs up slowly, but then I kicked up hard and backward. And missed. I flopped onto the second-floor landing without breaking the two-by loose.

She clanged up the metal stairs, firing up into the opening as she came.

Still on my back, I kicked blind but I kicked hard. My left foot found the two-by, flicking it away like a feather just as her head and her gun hand appeared in the opening.

The great iron stair-beast broke away, tearing her head and gun hand from my sight. She screamed as the staircase crashed deafeningly against the limestones and onto the concrete below. And then there was nothing.

I rolled onto my stomach, torn between scrambling up to escape to the stairs up to the third floor and needing to know where she was. I crawled to the edge of the landing and eased out just enough to look down.

She lay on her back, pinned by an iron step to the concrete floor. Her eyes were wide. Her chest heaved beneath the long coat as she labored to breathe, the wide-brimmed fedora beside her. She still clutched the gun. It wobbled in her hand as she raised it up to point at me.

The timbered door banged open. Frosty stepped in, gun drawn, and hurried soundlessly across the floor to kick the gun out of her hand.

Her hand fell. 'I just wanted what he said he wanted,' she said.

Frosty looked up at me. 'Cops?'

I stared but I wasn't seeing him. I was seeing evil in a long coat and a man's hat.

After a time, I stopped shaking enough to pivot around on my stomach and let my feet flail at the void below.

'Careful, careful,' Frosty called up. 'Push out a little more and I'll guide you.'

I did, and when he said, 'Drop,' I did that, too. My feet found the top step of the fallen staircase. I lowered myself onto it and slid down on my stomach, feet first, clutching each step with my hands as I lowered my knees onto the next. Frosty held my arm and helped me step off at the bottom.

'You can dispose of the gun?' I asked.

'We got a spot for the seized,' he said, crossing the room to put it in his pocket.

I looked over at my cell phone lying cracked on the concrete slab. 'Just call an ambulance?'

'No cops?' he asked again.

'Just an ambulance,' I said.

'I love this town,' he said, and went outside to call.

It took an hour for the fire department to extricate her. Amanda waited in her car by the curb. Frosty had called her, as I expected he would.

As the EMTs wheeled Julianna to the ambulance, I knelt to whisper in her ear. And then I walked to Amanda's Toyota and she drove us to Lake Shore Drive without saying a thing.

She wept at times. I did, too.

FORTY-TWO

I met with James Randeen and the Bohemian in the Bohemian's small conference room at 8:00 a.m., two days later.

'Thank you for arranging your schedules around your paying clients to accommodate my requests so quickly, though today I have the rare pleasure of joining them. As I insisted, I appreciate you charging your maximum billing rates for what you've done, up to and including four hours each for today.'

'Vlodek . . .' The Bohemian was still uncomfortable with that request.

'I will explain to Amanda, and she will enjoy the reason,' I said, because I suspected she would badger the Bohemian to bill her for his time, and he would badger back that he wasn't going to charge me at all. I supposed it was a joust that occurred every time he did something for me.

'You're relishing this?' Randeen asked.

'Squad cars have been slow-cruising past my turret, as the eyes of Mister Mayor, ever since the ruckus of the evening before last. Yes, I'm enjoying this.'

The Bohemian passed the first document across the table. 'The offshore account, funded yesterday via bonded courier in a private jet. As you desire, it's structured to disperse the principal deposit, plus earnings that accrue, less annual fees.' He glanced at his copy, looked up, and smiled. 'Forty-nine years, Vlodek?'

'Starting one year from today,' I said, unable to stop a grin of my own.

He nodded. I imagined he'd moved money offshore thousands of times, but perhaps not to perform in the same manner I'd requested.

'The new certificate of occupancy,' Randeen said, passing his document across.

It was the exact wording I'd emailed to him. 'This should stop Mister Mayor from sending over any more teenaged building inspectors with trumped-up violations,' I said.

'It's sure to delight,' Randeen said.

I stood up. 'Gentlemen, I've taken enough of your time.'

Randeen said, 'I do have one additional request.'

'Anything within reason,' I said.

'Or not?' he asked, looking over at the Bohemian.

The Bohemian smiled. Obviously, they'd already discussed the additional request. The Bohemian, smiling even more broadly now, motioned for Randeen to continue.

Randeen's face turned pink. 'May we be told when the next shindig at that clearing will be held?'

I left the two of them howling at the notion, not at all sure that Randeen was kidding.

*   *   *

The mayor had not been shy about telling his coppers to intimidate me with their drive-bys, and I'd not been shy about waving each time one passed by. But Mister Mayor stepped things up by calling the minute I got home from the Bohemian's office.

'You've been active,' he said.

'Any word on your mother's cat?' I inquired sociably.

'The search continues,' he said, which was no answer at all.

'And the depositor remains in good health?'

'As we agreed,' he said. 'He leads the search.'

'No one else is looking,' I said, 'except a few scattered residents, mostly children, who've paid no attention to the rumors . . .'

He chuckled a whispery, lizardly chuckle. 'About the activity at your place, night before last. We caught only the tail end of it, apparently, when the ambulance arrived.'

'A woman came with a gun, demanding your money.'

'My goodness,' he said. His voice picked up and I imagined his tiny pink tongue coming into the light, sharing the alarm.

'You made me earn my twenty thousand,' I said.

'Ten,' he said, because he couldn't help himself.

'We'll discuss that,' I said, warming to the ballet.

When I said nothing more, he said, 'Yesterday and today were also fraught with activity. A bonded messenger service came to you first thing yesterday, then a construction crew showed up, and this morning, you drove to Mr Chernek's office.'

I was not surprised he'd had me tailed that morning, but this time, he used professionals. I'd spotted no one.

'Yes, there's been all that,' I said.

'Is it resolved?' he asked, of the plate.

'Oh, my yes,' I said, and told him I'd be over. And I was, fifteen minutes later.

As when I went with Kowalski, a guard was waiting in front to accompany me to the door in the upstairs hall. Mister Mayor did not answer my knock on his inner door. Making me wait was gamesmanship and it was no matter. I lit a cigarette and amused myself by populating his anteroom until finally the door buzzed. Wisconsinites, no matter their genetic origin, are hardy travelers, reluctant to emerge, even days afterward.

'You've recovered my money?' He eyeballed the duffel calmly through the slits of his eyes, the way an ordinary lizard would savor the sight of a plump fly, but the pink tongue was hungrier. It darted in and out between his lips in a frenzy of anticipation.

I set Julianna's duffel, or perhaps it was Tripp's, on his desk so that he could admire it more closely. It was a cheap thing, made of blue nylon that had gone dingy with age. Being large, it was puckered and collapsed.

He pulled it to his lap, unzipped it, and began pawing inside like a dog or, I supposed, like Tripp had hoped I would the ground, when I spotted the bone he wanted me to think was his.

I lit another cigarette, reminding myself I wouldn't become addicted so long as I didn't inhale, or ever go back to Wisconsin.

'It's all there,' I said, crossing my right leg over my left and bringing forth the tip of the cigarette.

Mister Mayor looked up, his face almost purple. 'You'll pay, Elstrom,' he said.

'Do you have an ashtray?' I asked.

'Did you hear me? You'll pay.'

'Absolutely I'll pay.' I flicked ash on his carpet, and put the cigarette tip an inch from my skin. Such warmth felt good to me now, and apparently to the latest of the little travelers that had eluded me for days. It emerged to my welcoming fingers. Holding it gently in one hand, I put the cigarette to my mouth and took a small Ziploc bag from my shirt pocket and deposited the tiny thing alongside one I'd not released in the anteroom.

'I'd like an ashtray,' I said.

He pulled a heavy glass ashtray from his desk drawer and pushed it hard across the desk. I caught it before it fell to the floor, set it on the desk, and crushed out the disgusting cigarette.

'Absolutely I'll pay,' I said again. 'Every cent that's due you, plus interest. You'll end up with much more than you lost.'

Another spot began to itch, an inch above the first. There'd been many that had been slow to emerge. I lit another cigarette, aimed the tip, and out the critter came. I dropped it into the Ziploc to join its cousins.

'Let me give you a verbal accounting,' I said, 'but if you'd like it in writing, I can send you one of the photocopies I've placed in a lockbox in Chicago, attached to a very complete summary of our previous conversations.'

The tongue appeared as a speck of pink between his lips but then, sensing the charge in the air, quickly retreated.

'I recovered $2,960,000 in fifty and one-hundred-dollar bills,' I said. 'Since many of the bills were greasy, I assumed they'd not yet been laundered before being given to your depositor.' I looked up, not really expecting he would applaud my wit. He did not.

'Best guess is that the part-time teller took out forty or so thousand dollars to use as a down payment on her house in Weston, plus incidentals, leaving the bulk of it in the bank,' I went on. 'You would have every right to file a lien against the proceeds from the sale of that house, if you can show that the money she stole was from legitimate funds.' I arched my eyebrows like Leo but mine are insufficiently furred and the mayor seemed unimpressed.

'Next,' I said, 'there are my expenses. $20,000 for my finder's fee. $11,400 for consulting – the two gentlemen who met with us when I was released from jail, and who have set up the proper mechanism to make sure you and your heirs get paid promptly and fully, in the future.

'$5,800 for miscellaneous Italian food consulting, $54.60 for gasoline,' I went on, '$11.00 for tolls, $41.80 for cigarettes . . .'

I picked up the Ziploc bag I'd set on the edge of his desk and waved it in the air, enjoying his recoil.

'Ticks,' I said, 'little bugs that get under your skin. Tasty to the right—' I stopped. His little tongue had protruded and he wiped at his mouth angrily to force it back inside.

I set the Ziploc down and continued. '$9,600 for repair to my staircase from damage caused by the woman upset about not getting your money, $35,000 for security—'

He'd had enough of my show. 'What are all these charges?' he thundered. 'Security? Italian food consulting?'

'Security was needed, for the jet and the person to deposit your money elsewhere, plus I'm sure your slow-driving police officers reported the security I employed to keep your depositor available after he tried to break into my turret. That included detaining him overnight in a car trunk and for one of them to come to my rescue later, when that cranky woman showed up to take your money.' I said the last bit as self-preservation, to tell him that I had a team. Frosty and his sidekicks could be every bit as inventive as whomever Mister Mayor might think to throw at me in retaliation.

'Italian food consulting?' he repeated, but he was sputtering down, in defeat, I hoped.

'To reimburse a nice young couple for the street taxes you would have collected if they hadn't gone broke,' I said, as if that made sense.

'Anything else?' He almost spit the words out of his mouth, or would have, if they weren't intercepted by the little pink tongue dancing in a fury between his lips.

'Eight dollars for two bags of Oreos I bought when I stopped for gas and cigarettes. One regular, one thin mint.' I paused, and dug in my shirt pocket. 'Oh, and three dollars for this cigarette lighter, used to ignite—'

My other ankle had started to itch, and as I lit another cigarette, I was able to demonstrate the need for the lighter as being a reasonable expense as I bagged another Wisconsinite. This time, to extend the life of the lighter, I left the cigarette burning in the ash tray.

He stared at me, speechless. 'Are you crazy?' he said, finally.

'I've not been formally diagnosed,' I said, with some pride.

I took the envelope from my sport coat and withdrew the four documents. 'First up, your zoning inspector's . . .' I paused to shake my head in admonition. 'Excuse me, the young Derbil's inspection report that you sent to intimidate me.' I tore it into five strips and put them on his desk.

'Next up, the certificate of approved occupancy we first submitted to you, which I requested honestly, and which you had no intention of honoring.' I tore that into five strips, too, and placed them on top of the torn inspection report.

'Third, an accounting of the payments you are to receive.' I passed it across.

He picked it up. It was a simple document, quick to read.

'You will receive a base amount of something in excess of $57,000, plus accrued earnings, every year for fifty years,' I said. 'The first payment is in that duffel. You'll note that I've stipulated that if, for any reason, I decide to terminate this obligation, I may do so at any time without further financial obligation.'

'I'll get you for this.'

'Perhaps,' I said, 'but you won't get your fifty-seven thousand dollars, plus earnings, each year. You'll also note that it is your responsibility to collect the annual payment at the spot chosen by my off-shore representative. It will be paid in cash, like so much of your income. For many of the first years, you'll receive interest earnings that exceed the principal, so you'll be collecting well over a hundred grand, each year, for years to come. Investing with me is a wise investment, not to mention efficient laundering.'

The cigarette in the ashtray had burned out. I lit another to extract another tick, but this time, instead of depositing it with the others in the Ziploc, I dropped it onto the carpet, hoping it would scamper his way.

'You are crazy,' Mister Mayor said, but this time he said it in the softest of whispers.

'Probably best to not eat off the floor,' I cautioned, to the pinkness between his lips.

I took the last document out of the envelope. 'My revised certificate of perpetual occupancy, entitling me to any and all modifications of the turret, without approval of anyone in city government, most especially to include any teenaged zoning inspectors you might employ. Also, since you zoned my property a municipal structure, I've asked The City of Rivertown to pay the property taxes, also in perpetuity. There's a space for your signature, but you don't need to sign it right now. This document is really not necessary, given our financial agreement, but I like the idea of it. Sort of puts the cherry on the sundae, or if you prefer, the tick in the skin.'

I paused to reward him a smile at this new cleverness, and went on. 'You have a year to sign a notarized copy, or much longer, if you choose. But know that, without a signature, there can be no second payment.'

I stood up, wished him a good day, and left.

FORTY-THREE

Weeks passed, and October began.

It had only been a year since Sara Jansen was murdered. It seemed like a lifetime.

We gathered, lovers and friends, Amanda and I, Endora and Leo, on a Saturday afternoon at Kutz's clearing. Oak leaves had begun to fall, coloring the ground with reds and oranges and yellows, but most were still in the trees. The Willahock flowed peaceably, free that day of recyclables, and from the speakers, Astrud sang softly of Corcovado, oh how lovely. It was a perfect autumn day, the kind that makes the snows and frigid winds that follow an endurable price to pay.

On the table was a small Polish smorgasbord of kielbasas, pierogies, and some unpronounceable sausage Ma Brumsky had just added to her own menu board that now hung beside Kutz's original plywood. And beer; there was beer. Ma had surreptitiously hidden cases of the Miller that Kowalski had ordered for that incredible, diversionary evening, and was selling the cans for five bucks apiece. So long as the cops didn't complain, they ate – but not drank – free.

Our table was the one closest to the river. It was the table I'd seen two ancients swaying on, just a few weeks earlier. I wanted to find symmetry between their dancing and Amanda and me sitting at that same table, that when she and I got to be their age, we'd still need to dance on a table.

'I don't know, Dek,' Endora said. 'I'm still troubled by Julianna Wynton.'

'No, you're troubled by my not calling the police on Julianna Wynton,' I said.

She nodded, grateful but rueful at the clarification.

'I'm still troubled by it, too,' I said, 'but it was my way of inflicting the most pain.'

Amanda watched me. She knew why I'd suggested we get together that afternoon. She hoped it would be a sort of ending, as well as a beginning, but neither of us really believed that. There'd been too many nights when we sat late in front of one of the fireplaces in the turret, talking it all through, but we never found closure to any of it.

'It was a spur-of-the-moment decision,' I said to Endora, 'but it was right to tell Frosty no cops, to just call for an ambulance. I saw his confusion; he'd heard the whole story through the phone I'd kept on . . .'

'And so cleverly dropped,' Leo said.

'I was grabbing for the handrails,' I reminded. 'By then, Frosty heard all he needed, to understand.'

'He's got a wide view of the world,' Amanda said. 'He sees all sides.'

'But still, Julianna free, and out of the hospital . . .' Endora said.

'If I'd called the cops, it would have been my word against hers—' I said.

'Frosty could have corroborated you, since he'd heard it through your phone,' Endora said.

'Without knowing, in terms of a legally admissible identification, who he was hearing speak?' Amanda shook her head. 'And remember: Frosty's word is that of a four-time-arrested drug dealer.'

'Worse,' I went on, 'Julianna confessed to nothing. It was just me saying she killed Sara.'

'You knew,' Endora said. 'You knew.'

'Of course, as soon as I saw that fedora and long coat she was wearing.'

'That mysterious man in the shadows, that midnight,' Leo said.

'And earlier, that afternoon,' I said. 'The neighbor that afternoon thought she was seeing a man. The neighbor that night thought he was seeing shadows. Neither places Julianna at Sara's, either time.'

'As far as any district attorney would be concerned, the murder case was closed,' Leo said. 'Tripp confessed to the killing.'

'What if he could be tried as an accomplice, or a co-conspirator, for winding her up? Could he be forced to testify against her?' Endora was testing all the angles, needing to be sure that I'd tested every one of them, too.

'No one can prove anything anymore,' I said. 'No one can prove it was Julianna that afternoon. No one can prove Sara gave Tripp hell about his girlfriend stopping over. No one can prove Tripp saw opportunity in that, and no one can prove Tripp told Julianna they could be together if she put Sara out of the way.'

'While he'd be out that night, looking to be seen walking,' Amanda said. 'What a prince.'

'So now they're both free as birds?' Endora said.

'Free as birds trapped in tiny, tiny cages,' I said.

'Tell her what you whispered to Julianna, when the ambulance was taking her,' Amanda said to me.

'I repeated what I'd said on the staircase, and added that she should take comfort in knowing her man, Martin, would be enjoying the money he grabbed for the rest of his life.'

They all groaned. And smiled.

'You're sure he doesn't suspect you were in those woods?' Leo said.

'If he doubted the money burned up in the cottage, and guessed that I was there, he would have come for me by now.'

'But Julianna knew you were in those woods during the fire,' Endora said.

'True, but they'll never connect. Her coming for me was like Kowalski blowing the bank: a desperate last play after she knew Tripp was long gone,' I said. 'The sheriff told her I was in the woods but that didn't mean I had the money. She had nothing to lose in gambling that somehow I'd found it.'

'All for nothing,' Leo said.

'It must be awful for Tripp,' I said, 'thinking of all that kissing up to Sara, all that verbal abuse he took, only to see it all burn up in the cottage.'

'You're not blaming Sara . . .' Amanda looked at me, about to be furious, again.

'She didn't deserve murder, absolutely not,' I said. 'But I wish she'd had the kind of life that could have made her kinder.'

'To Martin Tripp? She brought it on?' Amanda said, watching my eyes.

'She toyed with Tripp,' I said. 'She must have known that he and Kowalski were drinking buddies. After she moved out to

Weston, she came back to see him at The Hamburger. She must have known Kowalski had suggested that she stole the dough.'

'It must have been horrible to think the only attraction she had for him was the money she stole,' Endora said.

'That had to feed the rage she dumped on him,' I said.

'Tell me again why she left most of the money in the lockboxes?' Endora asked.

'I can only speculate that she put it there, in batches, as she stole it. She was probably afraid she might get searched.'

'And the lockboxes were rented in fake names,' Leo said.

'She must have thought the banker would never think to look for it there,' I went on. 'And later, when Tripp moved in with her, she must have been afraid that if she kept it in the house, he'd find it, and take off with it. So it was easier to let it be, for the time being.'

'So she spent and spent, knowing she could afford it, but yet unable to pay for the stuff she was buying for fear Tripp would learn how she could afford it, and demand she retrieve it? And then grab it and leave?' Amanda said. 'I guess I'd scream too, if that's what I thought it took to attract a man.'

'Poor woman,' Endora said. 'All I can think is that she was killed by a knife, then killed in reputation.'

There was no answering any of it. I turned to look where the trees met the river. The Frenchman was there, on his knees, looking for a cat. After a moment, he straightened up and moved to the next clump of bushes.

'A victim, too,' Leo said, gesturing at Kowalski as he dropped to his knees to peer under the new shrubs.

'He's whistling,' Endora said.

'Happy to be back working for the lizards,' I said, 'even if it's just looking for Mister Mayor's mother's cat.'

'Ma saw his mother at the food store,' Leo said. 'She asked her about her cat. Mister Mayor's mother just smiled.'

'I heard the rumor, too,' I said. 'The cat was found but the mayor didn't want it known because Kowalski has to serve some sort of sentence for running out of town.'

'Where's Julianna now?' Endora asked.

'On the run, I imagine,' I said, 'feeling betrayed by Tripp and fearing that at any time I'll tell the cops what I know, and they'll come looking for her.'

'A lifetime sentence,' Amanda said.

'I want her to suffer forever,' I said.

'And Tripp?' Endora asked. 'Where's he?'

I pulled out the envelope I received, smoothed it, and set it on the table.

Leo picked it up. 'Postmarked Madrid, addressed simply to "Dek Elstrom, Rivertown, IL"'

He opened the envelope. Inside was the other envelope.

'I don't get it,' he said. 'An empty water bill envelope?'

'That envelope once held five hundred dollars that Tripp offered me. He needed to be seen as having a reason for hanging around Rivertown, and hiring me was it. He's telling me now that he's in Spain, or was. Beyond the reach of the law and that I should give up any hope of finding him.'

'He'll spend his life running, too,' Endora said, looking satisfied for the first time.

'One question remains,' Leo said, gesturing toward Kowalski. 'When you pulled him out of that trunk . . .?' His eyebrows rose and quivered below where his hairline would have been, if he'd had one.

'And his beret, having been dislodged . . .?' I said, coaxing.

'What is tattooed?' he asked, leaning forward for the revelation.

'I promised I'd never tell.'

Quick as one of Kowalski's cats, Leo reached to grab the paper boat that held my kielbasa. But I was quicker than the fastest of felines, and snatched the kielbasa out and took another huge bite.

'OK, I confess,' I said, though muffled by kielbasa. 'I didn't see.'

'You didn't see?' Leo said, keeping his incredulity low on account of the nearby Frenchman. 'You were inches from the top of his head!'

'He wouldn't climb out of the trunk until he found his beret and put it on.'

They groaned and then they laughed.

I leaned back, needing to enjoy their laughter, to banish the memory of Martin Tripp, Julianna Wynton, Mister Mayor and his darting tongue, and even of Sara Jansen, if only for a little while.

Up in the tallest oak, amid the glorious color, the pulley had been left strapped to the trunk. I wanted to tell Leo to never take it down, to leave it as a reminder of the irrepressibility of the never-defeated Mrs Roshiska.

'I'm grateful . . .' I said, and stopped, unable to find the words.

I felt Amanda's eyes on me, warm, in the silence that followed. She knows me best.

'I'm grateful for Julianna Wynton, destroyed,' Endora said, picking up my slack.

'For Martin Tripp, drifting around Europe, ruined,' Leo said.

Amanda said nothing. She just kept looking at me, and when I dared to look at her, I could see her eyes glistened, just a little.

'I'm grateful for this,' I said.